BIRTHMARK
KILLER

Writer Jaw Books, www.writerjaw.com

Copyright © 2018 J. A. Winrich

Cover design and interior format by Debora Lewis, deboraklewis@yahoo.com

ISBN: 978-0-9895650-4-2

Birthmark Killer

J. A. Winrich

For my Family, Friends, and Fans for their continued support.

Acknowledgments

Thank you to my Critique Group in Green Valley, AZ
for their insights, to Susie Walkey for her editing skills, to Bonnie
Papenfuss and for her proof-reading skills, to DP Lyle for his
valuable forensic expertise, and to my book cover designer Debora
Lewis, deboraklewis@yahoo.com.

1

Sam Volarie stared as the long, thin-bladed knife ripped the soft white underbelly open. Entrails spewed onto the Cabo San Lucas boat ramp from the cavity of the 496-pound female bull shark she had caught earlier. She gasped from the burst of putrid stench. At 10:15 A.M., just ten minutes ago, Sam had smiled as Captain Enrique snapped pictures of her standing next to the eleven-foot-long shark. She wanted to do a "happy dance," she felt so elated. The possibility of her winning the $50,000.00 dawned closer. But she remained calm, not wanting to blow it in front of the others. Only one boat left out fishing. If they didn't bring any shark in bigger than her bull, she'd receive the pot and then she could let loose, maybe.

She swelled with pride and pointed towards the shark. "Capitán, mí tiburón por ustedes." Sam nodded as the boat captain and his mate grinned. Then she climbed the ramp to stand behind the rock wall with the other fishermen.

"Gracías." Enrique and his mate thanked her for giving them her big fish. Then they reached into the cavity and pulled out the stomach, heart, and more guts. They hacked them free when necessary and tossed the entrails onto the cement.

Seagulls flew overhead, squawking and diving for the viscera, fighting for morsels with the vultures. Waves lapped at the sides of the harbor inlet and boat ramp. A black lab and a brown mangy dog raced by her, ran down the incline, and both snarled and gnawed at the stomach. They ripped it open. Contents exploded all over.

The first mate, with his fillet knife raised high, charged after the two stray dogs, yelling, "Vámanos!"

The pair hurried off with bits of entrails hanging from their jowls. Blood dripped along their path. One vulture dived in, grabbed a chunk, and flew off. Sea gulls chased after the bird.

"Sam, this is disgusting." Ed Johnson wrinkled his nose and looked away. "No woman should watch this." Her friend who'd joined her on this May shark fishing contest appeared as gray as the fish. He dabbed at his brow with his white handkerchief and undid two buttons on his shirt.

Poor Guy. The fishy smell and guts reminded Sam of many fishing trips with her dad. She'd filleted fish on her own. Never, however, this big.

Resting her palm on the rock wall, Sam leaned over and inspected the innards lying about the captain's feet. When she spotted it, she felt her body, hot and damp from the 100-degree weather, turn cold. She slapped Ed on his arm. "Hey, isn't that a man's high-top tennis shoe?" She directed everyone's attention to a spot near the captain.

The fish mess mesmerized her. Sam couldn't tear her gaze away. She eyed each piece and came back to the shoe. Then she realized what she tried to ignore. Sam clutched Ed's arm and squeezed tight. "Oh, my God, there's a foot still in that tennis shoe." Her stomach clenched. Bile rose in her throat, but she managed to swallow. It tasted sour. "Did that shark eat a human?"

2

Before Sam's friend Ed could answer, Mark Randall, the man who'd put this fishing contest together, peered down at the mess strewn over the boat ramp. He puffed on his cigar. A smoke ring drifted by. "Appears so."

Sam waved at the foul-smelling smoke and coughed. She clenched her teeth. *I can't stand his attitude. Mark's so cavalier.* Friction crackled between them, even when she first met him at the airport. He'd stood next to Ed, who introduced her to Mark Randall. The arrogance never let up. Mark towered over both of them. The dimple in the man's chin reminded Sam of her handsome father. She couldn't believe Mark's russet hair never blew in the wind. *I bet he uses a ton of hairspray.* It plastered the man's hair in place. And those hazel bedroom eyes didn't take Sam's breath away at all. Mark turned out to be Ed's old college roommate.

After spending time with him, Sam decided Mark's one redeeming quality—partnering with her despite the fact she was a woman. When she'd signed up as Sam Volarie instead of using her full name of Samantha, she hadn't thought it would make a difference. It shouldn't have. These professional men all worked in the contracting business. As a landscape architect, Sam toiled with many men who accepted her as an equal.

But this group...

Didn't they care about the foot?

She shook her head. Her short, dark hair bob didn't blow in the wind because of the broad-brimmed, tan hat she wore, tied on by a string under her chin.

"Señor Capitán, por favór, look at that tennis shoe." Sam ogled the grotesque sight.

"Dónde?" Enrique asked.

"Where? Right in front of you." Sam jabbed her finger toward the high top mixed in with the entrails.

The man glanced down near him at the guts and undigested pieces. The captain shrugged. With his foot, he shoved away another stray dog that tried to grab some fish.

A seagull flew so low, Sam ducked. Above her, a flock of gulls circled and squawked. Red-headed vultures perched on the boat ramp and surrounding rock wall, eyeing the shark. The overpowering stench from below, mixed with the sea air, forced Sam to hold back more bile that crept up her throat.

The other fishing competitors gawked over the wall at the innards.

"Hey, Volarie," Frank Collotti, the oldest fisherman participating in the contest, croaked in a hoarse voice. "Stop looking at that goop. No dang place for a woman."

When Sam kept pointing, Frank ran his weathered hand through his military cut gray hair. "That undigested stuff's not human." He used his other hand to throw down his smoldering cigarette. With the gravel-sounding voice, Sam figured he'd smoked too many. Frank stomped his boot down and ground the butt out.

"Couple of those pieces remind me of a shoulder and the hip area." Sam studied the freckled skin.

"Where did you catch this shark?" Frank pulled a pack of cigarettes from his gray T-shirt pocket. He shook out another one.

"Near where you'd fished earlier this morning. Before you moved on." Mark pushed a strand of hair away from his face, although the rest of his hair didn't move.

"I told her not to fish there." Mark puffed on his cigar. "But she insisted."

"And, she catches a big one in that spot," Frank muttered.

Mark gripped Sam's arm and tried to pull her away from the wall. "Ed, why don't you take Samantha back to the hotel with you? You don't look so good, and she doesn't need to be here."

Sam yanked her arm from Mark's grasp. Even though she was a foot shorter than Mark's 6'2", she had never let a man bully her yet. "I can't believe none of you are concerned with this!"

It surprised her that Ed wasn't interested. He cared for her and came on this trip because she dragged him. He'd found the website telling about this contest. When she signed up for it, Ed asked, "What are you up to? You really want to do this?"

"Yes. If I can get the $5,000 seed money, it would be fun."

"Maybe." Ed stroked his chin. "You know I had a roommate named Mark Randall in college. Wonder if it's the same guy who's putting on this contest?"

"I say, let's find out." Sam suggested Ed come with her.

"But I have an architectural conference the week before. I couldn't make it to Baja."

But Sam insisted he should come.

"Mark's right, Sam," Ed said, bringing her back to the present. "We should go back to the hotel." He wiped more sweat from his brow.

"I'm fine. But, Ed, you *do* look bad."

He wore round, wire-rimmed glasses that suited his face and behind those rims his green eyes usually sparkled. Now they lacked luster.

"You go on, Ed, I want to get a closer look." Sam jumped down over the wall, landing next to the boat captain, hitting a corner of the shark's huge liver. Guts and blood splattered onto her jeans and a bit onto her purple T-shirt.

"Señor, su cuchillo, por favór." Captain Enrique handed Sam his fillet knife. She leaned over and examined the tennis shoe and foot. Then, using the knife, she poked among the pieces from her shark's stomach, turning them over. "These undigested pieces look fresh. Bet she just ate."

"Sharks eat all kinds of things." Mark blew another smoke ring. "Their digestive juices are so powerful they can digest chunks of wood or even iron. What's the big deal?"

"This is *not* wood or iron." Sam understood sharks ate everything, including bottles, even flashlights.

One year she'd caught a shark, fishing with her dad. She'd researched the different breeds of fish, and read where even a raincoat had been found inside one. When the stuff in their stomach grew large enough to become a problem, the shark belched up the whole mass and swam off to dine again.

But this mess isn't junk. I think it's human flesh. She dug around some more.

"That *is* a foot in this tennis shoe." Sam poked the shoe with the knife. "This shark ate a person."

"Oh, come on, that can't be possible. Besides, if true, how the hell do we know where it came from." One of the men groaned.

A younger contestant nodded. "She has a point."

As Sam stirred the viscera around, the men shouted their opinions.

"What are you, nuts?" Frank tossed his cigarette into the water.

"Hunting for buried treasure?" another contestant asked.

The men laughed.

"Don't give her too hard a time." The youngest man leaned over the wall and motioned toward the mess. "That *is* a foot in that shoe."

While Sam poked around the fish guts, Mark spoke to the boat captain in Spanish. The man reached to get his fillet knife back.

Sam pulled away from the captain. "Hey, I understand Spanish. Don't tell him to get rid of all this stuff. Aren't you curious?"

On the chunk that reminded her of around the hip area, she used the knife and traced a discoloration on the skin. "This looks like a birthmark or something. Ed, hand me my camera."

"Are you kidding?" Ed's ashen color made Sam wonder if he might throw up.

"No. I want to get a picture of this. It's in the shape of a duck. Señor Capitán, llama la policía."

"Don't call the police." Frank pulled out another cigarette. "God, not only has she caught the biggest fish so far, but she catches a shark that ate someone. Mark, you assured us there'd be no press. If you report this to the police, reporters might get wind of it. My wife thinks I'm at a conference. We can't do anything about this."

"What's to report?" Mark pulled out a lighter from his pocket and leaned toward Frank to ignite his cigarette for him. "I suggest we let the captain finish with his shark and if he thinks he should tell somebody, it's up to him."

Mark turned to the rest of the men in the group. "Hey, isn't it cerveza time? Let's head to that little bar across the street where we can get a beer. We'll all wait over there for the last boat to come in. People are watching us from there now, so we will be able to see what's happening."

With one boat left to arrive in port, Sam hoped the $50,000 contest prize might be hers. She smiled. This shark could help save her from a financial disaster. Would the panga have a bigger shark? Pangas. *Of course, Mark Randall spared no expense.*

Instead of fishing from fancy motor vessels, he rented the best seaworthy ones for the Sea of Cortez—pangas. These Mexican-built, fiberglass fishing boats were open, with mainly blue interiors. They had four bench seats, and smelled of old fish. The captain ran the motor at the stern. It reminded Sam of an open row boat with a motor, but it measured twenty-two feet long. She and her dad had fished from them whenever they'd traveled to Baja.

"I'll wait here." Sam didn't budge.

"The bar will be more comfortable. We can still see the last panga come in. Let's go." Mark reached his hand down over the wall, as if he wanted her to grab it.

Looking up at him, Sam placed both hands on her hips. "Forget it." She spoke to the boat captain. "We really should call the police."

"Por qué?" Enrique scrunched his eyebrows together and tilted his head.

"Why, is right." Mark jerked his hand back and straightened to his full height. He waved toward the fish. "That shark could have come from anywhere."

Maybe. Why do I want the police called? From Sam's past experiences in Mexico, she knew they would probably do nothing.

"I realize that shark might have traveled miles." Sam shrugged. "But—,"

"You won't get much from the police here." Mark ran his hand through his hair. "At least not unless you pay them."

Last year Sam's friend had been shot on the Mexican mainland, and he had to pay the police for gas for their car before they'd come out to investigate. Everyone in town knew who had shot him, but nothing ever came of it. Her friend didn't have enough money.

"Well, at least we agree on something," Sam muttered.

Captain Enrique chuckled. Sam smiled. *Okay, he understands more English than he lets on.*

"Even our great boat captain is not concerned." Mark patted his old college roommate on the shoulder. "Ed, talk some sense into her?"

"Hey, she didn't listen to me when I tried to talk her out of competing here, so I don't have any influence over her."

Frank ground out his cigarette. "This was your idea?"

"Who cares about the contest?" Sam focused on the entrails. "My, God, you men are insensitive. There's a dead person involved."

"Oh, please." Frank motioned toward the guts spewed about on the cement. "It's a piece of flesh. Can't even be sure it's human."

A seagull swooped down and grabbed a piece of fish and flew off.

The younger contestant looked over the wall at the fish mess. "Remember the foot in the shoe."

Frank snarled at the young man. "So, *we* don't need to get involved."

"Proves that shark ate someone." Sam furrowed her brow. "What's your problem, Frank? Someone is dead. We need to notify the police."

Ed wiped the sweat from his brow. "Sam, honey, calm down. It's a gruesome sight. But leave it to the boat captain."

"Besides, this person could have been dead a long time." Mark blew another smoke ring.

Sam didn't like the cigar smoke, but it did mask some of the putrid odor of the guts.

A black Labrador ran down the gangway barking, chasing off a vulture that ventured too close to the entrails. *Was that the same dog that started this by ripping open the stomach?* The big black bird rose into the air and circled.

"You are all unbelievable." Sam wanted to beat on their chests to make them care. "You act as if you see body parts all the time."

Even though she sweated, a cold chill surged through her. She couldn't stand the thought of someone being missing.

Missing. She shivered, and thought about her poor cousin. *I've searched for you, Jennifer. Why'd you disappear? Just 'cause I can't find you doesn't mean I won't be able to figure this out.*

Now, here lies chunks of human flesh. It brought back all the old issues. This reminded her too much of abandonment and dredged up the hurt, not only from her missing cousin, but from being adopted. Sam had been found on a church doorstep. Abandoned.

"Please call the police." *Do I have to bat my big eyes to get these men to do anything?*

The captain referred to Mark. "Oh, do as she asks, Señor Capitán. Call the police. If you don't, she will."

Frank groaned. "Do we have to?"

Some of the others nodded.

"I'm sorry this bothers you." Sam felt flabbergasted. "But this is important to me."

"I go get the policía." Captain Enrique ambled off.

"I don't know what you think you're seeing." Mark glared at her while Samantha snapped pictures. "There's no telling how long that's been in the shark's stomach."

Ignoring him, Sam continued taking pictures from several angles and distances, and included the tennis shoe. "From the lack of breakdown of the undigested pieces, it hasn't been too long since she ate."

"Do we have to stick around?" Frank asked. "The putrid stench is getting worse."

"No." Mark slapped him on the back. "I suggest you all go back to the Hotel Finistera. Wait for us at the Whale Watch Bar there and drink a beer or have a margarita. Drown your sorrows."

"Great idea." Frank and the men cheered and wandered off. Ed stayed with Mark and Sam.

The boat captain came back and helped the mate cut up the shark. "Police here in couple minutes."

Fifteen minutes later two policemen ambled over. The biggest one asked in broken English, "Where's the body?"

The honcho of a man stood seven inches taller than Sam's five foot two. His uniform barely covered his round belly. From his right hip hung a pearl-handled pistol. The holster—hand-crafted from black leather. His ebony thick eyebrows and his mustache bobbed up and down, dancing as he spoke.

The boat captain zeroed in on the shark and guts.

"You called us for a dead tiburón?"

"No, no, Señor." Enrique widened his eyes and gesticulated both hands back and forth.

Sam moved closer. "Excuse me, officer, we didn't call you for the shark, but what she ate."

The policeman ignored her, eyed the boat captain, and then glowered at Mark.

Mark told the police in fluent Spanish about the shark and the tennis shoe. He pointed over the wall down to the boat ramp at the chunks of flesh. He told the two officers about the one undigested piece in particular and how Samantha wanted the police notified.

"And what did you expect us to do?" the big officer asked, still not looking at Sam.

"This shark ate someone." Sam tilted her head. "Shouldn't you find out who?"

The man sneered. His smaller sidekick kept quiet. The honcho again spoke to Mark. "Maybe in your country this does not happen. Many fishermen here fall overboard, disappear, who knows. Most go unreported." Pointing to the viscera, he continued, "There's no way to determine who... we don't even know where it happened. Sharks travel many miles."

"Sí, yo intiendo." Mark nodded. "Yes, I understand."

Sam opened her mouth, but snapped it closed. Was the policeman lazy or was there really nothing he could do? She couldn't accept that. "Well, I *don't* understand."

The officer raised both shoulders.

"Some family needs to know." Sam couldn't leave it alone. "This body could be one of your turistas. Wouldn't a missing tourist hurt your trade?"

The big honcho's face appeared a bit purple and his mouth puckered. Sam's heart pounded. Should she take a step back? She stayed planted in front of him. *Oops, wrong words to say to this man.* His raised eyebrow, gritted teeth, and firm stance showed he believed that women should be seen and not heard.

He again addressed Mark. "I do not see a body, but I will inquire at the hotels to see if anyone is missing. That is the most I can do."

Sam wanted to yell at him, but thought better of it. The idea of a Mexican jail turned her insides to jelly. Instead she asked, "Aren't you going to take pictures?"

"Of what? A tennis shoe with a foot and slabs of meat?"

"Officer, one piece has a birthmark." Ed nodded toward the incline.

"A what?"

"Marca de nacimiento." Mark blew a perfect smoke ring. "The señorita sees a mark and thinks you might identify the person by it."

The policeman laughed. He leaned over the wall and peered at all the mess. "I see a darker color on a slab of meat. Who knows what that is."

"Look closer. There's something imprinted on that one piece of skin. It appears to be a duck." Sam placed both hands on her hips.

"Un páto," the honcho repeated. He spoke rapidly to his sidekick. They both laughed. He talked to Mark and ignored Sam. "Gracías, for reporting this. Have a good vacation." He walked down the ramp, picked up the shoe with the foot in it, along with the piece with discoloration. He stuffed both in a plastic garbage bag and sauntered off, still chuckling.

"He thanks you for reporting it and does nothing?" Sam's cheeks burned. She knew they were bright red. "I find it hard to believe no one cares this shark gobbled someone up."

"The policeman's right, there's not much he can do." Mark lifted both shoulders, shook his head, and sighed.

Sea gulls called out and dive-bombed the guts and one vulture snatched a piece and flew off.

Reaching out, Ed touched Sam's shoulder. "At least he'll check the hotels. Let's not let this incident ruin our trip."

Mark clapped him on the back. "You're right, Edward. Tonight's our last evening, and I've a special dinner planned."

"Wouldn't want to spoil that," Sam muttered. *I bet the policeman will throw the garbage bag away. At least I have pictures of all of it and know what size shoe it is.*

Mark gazed out over the harbor and glanced down at his watch. "Ah, it's noon and here comes the last panga. Unless they've caught a bigger shark than your gambuso, Samantha, you'll win the fifty thousand."

"Gambuso?" Ed scrunched his brows together.

"The Mexican's word for a bull shark." Mark sneered. "To think, probably out-fished by a woman. We all fly out tomorrow. Please, don't let what the shark ate upset you. We've done what we can."

Sam studied Mark. *Why isn't he more curious?* She didn't ask. "We'll see about that."

3

Before leaving the dock, Sam spoke privately with the boat captain. When he agreed to what she asked, she smiled. "Gracías, Señor. Hasta luego." She'd see him later, but would make sure no one knew.

"What was that all about?"

"If you must know, Mark, I thanked him for being a great boat captain."

Sam, Ed, Mark, and the other two contestants who'd gotten back, scrambled into the waiting taxi and went to the Hotel Finistera and Whale Watch Bar.

In the yellow car, the men talked about the contest. Sam tried to think of a way to get back to the marina without the men figuring out what she planned to do.

"Well, Samantha, congratulations." Mark swiveled in his seat and smiled at her. "You won the fifty grand."

She grimaced every time Mark called her "Samantha." But this time, she grinned. "Yes." Sam remembered the look on Mark's face when he had caught his mako. He'd been sure he'd won the money.

As soon as they'd dropped off his shark, they had cruised out of the marina again, bouncing along in the panga, to go fish for her shark.

After putting a mackerel on her circle hook, Sam let the line out behind the panga, and wham! She braced her feet, arched backward, and held the pole, keeping the line tight. The rod bent as the line screamed off the reel. The tug at the end felt as if she'd latched onto a sea monster.

Mark reached over to help. Sam yelled, "I can do it!"

Catching the bull shark—not as fun and exciting as when Mark caught his mako. That shark leaped and thrashed, and they'd hoped it wouldn't throw the hook.

No, Sam's fish bit hard and swam with a steady pull, zigzagging through the water, trying to avoid coming to the boat. With the captain's skill in maneuvering the panga to keep the line taut, and Sam's determination, she had brought the bull shark near the boat. It took forty-five minutes, not long at all.

"What will you do with all that money?" Ed asked, bringing her back to the taxi ride.

"Not sure." *The money won't be enough to completely get me out of my financial jam, but... If it hadn't have been for that arrogant accountant. So, this money will help.*

The cab dropped them off at the hotel and they climbed the stairs to the open-air bar.

The men traipsed across the floor. Sam followed, but halted when she spotted the other shark fishing contestants. They sat at a table on the far side of the room. It overlooked the Sea of Cortez and Pacific Ocean. The men talked and gestured with their hands. *Are they discussing cerveza and women? I doubt they're thinking or talking about the chunks of human flesh or the birthmark.*

While standing inside the bar by the entrance, Sam admired the seven-piece mariachi band that strolled from table to table. Normally, they played later in the evening, but this bar must have them come in for the lunch crowd and work through dinner. They wore typical matching outfits—black bell-bottom trousers and black tunics with little silver hats for buttons, which also adorned the sides of their pants.

Atop the band members' heads were big black sombreros embroidered with silver swirls. The hats bobbed to the music's rhythm.

Each member played an instrument from strings to horns. Sam hummed along to her favorite Mexican song, Guadalajara. *Wow, for once this band is all in tune and singing in the same key.*

Mark, halfway to the contestants' table, spun around. Walking back, he squinted. "Samantha, what are you doing?"

Sam quit humming. "Can't help it, I love this song."

Ed, who followed Mark back, chuckled. "It does have a good beat."

Mark reached out and clasped Samantha's hand. "I think you're stalling. We'd better get over to the table and let the others know you're the winner." He pulled her forward a few steps.

Sam retracted her hand, not liking the tingling sensation that crawled up her arm, nor the little flutter in her heart when Mark came in contact with her skin. She marched toward the table where a few minutes ago the men were boisterous. But now, so quiet. If not for the other patrons and the band, you could hear Frank slurp his beer. Even their hand gestures stopped.

Frank ceased guzzling his cerveza, glared, and his gravelly voice grated out, "These two told us she won?"

"She did." Mark nodded.

"Oh, say it ain't so." Frank put down his glass and lit a cigarette.

"Sorry, gentlemen." Ed grinned. "Sam's bull shark wins, ousting all of you."

The table erupted with boos, hisses, and curses.

"Why thank you, gentlemen." Sam spoke in a fake Southern accent, giving a little curtsey. "It's always a pleasure dealing with such *gentlemen*."

Mark laughed. "She's right, you know. Show some sportsmanship. She won. The fifty grand is hers." He lit a cigar and blew a smoke ring. "Now, shall we *be* gentlemen and accept it as true sportsmen? Let's party!"

Sam knew Ed would back her, but found it hard to believe Mark supported her, not that she needed them to help. She inhaled the cigar smoke and coughed. That smell got to her. *Wish he wouldn't smoke.*

The young contractor of the bunch held up his hand. "You know, my wife usually catches the biggest fish when we go fishing. I'm happy for her. Sam, congratulations on winning all of that money."

"Thank you."

Another guy shrugged. "We should be big about it."

"I don't know." Another fisherman took a swig of his beer.

"Come on guys." Ed smiled at Sam. "She did win."

One by one the men hefted their beer bottles, or their margarita glasses. "Congratulations!"

"How's it feel being fifty thousand richer?" one of the men asked.

"Great! Can't believe I bested you all."

Frank mumbled, "I bet." Then he yelled, "Let's get drunk."

Before Sam could sit, she noticed Mark's girlfriend Linda, carrying shopping bags in each hand, enter the bar. All the men ogled her walk to the table. Her orange flowered spaghetti-strapped dress swayed as she moved.

Other than Sam, Mark was the only one who'd brought someone on this trip. *Amazing how it turned out that Ed and Mark were college roommates. If I hadn't insisted Ed come, they wouldn't have connected again.* He'd been very surprised about Mark being his old roommate. Didn't think it would be him. When they signed up, Sam said it might be him and she was correct.

Linda drew attention not only from the contestants but others in the bar, too. Sam saw one man sitting on a bar stool behind their table. He wore his baseball hat pulled low and he watched Linda's every step. Her long blond hair, perfectly styled, her polished nails, and flowery perfume that Sam could smell from the table, gave Sam an idea on how to get away early. The men and other patrons couldn't tear their gazes from Linda. *Perfect.*

"Hey, guys." Sam caught some of their attention. "Since I'm feeling grungy in these fishing clothes, if you'll all excuse me, I'm going to go freshen up."

"Good idea." Frank looked around the table and stood. "Before we get drunk, we should all do that."

Another man got up. "I agree."

"Great." Sam took a step back. "I'll meet you all here much later for dinner. I'm kind of wiped. Think I'll take a nap."

When the men snorted and winked at Ed, Sam wagged her finger. "Alone, thank you very much." She scurried past Linda who asked, "Was it something I didn't say?"

Most of the men followed Sam out and headed for their rooms. She thought even the guy in the baseball cap got off his bar stool and left. *Gee, I wonder why he didn't stick around to stare at Linda?* Of course, maybe he did. Lots of men wore the same baseball hats in the bar, since the management handed them out to all the patrons.

⸗⸎⸎⸏⸗

Inside her hotel room, Sam wriggled into her one-piece black swimsuit and tossed a purple-flowered shift over it.

She grabbed her dive gear bag that she'd packed in case the opportunity arose. *There's plenty of time to do this dive and get back for dinner.*

The men wouldn't approve of her next move and might even try to stop her. *That won't happen, of course, but why invite the hassles.*

After opening her door a crack, she peeked out. No one wandered the hallway. Sam stepped out, eased her door closed, and tiptoed past Ed's room. She heard what she figured to be water running for a shower.

She hurried down the hall.

Outside, taxis lined the hotel's steep, curvy, cobblestone driveway. Sam flung open the door on the first car, waking the sleeping driver. They wound down the driveway and over to the marina's dive shop. Sam paid the driver, picked up a rented dive tank, wiggled into her wet suit, and met Captain Enrique and his mate. When the boat captain saw her dive gear he shook his head. "No, no, Señorita, no busea."

"Sí, yo buseo." Sam nodded and let him know she scuba dived. With an additional $20.00 in his hand, he smiled and helped her and her gear back aboard his panga.

The minute she boarded, she put on a life vest because of her weird dread of boating. She loved to fish and scuba dive, but she hated being in a boat, and the irrational fear she had of falling overboard.

Even though she had on her wetsuit, she still felt safer with the vest on. It acted as her security blanket.

Captain Enrique guided the panga out of the harbor and out to sea. He assured her he could find the same spot she had first hooked the gambuso.

With the motor throbbing through the choppy afternoon water, Sam narrowed her eyes. Because of the dirt in the air, the sun shone bright orange and glistened on the water.

Driven to find out who her shark ate, she blanked out visions of its unfinished dinner awaiting her at the bottom of the sea.

4

I sit on the edge of my hotel bed and slam my fist into my hand, thinking about earlier that day. Even though I know it's risky and the gut stench is sickening, observing Sam lifts my spirits.

That new tennis shoe spills from the stomach of Samantha's shark. I nearly have a coronary.

From my vantage point, all I can do is watch her sort through the Gambuso's guts. Wish I could say something to stop her.

Why on earth is she allowed to compete?

The contest ad specifies ten fishermen. Can't she tell the difference? It doesn't say fisherpersons. Still, I admire her for using her nickname "Sam"—very clever. And getting her father and his friends to put up the $5,000 seed money—brilliant.

But why can't she be squeamish? What woman pokes through fish entrails?

I spot the big chunk of human flesh with the discoloration. My insides tighten.

I'm so careful. No one suspects me. And no one is supposed to ever find the body.

Of all the dumb luck.

And, she feels sorry for the crew, turning her fish over to them so they will eat for the next several days. Of course, they cut it open right then, and, in front of everyone. Then those two mangy mutts rush in and rip the stomach, so everything spews out. What a stench and a ghoulish sight.

Her curiosity almost drives me over the edge. There is nothing I can do but watch.

I wipe the cold sweat from my brow when she finds that chunk of flesh with the duck birthmark.

Is it possible for her to find any leads with that?

Does she have a plan? Telling everyone she'll take a nap. I don't believe it. Clean up, yes. Nap, no. I get off the bed and pace the room.

It's all going so well up to the moment she catches the bull shark. Oh, I'm happy that she won the fifty grand. But because of what's inside of her shark—I might have to stop her.

How?

A sound emanates from the hallway. At my door, I listen, then slowly open it a crack and peer out.

Is that Samantha getting on the elevator?

I rush down the stairs, following the direction of the elevator arrow. As I reach the outside door, she climbs into a taxi. She carries a big bag with her.

What is she up to? Ah, I bet I know. Her taxi drives off. I hurry over to the next car in line and throw open the door. The driver drops his cigarette out the window and stares at me. "Follow that cab," I say. What a cliché. The driver doesn't move. I bang on the back of the front seat and point. "Go!"

The driver switches on the key. The motor turns over and over.

"Let's go, now."

The engine turns over. The taxi driver chugs out. My heart pounds so hard in my chest, I hear it. I wipe beads of sweat from my brow. This excitement is getting on my nerves. I don't need this.

The cab winds its way down the street. Yes, her car in front is heading for the harbor, just as I suspect. Is she really going diving?

Her taxi stops in front of the dive shop and she enters. I tell the driver, "Hang back."

He pulls to the side and waits. I stare at the door.

Ten minutes later, she exits and heads to the dock with a yellow dive tank and her duffel bag that probably contains all of her dive gear. I wait and watch her climb into the panga.

When the boat leaves, I pay the taxi driver, go inside the dive shop and make arrangements. I know where she is heading.

I gather up all I need and rent a panga. Sam is definitely trouble. If I scare her enough, maybe I won't have to kill her.

5

The panga skimmed across the sparkling water for about twelve minutes. Captain Enrique pointed out a pod of large, gray dolphins bounding through the waves. He motioned for Sam to get in the bow of the boat.

Most tourists wanted to play with these graceful mammals. On a previous trip with her father, they'd encountered a pod. Those bottlenose were feeding and had ignored the boat.

Sam glanced at her watch, deciding she had plenty of time. She smiled and nodded at the captain. He sped into the pod.

Tightening her life vest, Sam crawled to the front, and, on her knees, gripped the rail so tight her knuckles turned white. Her broad-brimmed hat blew back and flopped behind, the string choking her. She held on as if her life depended on it.

She took up scuba diving because of that stupid irrational aversion of being on top of the water in a vessel. She rolled her eyes. *I'm so not a boat person.* Under the water—fine: on top—a different story.

As the panga pounded over the waves through the bottlenose dolphins, Sam stared down into the sea. Two of them swam along, inches below the bouncing bow, matching the speed of the boat. The front flew up in the air over a wave and rammed back down. Sam gasped and closed her eyes. Peeking through her lashes, she spotted the pair gliding beneath unharmed.

Through the crystal-clear water, Sam saw an old one, with scars on its body, roll and stare up. She swore it winked at her. As it veered off, it leaped from the water and splashed down. Another bottlenose took its place beneath the bow.

Dolphins jumped the waves alongside the boat. A few surfed the panga's wake. Others performed with tail walks, leaps, and spins.

For a moment, Sam ignored her anxiety, let go of the rail, and clapped. She grinned so much her face hurt. One gray bottlenose soared out of the water near the boat, spraying salt water over her face.

With the playful mammals, she momentarily forgot where she headed, and why.

Birds squawked and circled the pod. The sea air smelled a bit fishy, but fresh. Salt spray stuck to Sam's face. She smiled. Neither crew member smoked to stink up the sea air like Mark's cigar had earlier in the day.

That thought forced her to remember why she came out here at sea, bouncing along with the dolphins. The captain wove the boat among the pod, playing with them for the next ten minutes.

Sam shouted, "Capitán, are we going in the right direction?"

"Sí, Señorita."

When the gray mammals swam off, Enrique maneuvered the vessel in the same heading and soon slowed the panga. The mate and captain glanced around. A brief discussion ensued between them, and then Enrique changed directions. A few minutes later he cut the motor.

"Aquí." The captain jabbed his finger down at the water. "This where you catch gambuso."

The water lapped at the boat. Sam never could figure out how the Baja boat captains could find exact fishing spots without markers or global positioning systems.

On one trip to Baja, she'd plotted a spot with her handheld machine, and the next day the captain had found the exact place without looking at her GPS. It amazed her.

Sam gathered her equipment and looked out over the sea. She shaded her eyes and peered at another racing panga. It came roaring up and stopped, bobbing in the water three hundred yards away. Sam wished she'd packed her binoculars. She couldn't make out who sat in the boat or what they were doing. It appeared they had fishing rods. She didn't want to think about the drug smuggling that went on down in Baja.

While Sam hooked up her air tank, Enrique shook his head. "No, Señorita, no es una buena ídea para busear aquí."

Maybe not such a good idea to dive here. Didn't thrill Sam either, but she had no choice. If no one else would do anything, she had to try.

Her shark probably hadn't even eaten the person at this site. It could have ingested it several miles away. *Okay. Not a good picture. Get those big teeth and being eaten out of your mind.*

For some reason those images brought other thoughts: her own birth parents and what happened to her missing cousin Jennifer. *I can't stand the thought of someone never knowing what happened to their loved ones.* Sam took a deep breath. *I have to do this dive.*

Her parents had adopted her and loved her. They'd told her she was special from the day she could remember, but she never quit thinking about her birth parents or her aunt's missing daughter for that matter. Many nights she'd have this dream—shipwrecked on a deserted island, but no one ever searched for her. She would wake up crying and feeling cold.

Maybe Sam couldn't find Jennifer, but she had been kicking around the idea of hunting on the Internet for her birth parents for almost a year. If she could find out the identity of the dead person in this shark, maybe she would have the confidence to locate her birth parents. *Then, maybe later I might discover what happened to my cousin.*

"Está bién." Sam hoped diving here would be okay. She didn't relish the thought of meeting a shark below the cold water.

Sam set her tank and buoyancy compensator vest on the seat and put it on. She brought the regulator around over her shoulder and placed the mask on her face.

The last thing she saw: the captain and mate watching her as she sat on the side of the panga, held onto her mask, sucked on her regulator, and tumbled over backwards into the sea. She feared being on top of the water, but underneath, calm seeped into her body as the water engulfed her. Maybe it had something to do with feeling safe like a baby must feel floating inside a womb.

Under the blue-green water, she tried to feel the peace envelop her. But this dive gave her a different vibe. She had to concentrate on her breathing.

Yellowtail amberjacks swam past as Sam descended. Visibility—a good twenty feet or more. This still didn't quell her apprehension.

Sixty feet down, Sam floated above the bottom. She kicked her fins and disturbed a stingray. It dashed away, sending up a cloud of sand.

Her eyes widened and she bit hard on the regulator. Her scream under water sounded muffled and garbled. She grasped her chest and when her racing heart calmed, she did a three-hundred-and-sixty-degree spin to see everything around her. Then she swam against a slight current, dreading finding the rest of a body.

A tan rock wall rose twenty feet. Fan coral, waving back and forth, adorned its face. Kicking her fins, she glided above some rock and came to an edge. She peered down into a valley about another twenty feet below. Fish hid among the scattered boulders.

A large golden grouper darted out from behind a big rock. Sam sucked on her regulator and blinked. Had something scared it? *Guess I'd better check.* She bent from the waist, kicked hard, and descended into the channel. As she drifted down, she squeezed her nose closed and blew, clearing her ears.

Sam glanced often at her depth gauge and her pressure gauge to see how much air remained.

The floating flora and plankton mucked up the water. Three feet down the rock wall, she found a small cave-like opening and flashed her light into it. A big green moray eel popped out. Its head measured about the size of her leg. She back-pedaled, stirring the water. The moray gawked at her with its mouth agape. Sinister looking, but that's how the eel breathed. When Sam's light hit its eyes, the green-colored, snake-like creature slithered back into the hole. She swam closer, held up her light, and peeked inside. Red spiny lobsters, hiding at the back, clung to the rocks with their long antennae waving. The eel hunkered off to the side. She admired the symbiotic nature of the two. Well, actually three sea creatures. The moray eel would not hurt the lobsters because the favorite food of the moray equaled the octopus. The octopus loved to eat the lobster. So, the lobster and eel shared the same hole. However, if the lobster lost a leg or received another type of injury, the eel would eat it if given a chance.

No human body parts floated in this little cave.

As Sam turned around to descend further, something big, about the size of a man, went past the side of a large boulder. She'd seen a glimpse from the corner of her mask and couldn't tell whether it was a fish or another diver. No air bubbles interrupted the water.

What about the panga several yards away? Could it have had a diver? Were they just fishing? Oh, crap! Remove these ideas from your brain and search.

In and out, Sam weaved among the huge boulders. She swam a zigzag pattern, flashing her light into cracks, crevices, and under rocks. Small butterfly fish with yellow stripes and damsel fish darted around. But the only things she found: a few floating pieces of denim disturbed from the sand by her fins, an empty conch shell, a beer bottle, and a tangled fish line in one of the rocks with a green and white lure attached. She stuffed them all in her yellow mesh bag.

Swimming along the bottom, she noticed a blue Bic ink pen. When she went to put it in her bag with the rest of her treasures, she spied the imprint, but couldn't make out the words under water. *Maybe it's time I buy a mask with lenses.*

After dropping the pen into her bag, she locked the clasp, and glided past a large boulder with big waving fan coral. Her forward motion ceased. *Great*, she thought, tugging. *The coral entangled in the mesh.*

The regulator was yanked out of her mouth and the mask ripped off her face. She flailed her arms and kicked out her legs. Sam connected with a rock.

Think, she scolded herself. *Don't panic.* This had happened before on a dive a year ago.

I need to be calm. Think! Dang it, think! She reached around grasping for her regulator hose, found it, and put the mouthpiece back in. She held her nose, blew the water from the regulator, and took a breath. Through squinting eyes, she located her mask, and spent some time putting it back on, making sure she snorted all the water out.

Her eyes felt like sandpaper and burned from the salt. The sea water she swallowed made her cough and sputter.

She spiraled around in a 360. Up ahead a big blob went around a huge rock. She started to follow it, but got snagged on a piece of coral. She pulled free and started to continue when she peered at her gauge.

Eight hundred pounds of air remained. Seven hundred was the red zone where she needed to ascend to the surface and head back to the boat. Probably a piece of coral ripped off her mask and regulator. *But what about the blob?*

Had someone sneaked up behind her and done this?

Possibly. Her father dived with her many times in the past and as a joke, he used to swim up and grab her fins, scaring her. A diver's visibility was straight ahead, unless the diver swiveled his head or did three-hundred-sixty-degree spins.

Why would someone do this to me? Did any of the fishing contestants know how to dive?

As Sam drifted up, she continued spinning and scanning for anything big.

A huge shadow passed over. Above her, a large hammerhead shark swam in circles. Was that the blob?

Her breath came in quick and short. *I don't want to be fish food.* Images of being torn from limb to limb from sharp teeth invaded her thoughts.

"No!" she screamed.

She reminded herself to breathe. The shark continued circling, working its way down, closer and closer. Sam gripped her flashlight, holding it to use like a hammer. With her eyes wide open, she watched the predator swim, drawing closer in a zig zag pattern.

Banging and yelling filtered down through the water. The hammerhead swung around and swam directly toward her.

Water churned above Sam near the panga. She flinched, and the startled hammerhead swished its tail and darted faster. Her eyes grew wider. She elevated her flashlight.

The hammerhead zoomed past, missing her by inches.

She focused on the fish, then kicked with all her might for the surface. Sam had to stop at fifteen feet for three minutes for safety to help get rid of any nitrogen build-up absorbed while diving. The safety stop gave the body time to release the nitrogen at a slow pace. If it released too fast, bubbles could be created and lead to decompression sickness. Sam didn't need that to happen. She stared below her, spun 360's, and peered around. It took all her effort to stay the required time.

The entire stop she traced the area, telling herself to breathe and that hammerheads didn't like the taste of human flesh. *Oh, Lord, please let that be true.*

Down in the depths, she fixated on a dark blob. Was it heading up?

When she hit the three-minute mark, Sam kicked hard and fast for the last fifteen feet. She popped up near the motor.

The boat captain shut off the engine and smiled. "La señorita está muy loco!"

I'm not crazy.

At the back of the panga, the mate clutched the straps of her BC vest and hauled her inside.

Something brushed the boat and the mate fell on top of her.

Enrique yelled, "El tiburón?"

As she and the mate pushed up onto their knees, Sam saw a grey fin sink under the water.

Sam set her yellow bag on the bottom of the panga, unbuckled her weight belt, and grunted out of her buoyancy compensator vest. She tugged off her fins and mask.

"Gracías for starting the engine." Sam motioned toward the motor and smiled at the captain.

He grinned wide and nodded.

After gazing around, Sam discovered that the other panga no longer bobbed in the water. A dark spot in the distance raced toward Cabo.

"Were they fishing or diving?" She pointed at the speeding vessel.

"Watch you, not boat." Enrique shrugged. So did his mate.

The helper laid Sam's BC vest with the air tank on the bottom of the panga. The captain pulled the starter cord on the motor. The 70-horsepower engine coughed, sputtered, and then died.

Sam donned her life vest and rolled her eyes toward the heavens. Typical Baja outboard motors. One minute they ran, the next time they didn't.

Both Enrique and the mate tinkered with the engine a few minutes, and then the captain yanked on the cord again.

Nothing happened.

Thirty feet from the boat a grey fin disappeared under the water. *Why did the shark still hang around? Had I missed a body down there?*

The two men worked on the outboard some more. Wind whipped the waves into white foam. The panga bounced up and down harder, and the waves grew rougher.

"Señor, —" Sam cinched her life vest tighter and inhaled the smell of oil and gas.

"No problema," the captain told her.

Might not be a problem for him, but Sam shivered. She rubbed her stomach as it roiled with the motion of the boat.

Five minutes passed and she spotted another panga. "Señor, alla." She pointed over there. The mate stood and waved. The other vessel headed their way and glided into them. Fish littered the panga's bottom. When Sam smelled the stench, she wretched over the side into the water.

The men laughed, pointing at the "Gringa."

Sam glared at them and wiped her mouth. She must be a horrible shade of green.

Then all the men spoke in Spanish amongst themselves, pointing to the engine.

One of the other crew members bent down, picked up a rope and tossed it over. The mate tied it to the bow cleat and the two pangas sped toward the Cabo marina.

While being towed, Enrique and the helper continued working on the motor.

Now that they moved along, Sam felt a little less queasy. She packed her fins, mask, snorkel, regulator, BCV, and yellow mesh bag into her duffel.

When the two boats reached the opening to the harbor, Captain Enrique pulled on the starter cord. The 70 horsepower Johnson roared to life. The mate untied the rope and threw it to the other panga. The captain cruised through the harbor and docked at the boat ramp.

Sam climbed out and the mate handed over her gear. "Gracías, señores." Sam smiled. Enrique and his mate grinned. The captain saluted her.

Sam, happy to be on land again, lugged her duffel bag and rented equipment to the shop and turned in the dive tank.

In the restroom, she wriggled out of her wetsuit and peeled it down to her ankles. Then she stomped on one side and struggled a foot out. Tramping on the other side, she yanked her other foot from the wetsuit. She stuffed the neoprene suit into her bag. Her hands shook so badly, she found it hard to get dressed. *Am I shaking from the cold or the fright?*

With a deep breath, Sam calmed herself and threw her shift on over her bathing suit. She zipped up her duffel.

Outside the shop, she flagged down a taxi and negotiated a price. She had to hurry or she would be late for dinner. She didn't want the contestants to find out about her adventure.

The taxi driver pulled out and chugged toward the hotel.

Well, I didn't find a body, but did I have a run-in with a man or a shark? She didn't know for sure. She'd been scared. She loved diving and didn't get much time or chance living in Idaho to dive in saltwater. Being under the water refreshed her, but not this time.

Could the hammerhead have eaten the rest of the body? Too many questions and not enough answers.

The taxi drove up the winding, cobblestone driveway to the hotel. By the time the driver dropped her off in front, her body quit shaking. She took another deep breath and composed her nerves.

People milled about the lobby, some sitting in chairs reading newspapers, some heading to the restaurant and Whale Watch Bar—no one Sam knew.

In the elevator, she faced forward and smoothed down her wet hair. As the doors closed, someone partially lowered the newspaper they were reading, but quickly raised it again before Sam could see who it was.

She strode along the hallway to her room. A door opened. First instinct—freeze, but Sam tucked her head down and quickened her pace. An old, overweight Mexican, dressed in a business suit, walked out.

Whew. Sam exhaled and rolled her eyes. Not one of the fishing group. She unlocked the door and slipped inside her room.

In the shower, she rinsed her dive gear, laid it out in the bathroom, and stepped back in to rid the salt from her body. When she finished toweling off, she dressed.

Someone banged on her door.

6

Sam opened her bedroom door. Ed poised with an uplifted fist, about to knock again.

"Where've you been?" He lowered his arm.

"I overslept. Just finished with my shower." Not a total lie, but not the complete truth.

Ed ran a hand through his own damp hair. "Well, if we don't hurry, we'll miss the sunset and dinner."

"I need to dry my hair."

"Don't have time. Your hair looks fine."

They hurried into the Whale Watch Bar and restaurant. At the table, Ed pulled out a chair for Sam. "Sorry we're late." He sat next to her.

"Oh, look." Sam pointed out to sea. "The sun is going down."

Before the men could question her, the last of the big ball of orange sank into the vastness of blue, turning the horizon magenta. "Oh, my God, there's the green flash at the exact moment the sun vanished into the ocean." Sam clapped along with everyone else in the bar.

The youngest contestant asked, "What did we just see?"

"You don't know what a green flash is?" Sam couldn't believe he didn't know.

"No, I've never seen or heard of one."

"I have a few times." Sam smiled. "It's an optical phenomenon. Green flashes occur when the Earth's atmosphere causes the light from the sun to separate out into different colors. Usually happens just as the sun vanishes into the horizon. Sometimes it happens as it rises, too."

"Wow, an awesome sight. Thanks, Sam, for pointing it out." The contestant smiled.

The men appeared all clean and dressed in shirts and pants, some still had wet hair. Sam smelled different aftershaves, which mingled with the salty breeze and the cigar and cigarette smoke.

The purple sundress with a red sash that Sam wore didn't have flare like Linda's dress. But it still fit even though the extra ten pounds made it snug. If only she didn't overeat when she worried.

"You always wear purple?" Mark's Brut aftershave wafted over her, and his wet hair reminded Sam of hers and Ed's.

Had his girlfriend ever left the bar? Linda still sat with her packages next to her chair, or maybe they were new ones.

"Purple's my favorite color." Twenty years shy of being able to join the Red Hat Society, Sam liked wearing purple and red. She would blend right in with the group when she reached the ripe old age of fifty.

Frank frowned and mumbled, "Your hair's all wet. What have you been up to?"

"Dragged her out of the shower." Ed smiled. "She overslept."

The youngest man in the group winked. "Catching the biggest shark must have worn her out." The others laughed.

A tall, dark-haired waitress rushed over. "What may I get you?"

"Three pitchers of margaritas and a bucket of beer." Mark glanced around the table. "Anything else to drink?"

"That'll get us started." Frank grinned and held up his half-empty Corona bottle.

"How about food?" The server held her notebook, ready to write their orders.

"Yes, please." Sam studied the menu. "I'll have fish tacos."

"Me, too." Ed placed his menu on the table.

Mark ordered beef enchiladas, and the others ordered various Mexican dishes. Linda ordered a salad.

"Put the food and drinks all on one bill." Mark lit up a cigar and blew a smoke ring. "Tonight's all on me."

The men cheered. They discussed fishing the Sea of Cortez and drank until the waitress returned with their orders.

When it came, the men gobbled their food and drank their margaritas and beer with much lip smacking and belly rubbing.

Linda ate her salad, a tiny bite at a time, and listened, smiling and nodding occasionally.

"This meal is delicious, Mark. Thank you." Sam grinned, savoring her fish tacos.

After dinner, everyone lingered in the bar. The more the men drank, the better they accepted being beaten by a "mere woman," as they called Sam.

All of the men at some point left the bar, claiming they needed to use the bathroom.

The mariachis strolled by and stopped near their table. "Señor," the violinist called out, looking over their table, "you wish to hear your favorite song we play for you on Tuesday night?"

When no one answered, they played Spanish Eyes. Since the violinist surveyed each person, and even behind their table, Sam couldn't figure out who he'd been talking to. Mark said he came in on Thursday. The rest arrived on Friday. Could the band member be confused?

Sam sat between Ed and Mark. She sipped her beer, tried to ignore the smoke, and listened to the music. The men bragged about fishing and talked about construction.

Everyone at the table in some way or another worked in the building trade, except, of course, Linda, who sat on the other side of Mark. The woman looked around the bar, crossed her legs and swung her foot up and down. She rolled her eyes and sipped her margarita. When Linda laid a hand on Mark's thigh, she sighed.

Sam wondered how she could find out if any one in the group scuba dived. She came up with an idea. "Hey, Linda, have you ever gone scuba diving?"

"Oh, no, I could never do that. Don't really like the water."

"How about any of you guys?" Sam watched the men for their reactions.

"I went with my wife once." The youngest man frowned. "Didn't like it much."

Mark scuba dives." Linda patted his knee and smiled.

"Hey, Frank," one of the men said. "Didn't you say you dove in the Navy?"

"Yes, a long time ago." Frank lit another cigarette and grabbed another bottle of beer.

"Ed used to dive back in the day." Mark blew another cigar smoke ring.

It drifted toward Sam and she coughed.

Ed smiled. "Haven't done that for a long time."

I guess that's why I didn't know.

Around eight, the big honcho policeman ambled into the bar and came over to the table.

"Ah, señor, care for a cerveza?" Mark tipped his Pacifico beer bottle toward him in one hand and held the lit cigar in the other.

"No gracías, señor," the policeman answered. "We checked the hotels and motels. No one's missing, and no one has reported any accidents in this area. There's nothing more we can do."

"Thank you," Mark nodded. "We all appreciate your effort."

The policeman glowered at Sam, and waited for a reply.

"Gracías." For once, Sam closed her mouth and didn't say anything more than thank you.

The man sneered. "You're welcome. Are you staying over?"

"No." Mark puffed on his cigar. "We're flying out tomorrow."

The honcho smiled and swaggered away.

Mark turned up his mouth into his all-knowing grin that Sam detested. "See, no missing tourists. Satisfied?"

"No." Sam shrugged. "But at least he checked."

"And now, Samantha, I suggest you let it rest." Mark took a sip of his beer.

She cocked her head. *Wish he would quit calling me Samantha. Let him think I'll let it rest.*

Mark raised an eyebrow. He puffed on his cigar and blew a smoke ring that elongated and dissipated.

I hate the foul stench of that cigar. Does he have to blow those rings?

Five minutes later, Sam yawned. "Sorry guys, I'm beat. If you'll excuse me, I'm heading to bed."

Ed scooted back his chair. Sam held up her hand. "No, stay. I'm bushed. You party on. I'm going shopping first thing in the morning before we leave for the airport. I'll catch you later."

Linda leaned forward and smiled. "Good to know you shop too."

The men laughed.

Sam shook her head and walked away.

Inside her room, near the bed, cold seeped through her body. Her wide-open stare hurt her eyes. She stifled a scream.

A note lay on her pillow. She glanced around, scooped up the folded paper and opened it. The note read: Since you need the money, don't do anything further.

Sam spun a 180 and stared at her door. It had been locked. *Who knows I need the money? How did they get into my room?*

Thoughts of her dive and the shark's guts invaded her mind. Sweat broke out on her forehead and she felt it drip down. She wiped the beads away. Her heartbeat felt as if it revved up.

Is it possible for me to solve this? I'm not going to let some jerk tell me what to do. What if it's the killer? Killer? Where did that thought come from? Maybe someone murdered that person and fed him to the fishes? She shuddered, chewed on her lip, and then took a deep breath.

Should she call the police? The big honcho policeman's silhouette and facial expression came to her mind. He wouldn't do anything for her.

Footsteps resounded in the hallway. She wanted to crawl under the bed, but knew she wouldn't fit. She couldn't swallow. The footsteps receded. She sat on the bed and inhaled deeply.

Sam couldn't control her shaking hand. She stood, stumbled to the dresser, and put the note on top. *What am I going to do? Oh, for Heaven's sake, get a grip.* She ran out of her room and back down to the front desk.

"May I help you, miss?"

Should I ask how someone could get into my room? No, bribing a maid or telling the desk clerk about a lost key would be easy here in Baja. One time she'd stayed in a Baja hotel on the first floor where the window had been installed backwards so that anyone from the outside could open the window.

She blurted out, "Do you have a telephone directory of the area?"

"Yes." The clerk reached down and put one on the counter.

Back in her room, Sam placed a chair under the door handle. Then she called several hotels from nearby towns and even La Paz, asking, "Are any of your guests missing?" The answer—always a firm, "No."

Might be a dumb idea to call hotels, but I have to try. Maybe the police did their job, but... Someone wanted her to stop snooping. Who and why?

Being adopted gave her abandonment issues. She hated those feelings. Took away her confidence.

In a way, this piece of human flesh with a birthmark on it was like someone abandoned the person. Her parents loved her, but she could never get over the feeling of being discarded by her birth parents.

And when she lost her cousin Jennifer, who was still a missing person... how could she let this go?

She dialed another hotel. "Yes, hello. Are you missing any guests?" Another no.

An hour passed. She gave up calling, lay on the bed, and fixated on the ceiling fan going around. She won fifty grand, but at what price?

First thing she would do when she got home—pay back her dad and his cronies for the $5,000 seed money. Then she could work on her financial problem, she hoped. Maybe she could recoup some of the money from that stupid accountant for his bad advice. She wished she hadn't followed his investment idea. Lost too much, but she would have to try to retrieve some of it back. Sam stashed that thought away, and soon unbidden pictures of the bull shark's guts intruded.

Her happiness dampened as she focused on the duck shape. Did the dead person leave behind a loved one? How had he died? How'd he end up in the sea in that shark?

7

Sunday morning the alarm rang loudly. Sam startled awake, reached out, and slammed down the button on the black clock. A rooster crowed.

The chair she put under the doorknob still sat at an angle, wedged tight.

She felt her heart racing in her chest and breathed deeply. *My head feels like a man jack-hammering on cement inside my skull. I shouldn't have had that last beer. Is my headache from the beer, or the fact that someone has a strong interest in my not pursuing the mysterious death and has free access to my room?*

How could I have fallen asleep? What if someone tried to get in while I slept? Oh, my God, what have I gotten myself into? Get a grip, girl! She prayed Ed in the next room hadn't heard her alarm. It was early, but she needed time to get dressed, check a few more hotels, and purchase some presents, especially for Paula who agreed to babysit her dog. She wanted to go shopping without Ed.

Ed. Why'd she beg him to come on this trip? So she could sort out her feelings for him.

Their working relationship—perfect. He designed a house and she landscaped it.

Their personal life? She smiled, thinking about last Christmas when he'd played Santa Claus for the foster children. Helping him dress for the part, she only added a little rouge to his cheeks and a fake mustache, beard, and wig. A perfect resemblance in the face to a jolly old Saint Nick. She had to use a big feather pillow to fatten him up though.

He was three years older and, unfortunately, hopelessly in love with her. Sam cared for him, but she didn't feel she had been hit by lightning with Ed. When she'd been near Mark, the strikes felt too close, and she would get burned if she didn't jump away. Thankfully, Linda saved her from the danger.

Sam shook off thoughts of both men, threw back the covers, and climbed out of bed. She splashed cold water on her face and shimmied into a clean pair of jeans. After slipping her purple-flowered blouse on, she dabbed on a touch of makeup and combed her hair. The chair under the door knob made her feel a bit safer, and she set it aside. The bedroom door creaked as she opened it. She sneaked along the hallway, crept down the steps instead of using the elevator, and hurried out of the hotel's front door. She hoped no one from the contest saw her leave.

Men and women opened up their shops as Sam strolled by. A few swept the sidewalks. She sauntered along the streets, stopping to inquire at some of the hotels she passed. "Excuse me, are you missing any guests? Any of the locals gone?" Most of the receptionists looked at her as if she was an alien.

At the last hotel, she asked the receptionist, "How do I find the glass factory?" Sam knew about it and wished to buy blown glass for her best friend Paula. The woman wanted children so badly that she even babysat Sam's dog, Goldie, to get practice in nurturing.

Since Sam made no headway on discovering if anyone was missing, she took a minute to refresh her thinking at the glass factory.

The glass blowers blew down tubes that created different shapes. The performance filled her with a bit of peace.

The molten glass of various colors twirled and bulged and formed bottles, jars, and glasses. Even standing behind the rope, heat burned her face. Beads of sweat glistened off the blowers' foreheads.

Sam wandered through the shop, admiring the many shelves with colored bottles, jars, bowls and different shaped glassware. She found the perfect gift for Paula and a few other friends.

Outside the shop, a taxi drove away and no others were in the parking lot. Sam hefted her bags and trudged toward her hotel, confident she could flag down a cab.

A block away, she stepped off the sidewalk to cross one of the paved streets. She heard the whine of a car engine racing. Tires squealed. Sam stopped, paralyzed. A van sped toward her at top speed.

Move.

She lunged out of the way.

One of her bags swung upwards and the vehicle hit it, spinning Sam. She heard glass breaking, lost her balance, and fell. She hit the ground and glanced up. No brake lights came on as the van sped down the street, rounded a corner, and disappeared.

She always considered that Mexican drivers were irrational, but this felt deliberate.

"Are you all right?" someone asked her.

"I saw the entire thing." A woman dressed in shorts, a flowered blouse and a big, floppy hat pointed down the road. "That van headed directly for you and didn't even slow down."

A man reached down, gathered up her purchases, and helped Sam stand. He handed her the bags that had been strewn around. "You could have been killed."

Sam, too stunned to speak, only nodded. The truth—she'd thought the same thing.

Had someone seen me leave this morning? Sam told the contestants last night she planned on going shopping. She thought about yesterday afternoon's diving incident with the regulator and mask. Maybe the coral hadn't ripped it off. Maybe the shadow she'd seen—not the hammerhead shark.

Another person asked, "Are you all right?"

Sam nodded. "I'm, I'm okay, everyone. Thanks so much."

Her packages had been strewn about. The lady at the glassblower's factory had wrapped her purchases with bubble wrap, but that breaking glass sound concerned her. Sam jiggled one bag and glass rattled. The other one sounded secure.

"You should call the police," the tourist-looking woman said.

A picture of the big honcho officer popped into Sam's head—his sneer and the way he treated her. She shivered. A knot formed in her stomach. She didn't want to have another run-in with him.

"Did anyone see the driver or get a license plate number?" Sam waited for the few people around her to answer.

No one did.

"Thank you all so much for your help. I'm okay. I'll just flag a taxi." Sam waved her arms and a yellow cab pulled over.

She sat in the back seat reliving the incident. She chewed on her lip. Could any of this be related to the birthmark? Or simply an accident?

The driver parked in front of her hotel. She reached over the seat and paid him. Then she rushed up to her room, not spotting anyone she knew, but didn't look too closely.

Her heart still beat wildly from the brush with the van. She'd lost some presents, but not her life. *If I hadn't moved when I did...*

Bile rose in her throat. Sam ran to the bathroom and vomited. At the sink, she rinsed her mouth out. Not able to sit still, she paced her room.

After glancing at her watch, she realized she had to get ready to leave. She threw clothes and her toiletries into her suitcase and gathered up her dive gear from the bathroom. All the items went into her duffle, except for the mesh bag. She remembered the pen and piece of denim she'd found and stuffed inside. With all the exciting things that had happened, she'd forgotten.

She grabbed the bag to open its clasp.

Someone banged on her door.

Sam shoved the yellow bag in with her gear. She went to her door and whispered, "Who is it?"

When no one answered, she boosted her voice and asked again.

"Me," a man answered.

"Ed!" Sam yanked open the door.

He stood with his fist uplifted to knock again. "Where've you been?"

Sam peered down the hall both ways, jerked Ed into her room, and shut the door.

"I went out this morning."

"Oh, that's right." Ed studied the room and her packages. "You did say you were going shopping."

"Yes, I did, and someone…" Sam took a deep breath and muttered, "tried to run me down."

"What? Are you okay?" Ed clutched Sam's shoulders. "You should have taken me with you. The people in this town drive crazy. I shouldn't let you out of my sight."

"No, Ed." Sam opened her eyes wide. "You don't understand. Someone *deliberately* tried to run me down."

Ed blinked several times and dropped his grasp on her shoulders. He plopped down on the bed. "Sam, I know these guys weren't happy about you winning the contest, but they wouldn't try to hurt you."

Sam sank down next to Ed. "I hadn't thought of that reason."

"What other reason would there be?"

"The body parts in my shark." Sam gazed at Ed. "Someone even left me a message saying to back off."

"Where is it?"

At the dresser, Sam ran her hand over the top. Nothing but dust. No note sat on top.

"It should be right here." She fell to her knees and scanned under the dresser. Then she pulled it away from the wall, and peered behind it.

Nothing there.

She rummaged through each drawer, finding no trace of the threat she'd seen. Had she packed it? She spun and stared at her suitcase near the bed. "Where is it?" She hurried over to the nightstand, she lifted up the lamp.

Nothing.

BIRTHMARK KILLER | 45

The entire time, Ed sat watching her with a furrowed brow.

When she straightened up, Ed raised an eyebrow. "Are you sure there was a note? You were pretty tired and had a few beers last night. Maybe you dreamed it."

"No, I saw and read the message, I think."

"You don't sound convinced. It's ridiculous. Why would anyone want to hurt you because of what your shark ate?" Ed rubbed the back of his neck. "I think you're getting paranoid."

Sam focused on him. Could he be right? *No, look what happened on my dive.* For some reason, she held back telling Ed all about these incidents.

He and Mark were good friends. Sam didn't want Mark to know anything. *Besides, Ed might think I'm nuts and figure I belonged in a mental institute.*

"Maybe I should stick around another day or two?" Sam wondered if that would do any good.

"Look, if you're right," Ed said, "and I'm not saying you are, but number one, the guys in the group are all leaving today. If this is about the shark, one way or the other, there's no one here to care, so you might as well leave on the plane."

"I guess you make a good point." Did someone need that prize money more desperately than she? If the van almost mowing her down had nothing to do with the contest, then what?

Could one of the contestants have something to do with the death of who got eaten by my shark?

"Maybe getting out of Baja is a good idea. I do miss my home in Sandpoint." At least there, she could search the Internet from the safety of her own home.

"Yes." Ed smiled. "Going home is good."

"You're right. I'm anxious to get back."

Ed nodded and smiled broader.

They went downstairs to the open-air bar and restaurant. The men sat near the table they'd occupied last night. The ocean waves lapped at the shore down below. Rock and roll music blared from the T.V. above the bar. The slight breeze wafted in the salty, sea-smelling air.

Mark spotted them and waved them over. "Hey, Samantha, where've you been?"

"Shopping." Ed shrugged his shoulders. "Remember, she told us last night."

"Didn't know I was keeping you waiting." Sam licked her lips. "Where's Linda?"

"Sleeping in and packing. She doesn't eat breakfast."

"Well, I'm sure you're all starved, so let's eat." She loved huevos a la Mexicana, a favorite for her breakfast. But the brush with the van killed her appetite. Now all she wanted—to hurry up and get out of Baja.

Most of the others ordered huevos rancheros. Sam ordered toast and fresh-squeezed orange juice.

She took a bite of her toast and noticed Frank glaring at her, but he didn't say anything.

One of the fishermen continued the whining from last night about losing to a woman, and drew the rest of them into a lengthy discussion about women versus men in sports.

While they talked, Sam eyed each man. When her gaze landed on Mark, he smiled.

She shivered. Why did he make her nervous?

Sam munched on her toast and listened.

They avoided any mention of the chunk of flesh with the birthmark on the skin, which established questions in her mind.

When she polished off her toast, she took a sip of orange juice. Frank still ogled her. "Something wrong, Frank?"

"No, not at all." He finished his meal and lit a cigarette.

Linda sashayed in, and Mark pulled up a chair for her.

Ed cleared his throat. "So, what did everyone do this morning?"

Linda grinned. "Mark and I slept late."

Frank growled. "You call that sleeping?"

Not everyone answered, but most of them informed her they'd packed and prepared to leave.

They boarded the airplane after brunch and flew toward the layover in L.A. Sam sighed with relief. From L.A., they'd all go their separate ways. When home, Sam would start her search. Would she be able to find out anything?

8

That woman stays so calm.

Last night, she covered the reason for her wet hair without divulging her diving expedition. She is too clever. Who goes diving for the rest of a body? I guess Samantha does.

I think back.

Yanking the regulator out of her mouth and unmasking her—no deterrent.

I leave a note for her to back off.

Then this morning I decide to scare her while she's shopping. Unbelievable she's checking the hotels for missing people. She's not going to give up.

I can't let her figure this out.

The glass blowing factory—I like it. Very interesting. I see why she enjoys it. I leave before she spots me—although with my disguise, she cannot recognize me. I walk down the street. *Ah, someone's forgotten to take the keys in this van.*

Convenient. And, perfect.

I start the vehicle. I spot her walking down the street. I race the engine and peel out.

Whew! That's close. If that does not scare her, nothing will.

I take the note from her room. This should upset her even more.
If it's avoidable, I really don't want to kill her.
But I have to stop her from searching.

9

Sam sat near the airplane window, Ed in the middle, and Mark on the aisle seat. She gazed out as the plane taxied away from Cabo. Pictures of her shark and dead body parts invaded her mind.

"You okay?" Ed patted her hand.

"Yes, just reminiscing."

"I know you were brave to go out in that panga with your fear and all."

"Those boats are quite sea-worthy." Sam smiled at Ed.

"Right." He raised an eyebrow and nodded. "You saw how the mate rode standing in the front and bounced with the panga, holding on to a flimsy rope? I would think lots of fishermen fall overboard. And, you know, sharks eat anything."

How did Ed figure out she was thinking about the dead person? Those Mexican pangas were safe. But, the boat captain's mate did almost fall in when Mark brought his mako alongside and that shark went ballistic.

When Captain Enrique had reached down to kill Mark's mako, it thrashed and gnashed at the fiberglass. Its sharp teeth chomped into the side and the panga had rocked sideways, almost knocking the mate overboard.

"I understand sharks eat all kinds of things." Sam bit her lip. "But the police honcho told us no one was missing."

"You said yourself sharks swim for miles."

"Ed, aren't you curious?" Sam furrowed her brow and waited for his answer.

"In a way. But nothing can be done. How come it bothers you so much?"

Could Mark or any of the others sitting behind and in front hear her? The air swished down from Sam's vent. The roar of the engine made her head ache. A soft snore erupted. When Sam leaned forward, she noticed Mark's closed eyes. Across the aisle, Linda read a book and wore headphones. Sam rested her head back against the seat and sighed. "I'm sorry, Ed. It does upset me; can't help it."

"Is this eating at you because of your cousin's disappearance?"

"Yes. Partly. Can't stand not knowing what happened to Jennifer. It's been over two years."

"And still nothing." Ed clasped her hand. "I'm sorry this is hard for you."

"It eats away at my heart every day."

Ed nodded. "You said partly. What's the other reason?"

"My being adopted."

"What's Jennifer's disappearance or your adoption have to do with you finding out who's in your shark?"

"The adoption thing is a complicated abandonment issue. But think about it. If you were home waiting for your loved one, wouldn't you worry? Want to know what happened?"

"Of course—"

"Well, I know what it's like to feel abandoned. It's no fun. All those questions."

"Yes, but—"

"It's not my nature to let it rest, Ed. I have to figure this out. The person in my shark must have had someone, somewhere who cared about him. The one left behind will always wonder why he didn't come home, and will never have closure. I need to help."

Ed inclined his head. "Did you ever learn about your birth parents?"

Oh, boy, that's a loaded question. Sam still wondered if anyone searched for her. She didn't want to hurt her parents who loved and cherished her; they were so good to her. But that didn't stop her from being curious about her roots.

She'd placed her name, birthdate, and place of birth out into the Internet highway to see if anyone showed any interest about her. A year had passed; nothing happened.

In the state she was born in, adoption records were still kept sealed. She would have to do some serious digging. Maybe engage a search angel: those wonderful people who helped you search. It was free, or you could donate if you wished. In some states and cases, it wasn't that easy to discover birth parents.

Maybe the time had arrived to pursue it further. This piece of skin with a mark on it showing up—a definite sign. Sam shuddered at the thought of abandonment issues assaulting her all over again. The one thing that made her feel insecure—when no one wanted her.

"You don't look so good. A bit pale. You sure you're okay?" Ed squeezed her hand.

"Yes." Sam told him about her attempted search.

He remained silent.

"Have to do this," Sam whispered. "Need to try and find out who my shark ate."

"Yeah." Ed rubbed the back of her hand with his thumb. "Guess I see your point. Where do we start?"

"You'll help?"

"Of course."

Sam leaned forward again and peeked at Mark. His eyes remained closed, his breathing slow. "Let's not mention this to anyone. My curiosity seemed disconcerting to them."

Mark scared her. When he looked at her, her heart raced. Sam didn't appreciate those looks. She couldn't understand if those feelings were an attraction or if he.... Could Ed tell? She'd breathe easier when Mark parted their company.

When Sam glanced over at him, Ed scrunched closer to her. "Screw 'em. They don't believe it's possible to figure this out. Most of these guys do things for profit. If there's none, they won't be bothered."

"Maybe. Weird it turned out this Mark Randall was your old roommate. Anyway," Sam continued, "finding out who this person is— it's the right thing to do."

Ed straightened in his seat. "You have any ideas on how to do this search?"

"A piece at a time."

"I enjoy putting jigsaw puzzles together."

"Good." Sam rested her head against the seat and closed her eyes. She remembered her father's dermatologist had taken a picture of her dad's birthmark and wrote an article and published it. Maybe some doctor had done the same with this one. "First thing, I'll look for any published articles or books on birthmarks."

The smell of Ed's Brut aftershave drifted past. That odor reminded her of her teenage years. Brut always revved her insides—not for the man, but for the scent.

Sam thought about Ed. He played jazz on the piano and Sam enjoyed listening. He did try fishing with her in Idaho around Lake Pend Oreille, and in the streams in the mountains, he was a trooper. Years ago, he scuba dived. Wonder if he'd take it up again and go with her. And, besides, the man liked to solve puzzles, same as she.

At least he was willing to help, unlike his friend. Maybe Mark worked too much, or money equaled the only important motive to him, but couldn't he have been more curious?

"When we get back to Sandpoint," Sam said in a low voice, "I'll start with the library. See what they have on them."

"Why don't you look on the Internet?" Ed asked.

"I'll do both, but I love the atmosphere of the library, browsing through books and turning pages in a magazine, feeling the textures. And, I savor the smell of books."

At LAX, Sam scanned the screen for their departure gate to Spokane, Washington. One by one the other fishermen nodded as they sauntered off. A couple of the rivals managed a good-bye.

Ed and Sam had a long layover in L.A. She wondered how she would tell him she planned to meet a friend, when Mark, Frank, and Linda stopped near them.

Frank asked, "What flight are we on?"

"We?" Sam gaped at him, her mouth wide.

Frank laughed. "No one told you you're not rid of me yet?"

"Nor me." Mark grinned. "I've wired the fifty grand to your bank in Sandpoint. I have to sign some papers before the money is officially yours. I've changed my flight. I'm traveling with you."

"You're all flying to Spokane on American at 9:12 P.M. with us?" Sam had her fill of arrogant, macho men, specifically Mark. He made her feel as if she walked on sharp rocks barefoot.

"Sort of." Mark slapped Frank on the back. "This man's a contractor in Spokane. He and Ed talked so much about Sandpoint, I decided to look the area over. I'll stay at the Edgewater Resort."

"Not me." Linda kissed Mark. "I'm going home." She told the rest good-bye, and sashayed off, pulling her red carry-on, heading for baggage claim.

The thought of Mark's flying to Idaho made Sam cringe. It didn't have anything to do with his handsome features; more like the sinister look she received when talking about the birthmark in her shark.

This contest had been a fishing challenge for Sam. It surprised her she'd won, but the windfall would help her out of her jam. One that somebody knew something about. Had someone known her so well, that by leaving her that note, they knew she would do the opposite and look deeper into who her shark had eaten?

Did Mark leave me the message? Why did he have to come to Sandpoint?

Sam observed Ed's expression. "You knew?"

He stared at his shoes and mumbled, "Yes."

"This works out perfect then." Sam grabbed her purple carry-on. "I'm supposed to meet an old college friend here. You, Mark, and Frank pal around until our flight. Meet you back here later." Sam marched off before anyone could answer.

While going through the airport, she thought she saw her friend Paula's husband Jim, but knew it couldn't be. They were home taking care of her dog. Then she realized the man only resembled her friend. His hair was styled different than Jim's. After all, she only saw his back. *What's wrong with me? I have to get my paranoia under control.*

10

At the Spokane airport, Frank slapped Mark on the back. "Thanks for a great trip. See you later. Bye, Sam. Congrats on winning." He marched off.

Mark insisted on driving Samantha's Ford Ranger. She climbed into the jump seat behind the passenger side and when Ed didn't object, she felt miffed. *Why is Mark so controlling? I despise it.* She kept her mouth shut.

"Okay if I smoke my cigar?" Mark pulled the stogie out of his pocket before starting the engine.

"Not in my pickup."

He placed the cigar back in his pocket, started the Ranger, and drove out of the parking garage.

They proceeded east on I-90 from the airport. Spokane's skyline shone bright. Tall buildings, their lights twinkling in the night, stood against the clear starlit sky.

On the drive to Sandpoint, Sam dozed, but woke when they hit a pot hole. She spotted the long bridge going into her hometown.

Moonbeams glistened off the rippling water on the east side of the bridge. Lake Pend Oreille, carved during the ice age, stretched northeast. A train rumbled across the railroad bridge angling away from them. To the west of the long bridge, the Pend Oreille River flowed so wide, it appeared as if it were part of the lake.

"What are the mountains called rimming the lake?" Mark asked.

"The Green Monarchs." Ed motioned toward them. "Sam does a lot of hiking, fishing, and hunting in there."

"You hunt?" Mark asked.

Sam folded her arms over her chest. "Don't sound so surprised. I can shoot the balls off a deer at a hundred and fifty yards."

"Really?" Mark gawked at her in the rearview mirror.

"It's true." Ed laughed. "Last year hunting with her father, she shot a buck. It ran off and her dad chased the deer, and eventually put it down. Said the animal ran up the hill, stopped and would turn and stare at him, practically begging to be shot. When he went to gut the deer— no balls. Figured her shot castrated the poor thing."

Mark didn't say anything.

They crossed the bridge and followed the highway through downtown. Mark waited for one old guy out late to pass through the crosswalk before turning from First to Cedar. "That building is lit up. Looks interesting. What is it?"

"Used to be called the Cedar Street Bridge." Sam nodded toward the shops. "Coldwater Creek, a mail-order giant, took the bridge over and put in outlet stores and a deli. Cedar Street Bridge is built with massive tamarack logs and passive solar windows. Now it's the Cedar Street Bridge Public Market. All the shops overlook Sand Creek. It's the only marketplace on a bridge in the United States."

Mark pulled into Samantha's driveway next to Ed's truck. The car headlights lit up the columned front porch of her little Queen Anne Victorian house with a widow's peak and stained-glass windows.

"This must have set you back a piece." Mark exited the truck. He studied the house and nodded. "Nice."

Sam gazed heavenward after she scrambled out. Did everything have to be about money with this guy? While Mark and Ed retrieved her bags from the truck, she hurried up onto the porch. The scent from the lilac bush at the side of the stairs welcomed her home. Quickly leaning down, she wrenched the key out from under the potted lemon geranium, hoping the darkness prevented Ed or Mark from seeing. With the help of her pocket flashlight, she unlocked the door.

The men came up the steps with her bags and into the front hall. The hallway's medium-colored oak floors stretched down the hall and into the back bedroom. The living room off to the left had the same floors, but with a blue, green and brown, wool area rug. The same flooring extended into the room across the hall from the living room.

"Great wood floors." Mark tapped his foot on them. "What time do you want to meet at the bank?"

Never. "How about around eleven?"

"Fine, Samantha. Before Ed takes me to the resort, may I use your bathroom?"

"Yes. And please bring my dive bag to put in the laundry room, and then I'll show you the bathroom."

Sam strolled back from down the hallway. Ed remained standing at the base of the stairs still holding onto the handle of her carry-on. He reminded her of a lost puppy. "Leave that there. I'll deal with it later."

They wandered into the living room to wait for Mark. Sam wanted to go into the parlor room across the hall, now the office, and open up her emails off the computer, but she'd have to be at work in a couple of hours. *I'll wait 'til later.*

"You look tired." Ed leaned closer to her.

"I'm bushed. I've a big day ahead of me tomorrow."

Ed looked at his watch. "You mean today. The Lowell landscaping?"

"Yeah, and get to the library to do that research."

"What about Goldie?" Ed asked.

Sam pictured her red-haired whippet crossed with lab dog jumping up and down, with tail wagging non-stop. She smiled. "I'll pick up Goldie tomorrow after work."

"Are you sure doing that research is wise?"

"Ed, I thought you agreed with me?"

"I know, I know. But Mark—"

"You weren't supposed to discuss it with anyone."

"Don't get excited. He brought it up. Not too keen on the idea."

"It's none of his business." Sam didn't want Mark to have any opinion. "Don't say anything more to him about it. I'm doing this. If you're still going to help, how about meeting me at the library around noon, and then we'll go to lunch?"

Ed kissed her on the cheek. They hadn't progressed much further than that in this relationship and Sam felt thankful. Since her last bad relationship, she wasn't in any hurry to jump in and get hurt once more. "Sure, how about twelve-thirty?"

"Fine. I should be through with Mark at the bank by then."

"You're not inviting him to lunch?"

"No. And don't you do it."

"Sure, Sam, whatever you want."

Ed hugged her. Over his shoulder, Sam spotted Mark leaning on the living room door jamb, his arms folded, one foot crossed over the other. He wore a sneer or a grin, she couldn't tell which.

"Thanks for the use of your bathroom. If you two aren't ready, I'll wait outside."

Sam pulled back, her face growing hot.

Ed smiled. "No, I'm ready. Bye, Sam." He strutted away.

"Good-bye, Samantha." Mark followed Ed out.

Sam locked the door and trudged upstairs with her small suitcase. She dropped it on the floor and fell on the bed, too tired to change her clothes or unpack.

Would the birthmark lead her to a name?

11

The next morning, the snooze alarm sounded, waking Sam with a start. She eyed the clock and jumped out of bed. *Must have hit the snooze button a couple of times before and fallen back asleep.* Now if she didn't hurry, she would be late. Her father had drilled into her the importance of never being tardy, a truth she normally followed.

The suitcase lay on the floor and she almost tripped over it. She stood it up and put the purple carry-on over in the corner. She'd deal with it later.

She changed into a pair of blue jeans and a flowered shirt. She took the stairs two at a time, and rushed out the door. Sam climbed into her pickup and took a few minutes to drive to the one-hour photo shop on Fifth Street. She didn't have any photo paper and wanted printed pictures as well as a C.D. They had an outside drop slot, and she deposited her camera's digital chip with instructions.

The drive to her office didn't take long and she arrived one minute before her usual time.

"Hi, Sam, welcome back. How was Baja?"

She smiled at Hank who sat in a truck about to leave. "I caught the biggest shark. Had a great time. How's the Lowell project going?"

"On my way there now with the crew. We're on track. You coming out?"

"Do I have paperwork?"

Her right-hand man smiled. "A bit."

"Maybe I'll catch you this afternoon. Tomorrow for sure." Sam watched him drive off.

A mound of paperwork stacked on her oak desk awaited her. She sat in her swivel chair, took a deep breath, and delved into it. When finished with that, Sam went over landscaping plans until 10:30.

While looking at plans, images of tennis shoes and chunks of human flesh spilling out from the shark kept invading her thoughts. So many questions—her insides churned and she fought back bile. Her shoulders ached. Could she find the answers? Did she want to?

At 10:40, Sam left the office with plenty of time to stop at the photo shop. She retrieved her camera chip, a C.D. and two packets of the pictures she'd asked them to print out. Before heading to the bank, she took a moment to glance at the prints until finding the one she wanted. The close-up showed the brown mark. *That definitely resembles a duck.*

<hr />

The public parking lot had one spot remaining. She shut off her pickup, put the chip, C.D. and photos in her purse, locked the doors, and headed for the bank. From half a block away, Sam spied Mark, dressed in Levi's and a crimson Polo shirt. He paced outside the bank. As she got closer, smoke from his foul-smelling cigar drifted into the air. "How do you find Sandpoint so far?" she asked.

"Quaint little town. Friendly. Linda would love shopping at the Cedar Street Bridge Public Market. All those boutique shops, local artisans, bistro and coffee shops."

Sam laughed. Mark ground out the cigar on the sidewalk and held the door open for her to enter the bank. The squashed brown mass disgusted her. Not moving, she crossed her arms and tapped her foot. Mark didn't take the hint to pick it up. She stomped over, leaned down, and with two fingers, snatched it up and threw the stogie in the trash can. Mark still held the door. Sam marched through and heard him chuckle. Why did she let him irritate her?

At the manager's desk, Mark took charge. Samantha sat tapping her foot, biting her tongue.

When Mark finished, Sam asked, "Could you wait over there, please?" She waved to a seat by the front window. "I've some banking business to take care of."

"You want me to leave after all we've been through?" Mark lifted an eyebrow and smirked.

"Yes." Sam smiled, knowing he wasn't as shocked as he made out to be.

Mark sighed. "Independent, aren't you? I'll be right over there." He took a seat near the front.

Sam made arrangements to pay back her dad and his cronies. She put the balance in her savings account. Later, she would come back when Mark wasn't near her. First she had to decide how to deal with her financial problem.

Sam exited the bank with Mark striding right behind her.

"What's got you smiling like a Cheshire cat?" Mark cruised alongside of her down the sidewalk.

"Nothing. Feeling flush. I think your men feel quite disappointed that a woman won the money."

"First, they aren't 'my' men. Second, too bad; they'll get over it. I enjoyed myself. Let's go to lunch and celebrate your winnings?"

"Sorry, I've made other plans."

He frowned. Sam bit the side of her lip and glanced heavenward. A stranger in a strange place. *I should be more considerate. Just because I don't appreciate how he takes command of situations, and how he sets my skin crawling, doesn't mean I should be rude.*

"Plans you can't change?" Mark asked, disturbing her thoughts.

"I'm meeting Ed at the library, and then we're off to lunch." *Why did I blurt that out?*

Mark nodded. "I'm sure he wouldn't mind if I tagged along."

"Probably not." Sam wanted to add, *but I would.*

"Well?" Mark stared at her with his eyes half closed looking sexy. *Whoa, where'd that thought come from? He's not sexy.* She lowered her head and chewed on her lip. *I relieved him of fifty grand. But, I don't want to send the wrong message.* "You couldn't possibly want to go to the library."

"Well, I would like to check on my stocks. They have Internet access, don't they?"

Sam rolled her eyes heavenward again. He had a laptop computer and cell phone. Couldn't he use one of those? "Yes, they do." She held up her arm and pointed. "My truck's over there."

They strode up to the driver's side, and when Sam unlocked the door, Mark grabbed the handle. As he opened the door, Sam slipped quickly into the seat behind the wheel. "Thanks." She smiled.

The sardonic grin appeared on Mark's face as he slammed the door. He went around to the passenger side, sank into the seat, and closed the door.

"Buckle up." Sam smiled and drove off.

It was too early for Ed to be at the library, but Sam thought she saw his vehicle in the parking lot. She didn't spot him inside. At the computer index, she wrote down the numbers for any books or magazines on birthmarks. Mark signed up to use the Internet and sat at the last vacant computer terminal.

With the index numbers in hand, Sam searched for pertinent books, deciding to go online later at home to look at magazines.

She ran her finger across the spines of the books, searching for the ones on her list.

Ed strolled around the corner. "Hi! Finding anything?"

"No. By the way, Mark's with me. He sort of invited himself along. I couldn't refuse."

Sam directed his gaze toward the computers. "He's over there checking out stocks. Here." She handed Ed a title and number. "See if you're able to find this book. So far, I don't see any of the ones I'm looking for. According to the computer, they're here."

For five minutes, they scanned each aisle, running their fingers along the books. No luck.

"I don't understand it." Sam squinted at the titles. "I was going to go online to look at magazines, but let's check them out here."

No magazines on the list could be found in the library.

"This is odd."

Ed shrugged. "I'm starved."

"Oh, sorry." He had such an appetite, but when Sam got on the scent of something, she forgot to eat. They walked over to Mark. "Are you hungry?"

He shut down the computer and grinned. "Hungry as a shark. Where are we going?"

With her eyebrow raised, Sam wondered why he mentioned shark? *Maybe he didn't mean anything by that.*

"We're going for Mexican food at Jalapeños." Ed led the way to the front of the library. "You'll enjoy it. Their fried ice cream is something I could make a meal on."

"Fried ice cream?" Mark leaned his head to one side and furrowed his brow.

"Yes." Ed laughed. "They take a big ball of hard vanilla ice cream, roll it in corn flakes with cinnamon and sugar, and deep fry it."

"That I have to try." Mark and Ed passed the front desk.

Sam lagged behind. She wanted to stay and browse the books, but felt she owed these guys a meal. She stopped to talk with the librarian. "Excuse me. I'm looking for these books." Handing her a list, she continued, "The computer reported they're here, but I can't find them."

"Then they're here somewhere."

"Could you check?" Sam waited for her answer.

"We're short-handed today. If it's not urgent, I will look later."

"I'll come back this evening."

"Call me first. Ask for Yolanda."

Mark and Ed were not too far away and both scrutinized Samantha. Mark didn't say a word. She hoped he couldn't see the names of the books.

Downtown at Jalapeños restaurant, the three of them sat outside at one of the few tables set up on the sidewalk. As they were about to order their lunch, Frank Collotti, with a cigarette hanging out of his mouth as it did at the contest, sauntered over to their table. "Well, if it's not the shark winner and her sidekicks. Didn't expect to see you three again so soon."

Mark arose and shook hands. "What are you doing in Sandpoint? Sit down, join us."

Frank pulled out a chair. "Had some business over here. How do you like this town?"

With notepad poised to take their order, the waitress stood by the table. "Hi. I'm Waunita. May I take your order?" She scribbled down what they wanted to eat. When she left, Mark, Ed, and Frank talked about the area. Sam chewed on her lip and studied each man. *Wonder why Frank didn't tell us he'd be over today from Spokane.* Then she thought about her upcoming research.

Waunita served the hot and spicy chicken enchiladas to Mark and Ed. Even though Sam wasn't too hungry, the aromas made her stomach grumble and reminded her of how much she liked Mexican food. When the waitress delivered the veggie burrito to Sam, she wished she'd ordered something more.

"Need anything else?" Waunita asked. When no one answered, she went back inside the restaurant.

Frank wolfed down his carne asada. *How long has it been since the man ate?*

Sam dug in her burrito, taking a few bites. Her taste buds watered at the flavor, but she couldn't stop thinking and seeing the grizzly picture of the guts of her bull shark. She stirred the rice around on her plate.

"You're not eating much." Mark sipped his beer.

Sam pushed some more food around.

"Are you thinking about that guy?" Ed took a bite of his enchilada.

Mark set down his beer bottle. "What guy?"

"You know." Ed swallowed. "The piece of back with the birthmark."

Frank choked, and took a drink.

Mark groaned.

"You still thinking about what came out of your fish?" Frank asked.

"Yes, she is." Ed shivered and grimaced. "I should never have suggested that Baja contest."

"Nonsense." Sam put down her fork. "I had a great time. Besides, I won. We should go again with my folks."

"Okay, but no shark fishing." Ed waved to a car's passenger that passed by going down the street. The guy stuck his arm out with a thumbs up sign.

"What would the chances be to find another body part?" Sam smiled.

"With you—excellent." Ed took another bite of his enchilada.

Mark chuckled, and then tilted his head and frowned. "Samantha, don't you think you should let it go? I mean, really, there's nothing you can do about it."

"Yeah, Sam." Frank gulped down his beer. "Thought you'd have given that crazy idea up by now."

"Oh, no." Ed leaned over and patted Sam's shoulder. "She thinks she's a detective and will discover who this guy is through that mark."

Sam kicked Ed under the table, connecting with his shin.

"Ow!" He leaned over and rubbed his leg. "What was that for?"

"For blabbing her plans in front of us." Frank got Waunita's attention and ordered another Corona beer.

"This crusade you're on is pointless." Mark clanged his fork on his plate.

"So, what's it matter what you think?" Ed leaned back in his chair and crossed his arms over his chest.

Another car drove by and Ed waved again. Sam realized he knew a lot of people in town.

"That's true. I don't care about your opinions." Sam looked at each gentleman and settled on Mark. "But I want to know why are you so against it?"

Mark shoved his plate away and reached for a cigar. "If you're going to invest your time on something, you should make money."

The waitress placed another beer in front of Frank. He picked it up and tilted it toward Mark. "I'll drink to that."

Mark lit his stogie and blew a smoke ring.

Sam coughed.

The server cleared their plates and delivered fried ice cream to their table.

"Did you make money on the contest, Mark?" Sam tasted a spoonful of dessert, trying to ignore the cigar stench.

"No, I lost my seed money like the rest of the men, but I made some good business contacts."

"That's true, my boy." Frank toasted his beer again.

"Aren't you curious who that birthmark or foot belongs to?" Sam contemplated their faces for any reaction.

"A little." Mark held his cigar to the side and tried a bite of the fried ice cream. "This is great. Odds are you'll never know who, so why waste your time?"

Frank took a scoop of the dessert. "Aren't you a landscape architect or something?"

"What's that have to do with this?"

The man swallowed. "Samantha, I'm trying to change the subject." He smiled.

They finished devouring the fried ice cream and Mark insisted on paying the check.

"But this was my treat." Sam dug in her purse.

"No, you get the bill next time. I'm paying." Mark blew another smoke ring and grabbed the bill. He put his credit card with it.

"Thanks, Mark." Frank shoved back his chair and got up. "Well, good seeing you all again, and enjoy the area. Sam, concentrate on work. Forget the stupid shark. See ya." He lit a cigarette and strode away.

Mark signed the statement and put down a cash tip. "I'll see you both later. I want to check with a realty company. Sandpoint and the surrounding area intrigue me. Appears it's growing." He puffed on his cigar, and wandered down the street. A smoke ring rose above him.

Ed and Sam meandered toward her pickup. "Don't you think it's odd, the books I needed couldn't be found in the library?"

"No, the library never has anything I want. That's why I stick with the Internet."

"Guess I'll use my home computer. Want to come help?"

"Sure." Ed opened her pickup door for her. "Seven o'clock early enough for you?"

"Paula and Jim still have my dog. I'm having dinner with them before I take Goldie home. How about 7:30? And, don't bring Mark."

12

The afternoon sped by. Sam finished the tasks that had piled up while she was gone and called Hank to check on the Lowell site.

"All well here," Hank said.

"Okay, I'll get out tomorrow." Before Sam left the office, she called Yolanda at the library.

"Not sure what happened to those books," the librarian said. "I'll keep hunting."

"Thanks. I'll search the Internet for articles and stories I'm looking for."

"Give me your email. If I find them, I'll email you."

"Thanks, Yolanda." After she hung up, Sam locked her office and walked to her pickup. Inside, she started the engine and took off for the home of her best friend to get her dog Goldie.

She'd known Paula for years. They'd gone to college together. Her friend married Jim two years prior. He was a good psychologist, always helping someone. Didn't make much money, but invested and was looking into another area of work to earn more income. Sam served as the maid-of-honor at their wedding and, now, Paula desperately wanted to have a child. She would babysit for all of her friends, and that included watching Sam's dog. Said it gave her practice in caring.

Sam parked in front of Paula and Jim's house. Their Queen Anne Victorian had one more bedroom than hers, with more ornate carvings, and a tower with a dragon weather vane on top. She hurried up the porch steps, admired the old wooden swing that Paula had painted white hanging from the porch rafters, and punched the doorbell. The chimes played Beethoven's 5th.

When Jim opened the door, Goldie dashed out and jumped up onto Sam. The dog's tail wagged so fast her little butt wiggled.

Paula came out and hugged Sam. "Come in." Before Sam could sit down in the living room, Paula clutched her shoulders and held her at arm's length. "Well, did you win?"

"Yes. I'm fifty grand richer!"

"Oh, Samantha, that's great." Jim sat on the couch and patted the cushion. "Let's sit and you tell us all about it."

Sam admired the living room. Paula had decorated it with earth tones and leather furniture so Jim could claim it for himself. She designed the tower room for her room to escape to. One wall contained numerous books on shelves and she'd painted it a pale-green with pink pillows. A restful place.

While sitting on the brown leather couch, Goldie climbed into Sam's lap, and if her dog had been a cat, it would have purred. Sam didn't mind the short, reddish-gold hair that rubbed off and clung to her blue jeans. She loved her 35-pound dog; such a cute whippet crossed with lab. Even though Goldie wasn't big, the dog's strength and energy kept Sam fit. Goldie was good company.

"So, spill the beans." Jim eyed her, waiting to hear.

Sam told her friends about Mark Randall, his being an old-time college roommate and friend of Ed's, and the band of men that she out-fished. "Ed stayed on shore. After Mark landed his mako shark, I caught the biggest, a bull shark."

"With all that money you won, we can go shopping." Paula grinned from ear to ear, similar to a kid seeing presents under a Christmas tree.

"No shopping." Sam laughed. She pictured her friend at the Spokane mall with dozens of packages. Paula spent hours there—her favorite pastime, but not Sam's. "Money's in the bank for now. Can't think of anything I need at the moment." *Except paying off my debt.*

Paula and Jim didn't know about her financial problems—no one did. *Well, I guess someone does. Whoever deposited that note in Baja in my room. Wonder what happened to it?* She'd been so careful, not even her best friend knew about the jam she found herself in.

Sam reached over and popped a jalapeño pepper oozing with cream cheese into her mouth. Her eyes watered from the spicy flavor. She reached for a wheat cracker to help put out the fire.

"Cabo changed much?" Paula asked. "Jim says it has."

"Hawkers everywhere on the streets, trying to get you to browse in their shops, eat in the restaurant, or listen to a condo presentation." Sam sighed. "Not like it used to be when it existed as a sleepy fishing village."

She reached into her bag and brought out a gift. "This is for you for taking care of Goldie."

"You shouldn't have. Goldie's a pleasure and she kept me company when Jim wasn't around. He and I checked on your house a few times."

"And, Paula, I appreciate that, so here." Sam held out the gift.

Paula snatched the present out of her hands and ripped open the wrapping.

"The jar was blown at the glass factory." Sam remembered that day. *At least this present didn't get busted up.* "It's filled with local honey."

"Thanks," Paula hugged Sam. "Did you take pictures of your trip?"

"Yes. Have some with me." She pulled the two packets from her purse.

They shuffled through the photos. Jim ogled the one with the spilled guts and tennis shoe. His face paled. "Sam, that's a tennis shoe. Looks close to the ones that—"

"Oh, yuck!" Paula ripped it from Jim's grasp. "What is all that stuff?"

"Oh, Paula." Sam tried to reach for the print. "I'm so sorry. I forgot how squeamish you are. I should have taken those out."

Jim plucked the picture away from Paula and studied it. "Those chunks of flesh? Samantha, they're not human, are they?"

"Oh, please." Paula shuddered. "You'll spoil our dinner."

"Sam?" Jim tilted his head. "You look pale. What happened down there?"

She told them about her trip. How the other contestants complained about what she'd found, and how the Mexican police did nothing. "I plan on finding out who the person was."

"That's ridiculous." Paula shivered. "That shark could have traveled miles. I watched a documentary on them. They don't stay in one place."

"Besides," Jim added, "that person could have been in Baja or maybe the mainland or even have fallen off a cruise ship. Who knows what country the person is from?"

"I expected more support from my best friends."

Paula arose. "I have to agree with what that Mark told you. It's impossible. Why bother with such a waste of time?" Her friend must have realized how she sounded, or noticed Sam had dropped her mouth to stare, because she bowed her head. "I'm sorry, but it's true. I'll go finish up dinner."

Sam closed her mouth as Paula strolled around the corner, amazed at her lack of support. The woman knew how insecure she felt about being adopted and how her cousin's disappearance had affected the family. They talked for hours about both. Couldn't Paula understand her reasons?

"My lovely wife has a point." Jim perused another photo. "Maybe you should drop the idea." He took a long time with the picture of the tennis shoe, and shuddered.

Abandonment. Sam remembered when her boyfriend dumped her two years ago without saying a word. She'd finished a hard day at work and come home to an empty closet. All his things gone. She hid up in the turret in her Victorian house for two days. Being abandoned by him had almost undone her. He deserted her a month after Jennifer vanished. Both losses ate at her insides.

"Maybe Paula is right. But, Jim, it's a little more to me." Sam frowned. "Hey, have you ever worn your hair any different?"

"What?" Jim wrinkled his brow. "No, why?"

"Thought I saw you in L.A. yesterday."

Jim laughed, but before he could say anything, Paula yelled from the kitchen. "I can't hear you guys. Come on in and help so I don't miss anything."

A long sigh escaped Sam's lips as she jumped up and headed for the kitchen. Goldie trotted beside her. *Guess Paula's a little curious.*

At the glass-top table, the dog curled up at Sam's feet. Dinner consisted of homemade lasagna, salad, French bread slathered with butter, and fresh apricot pie. *Great, I figure this will add at least five pounds to my girth.* Sam took her last bite and pushed back from the table. "Thank you, dinner was great, but I have to go." She didn't tell them she would meet Ed later.

"So soon?" Paula complained.

They walked together down the hall to the front. Goldie traipsed alongside of Sam.

"We didn't get enough time with you." Jim leaned down and petted Goldie on the head. The dog's tail wagged, thumping against Sam's leg. "Why don't you come tomorrow night for dinner, too?"

"A great idea." Paula smiled, nodding her head.

I should do my search, but she cooks mouth-watering meals that I love to eat. Sam didn't cook, but enjoyed eating. Food reminded her of happy memories of the good times with her parents. She could talk about everything with her folks every night. Now they lived far away. She missed them. Paula and Jim were the same as family. "All right."

They loaded Goldie's stuff into the truck and Sam drove home. In the driveway, she parked next to Ed's truck. He sat on the top of her porch steps, elbows on his knees, chin resting on his hands.

"Any problem ditching your friend?" Sam sauntered up the treads. Goldie raced ahead of her, ignored Ed, and waited by the front door. The dog wagged her tail, so much so, the little red butt wiggled in excitement.

Sam laughed. Her dog always wiggled in joy.

"No." Ed raised up and dusted off his pants. "Mark had a date with a real estate agent. May be buying something around here. He's pretty impressed with the area."

"Can't blame him for that."

Inside, Goldie ran around, and Ed went to the bathroom, while Sam put away her dog's bowls, food, and toys. When she finished, she hunted for Ed, expecting to find him in the front room. He stood inside her office door next to her old, oak desk. She had found it at an antique shop. The desk was perfect for her computer and fit in her Queen Anne parlor that she decided to use as her home office. She enjoyed sitting in the comfortable, brown leather office chair. A shelf above her desk held her landscaping books. Opposite her desk she'd discovered an old wooden picnic table where she placed her drawings and magazines. She covered most of the wood floor with another geometric-patterned wool rug with orange, red, brown and yellow colors.

More stacks of magazines piled on the floor. She put her grandmother's high-backed floral chair in the corner. Couldn't sit on it because it, too, was littered with Sunset magazines.

Sam sat in her chair and switched on the computer.

Nothing happened.

"What the..." Sam banged on the side, shut it off, and then back on again.

Still nothing.

The dog rushed to the open doorway and cocked her little red head.

Ed stepped around closer to Sam's chair. "Is the computer plugged in?" he asked.

"Very funny."

"No, seriously. When I go on vacation, I unplug my system. Didn't you?"

Sam bent down and looked under the desk. The surge-protector bar was unplugged and off. "I don't remember doing this." She plugged it in and turned everything on. The computer whirred to life. "That's better."

They stared at the black screen, Sam tapped her foot. She wanted to check her emails, see if the librarian contacted her, and, if she'd heard from that stupid accountant.

The screen remained black.

"What's happening?" She bit her lip and hoped Ed had an explanation. She was no computer expert.

He shrugged.

Words popped up on the screen saying: 'going to Windows,' but nothing came on.

Ed rebooted it, and a blank screen still appeared on the computer, as if the system had been wiped out.

"Now what?"

"Not sure, but something's wrong."

"Ed, can you fix it?"

He shook his head. "Sorry, not me, but I know a guy who can. I'll take your computer to him, if you want."

"Guess I have no choice. What else will go wrong?"

13

At home, I make a phone call. Then I pace the room, counting my steps, losing track and starting over. I sigh. She's unbelievable. Of all the luck.

I slump down in a chair, tapping my foot to the pounding rhythm of my heart. If I'm not careful I'll have a heart attack. Stress—I hate that word. But, it comes with the job and accumulating as much money as possible. I work hard for the bucks.

Why'd Samantha have to catch a shark that just happens to eat... I'm beginning to believe it's not possible for her to let it go. Sam is too smart for her own good. No raving beauty—at least not like Linda. Now she's a knockout. What every man should have on his arm. I can't even picture her digging through fish guts.

This is getting me nowhere. Okay, so the regulator/mask thing didn't scare her off. The hammerhead didn't do its job either. How did she evade the van? What should I do next? A closer eye on her proves necessary.

This search she plans on doing—will it lead her anywhere?

All I want is to protect my business and the people around me. It isn't personal. I justify it. Like putting a puzzle together where all the pieces fit. Now, there is one missing.

As long as I'm aware of everything she does, maybe I can keep the puzzle together and prevent her from finding out anything. It all boils down to luck.

And skill.

Samantha must have a four-leaf clover. Catching the shark with pieces of human flesh and a man's tennis shoe with the foot still inside, so lucky. Managing to grab the regulator and mask at sixty feet without panicking—okay, she's a good diver. Avoiding the hammerhead, and jumping out of the way of the van at the last moment, man, I'm not lucky like she.

I laugh. Luck! Mine better turn. Hers makes me shudder. I have to discover how to keep close tabs on Sam. Maybe my talent will come in handy?

Back down in my chair, I look at the ceiling fan going round and round. All my hard work. The planning. How meticulous I've been.

I lean forward in my chair, grab my phone, and search through names.

I find the name and address, and send an email.

Within an hour, I have an answer. Contacts are important; now they pay off. This will be helpful. It will bring in money, create jobs, and keep her busy.

14

Tuesday morning Sam awoke early. Since Ed took her computer tower to some guru named Don to get fixed, she couldn't work on any research. So, after grabbing a piece of toast and some tea, she decided to do the important things first—rewash her dive gear. Unpacking her suitcase could wait. In the laundry room, when she unzipped her dive bag, the salty, dead sea foul odor almost knocked her over. Goldie barked and went into the hallway and sat watching.

Sam hung the rinsed gear and bag out on the back porch. Inside the laundry room, she emptied her yellow mesh bag, which held her findings. She put the seashells in a pan and, in the kitchen, boiled them in a little bleach water, setting the shells outside on the back porch to dry.

The dog curled up in the kitchen and fell asleep.

The denim piece and lure from Sam's dive caught her attention. She rinsed them in the laundry room sink with fresh water, didn't see anything to identify them with, and laid the denim out to dry. Then she cut the fishing line off the green and white lure and studied it. Nothing fancy. No identifying marks. After washing the Bic pen, she examined it. But needing her reading glasses for the writing, she set the pen down behind the faucet and headed for her office to get her cheaters.

In the hallway, Goldie rushed up with the leash in her mouth and jumped on Sam. "Oh, all right. A quick walk before I go to work."

She set her reading glasses next to the computer screen and they walked around the block. Old-man Rogers sat out on his porch. He beckoned them to come up. "Hey, Goldie, I have a cookie for you."

The dog tugged on the leash toward the steps. Sam unhooked Goldie and the dog ran up and delicately took the treat from the man's hand.

"Thanks, but we can't visit. Have to get to work. Another time. Come on, Goldie."

The dog ran back and sat while Sam hooked up the leash.

The old man smiled. "Another time then," he called out.

Goldie took longer than the usual fifteen minutes. When they got back to the house, Sam raced to her job.

~~~

The work day sped by. An hour remained at the Lowell site before Sam could head back to the office. A worker dug a hole. Sam, standing next to it, opened her cell phone to call about the progress of her computer. The phone was dead. If her computer wasn't fixed, she would have to go to the library and use theirs.

A horrible crack sounded. Sam spun toward the hole. The worker had pushed his shovel too deep. Water from the broken pipe spewed into the air, raining down and soaking them both.

The man cringed when he glanced at Sam. He hurried from the hole to turn off the water. Droplets dripped off her nose, and her drenched purple T-shirt clung to her wet skin.

Before she opened her mouth, Mrs. Lowell ran out of the house, yelling, "My God, how incompetent! Can't you people do anything right? The wedding's in a week. This yard must be perfect!"

The water stopped gushing.

"It's all right, Mrs. Lowell." Sam used her best calming voice, wiping the water from her face. The Lowell's, a prominent family, generated lots of business for the nursery. She couldn't afford to have the woman upset.

"Hank, get over here," Sam called. "He'll have the pipe fixed soon. The yard will be finished on time as we promised. This dogwood will look great here."

"I don't want that white-flowered bush. I want something else."

Sam turned her back to Mrs. Lowell, faced the worker, and rolled her eyes. He snickered.

Hank arrived and knelt down to inspect the broken pipe.

After appeasing Mrs. Lowell with a new Korean Lilac plant, Sam told Hank, "Go back to the nursery and get the stuff to fix the pipe and bring the bush or rush-order it. Fix everything and plant the dogwood over in the corner."

Too bad Sam's battery in her cell phone died. She read her watch and sighed. She'd taken the charger out of the pickup when she had gone on her Baja trip and forgot to put it back.

She rearranged some plants, letting the dirt and smells of Mother Earth soothe her. By four-thirty, she escaped from Mrs. Lowell and drove to the office. There, she checked messages.

"Call me back as soon as you get this," came Ed's urgent voice on her machine. *Great, now what?* Sam dialed his cell phone number.

"I thought you'd never call." Ed asked, "Did you forget your cell phone?"

"No. Dead battery."

"Where've you been?"

Sam sat at her desk and glanced at a bill. "At the Lowell site. Just listened to your message at the office. What's up?"

"I talked with a Mr. and Mrs. Turkwood. They bought a piece of property out in Clark Fork off Lightning Creek Road on Cascade. You know the place."

"Yes." Sam set the bill in her 'to do' basket and raised her gaze to the heavens. Then she tilted her head. "Hey, Ed, listen, do you know if Don fixed my computer?"

"No. Anyway," Ed continued, "there's a cabin on it, but they want to renovate it and build a home. Eventually, they'll use the cabin as a guesthouse. It's semi-livable now."

Sam heard, "Let me tell her."

Ed said, "No, I'll tell her, okay? Sam, are you going to be in your office for a while?"

"Why?"

"Mark and I need to talk with you about this Turkwood project. They know Mark and want him as the contractor, me as the architecture, and you the landscaper."

"Me?"

"I highly recommended you. They insisted on only you for the job. Anyway, we'll be right over. Wait there."

"Can't this wait 'til tomorrow? I've a dinner date with Paula and Jim."

"Sam, this is important," Ed said. "Please."

All she wanted to do was her research, but the nursery could use the money. "All right, but make it quick."

Sam hung up, tried calling Don the computer guru, and received a busy signal. She shuffled paperwork around on her desk and found herself staring at the same paragraph on a certain page. Her parents' photograph sitting on the desk drew her attention. She reached for the phone, but withdrew her hand.

Instead, she pulled out the phone book and flipped through the pages to "Dermatologists." Two listings for Bonner County. She dialed the first number. The phone rang five times.

"Dr. Mallor's answering service. How may I help you?"

"Is his office closed for the day?" Sam asked.

"No, ma'am. He's on vacation and the office is being remodeled."

"When will he return?"

"The office will re-open in a couple of weeks. Is this an emergency?"

"No, I just wanted to ask him a question."

"Try calling Dr. Vinde. Or you can call back in three weeks to make an appointment."

"Thank you." Sam hung up and started to dial Dr. Vinde, thinking she would call the computer guy when she finished with the doctor.

A knock on the door startled her. She slammed down the phone.

"Hi! We're here. You're not busy, are you?" Mark stepped inside, not waiting for an answer.

Ed entered behind him. "Yes, I'm busy." Sam motioned to the two chairs in front of her desk. "But have a seat."

Ed nodded and sat. He dropped his briefcase on the floor next to him.

"Is the Lowell project almost finished?" Mark asked.

"Yes, thank God."

"Good." Mark perched on the corner of her desk. "The Turkwood's have a big proposal. Ed says one of the biggest projects for this area he's seen in a while."

"What's it entail?" Sam half-listened to Mark as he talked. She thought about her computer, the library, the birthmark, and her birth parents. When she finished the Lowell project, she would seriously do her search.

"... and of course, we'll spend some time with them at the cabin."

That brought her attention back to Mark. "What?"

"You're not listening." Ed cocked his head and furrowed his brow. "What are you thinking about?"

Sam lowered her gaze, feeling bad. "Sorry, my mind wandered."

Mark arose. "Please pay attention. We can't afford to daydream." He slapped his hands down on the desk and leaned over. "We need you focused—totally. If you have any other projects, you'll have to pass them on to someone else."

Sam noticed his blazing hazel eyes. His red polo shirt smelled like cigar smoke. He straightened, then paced back and forth. She took a deep breath. "Please, sit. I'm sorry. I do have somewhat of a personal life and apologize for thinking of it."

Mark stopped in mid-pace. "Are you thinking about... No, never mind. We need you on this."

"Oh, for Heaven's sake, sit down." Sam jabbed her finger toward the chair. "I'm listening now. Please start over."

The man sat, crossed his arms, and glared at her.

Ed cleared his throat. "Sam, the Turkwood's want us all to go to their cabin, spend a few days going over the property and discuss plans with them. They're here in Sandpoint for another week, or two at the most."

"Yes." Mark uncrossed his arms and placed his hands on his knees. "When the Turkwood's ran into me, they told me they'd talked with Frank in Spokane and called Ed. When they found out I was here looking at property, they wanted me in charge and to start this project now. I worked with them in Southern California."

"But why stay at their cabin?" Sam didn't want to be gone again.

"It's a rush job." Mark slammed his hand against his knee. "They want you and Ed on-site for a few days to get your ideas. They'll pay whatever it takes."

"How much are we talking?" *I could use the money.*

"Three million for the entire project." Mark sat back in his chair and smiled.

Leaning back in her seat, Sam's mouth dropped open and she stared, for once, speechless. For this area, one house, that was a lot. Her mother used to say something about catching flies. She snapped her mouth shut.

"And," Mark shifted in his seat, "they want you to get the feel of the place. Work with all your senses tuned in with their project."

He shoved a stray hair out of his face. That russet strand always kept falling. *Why did I notice that?*

"Besides the house and guest cottage, they'll be putting in a pool." Ed disrupted her thoughts. "Which you'll create all of the landscaping for. They want the place to blend with the area, and feel seeing the site isn't enough. They requested you live there, so your designs will reflect the setting."

Incorporating the landscaping into the beautiful setting where their property sat would be a challenge for her. "But I have the Lowell project to finish." What Sam didn't say was, 'and my computer research.' She knew she could do the computer stuff anytime, but the thought of someone never knowing what happened to their loved one made her feel it was a rush.

"This project sounds great, but—"

"Look, Sam." Ed interrupted. "I don't know about you, but I could use this job. Be good for our reputations. It's a week or two out of our lives."

"True." *Would postponing my search for that long make that big a difference?*

Mark jumped to his feet and paced again. "I understand you have a dog." He stopped near her and studied the floor. "You can even bring the mutt. So, what do you say?"

"When do they want to start?" Sam felt her face flush with Mark's stare.

"Yesterday!" Ed grinned. "But they'll settle for tomorrow."

"Tomorrow?" Sam shook her head. "Impossible."

"Charles and Barbara Turkwood are ready to go." Ed adjusted his wire-rimmed glasses. "They're heading for Europe soon and want this underway before they go. You know Hank is capable of finishing the Lowell project. But if you don't wish to do this, don't worry about us. We'll manage."

That man is so understanding. How can I let him down? This job will bring in big money, and it would be good for Ed, not to mention me.

"Do they have a computer at this cabin?" Sam read her clock. Too late to call Don or make the library and still get to Paula and Jim's in time for dinner.

"No." Ed frowned. "There's no electricity yet. It's just a camp cabin now."

Mark continued to glare at her. "But, you can do tentative plans by hand."

"Okay, I'll do the job. But why not meet them at the cabin every day?" Sam pictured driving out to the site. "It's not that far and takes about a half hour."

"Clients requested us to stay with them at the cabin." Ed shrugged.

At least the Turkwood's will be there, too. Thank God. I'm not keen on the idea of being alone with Ed for some reason. Now where had that thought come from? What was wrong with her?

This project might be what she needed to pay off her financial mess.

"Thanks, Samantha." Mark patted her shoulder and continued glaring at her. "The potential for future income is a good investment here. This project would start me off."

"So, you're moving?" Sam shuddered at the idea of him living here.

Mark took a step back and folded his arms across his chest. "At least part-time."

His sardonic grin sent chills down Sam's back.

"With you on board, we'll get this Turkwood contract." Mark grinned wider.

Since Sam's dad knew about the shark money she'd won, this project money would be useful. She could funnel the money back in gradually, and no one would know. If it hadn't been for that accountant's bad advice, none of her problems would exist.

Why'd Mark have to be with Ed? Sam sighed. "When you call the Turkwood's, tell them thanks so much for requesting me—"

"But?"

"Oh, for heaven's sake, Mark, there's no but. I told you I would do it. Why so pushy?"

"Time and money."

That's all Mark ever thought about. Didn't he know there was more to life? Sam nodded. "I guess we're all on board and will go out to the cabin to stay."

"Great!" Mark grabbed her and lifted her out from the seat, hugging her so tight she thought she might lose her breath.

The tingles ran through Sam's body. She didn't appreciate those feelings. Then she spotted Ed's raised eyebrow.

"Come on, Mark, let's get out of here so Sam can get to Jim and Paula's."

"Oh, of course." Mark released Samantha and shifted a step away. "We need to go make some phone calls."

"Yes." Sam pushed her chair back and stood. "And I have to go to my friends' for dinner. They'll be excited for me when I tell them all about this new project."

Sam watched the men leave. Mark looked back over his shoulder and smiled. "Thanks. You won't regret this decision."

She prayed to God he was right.

15

So, Samantha is willing to meet with the Turkwood's. Relief floods me. I'm very clever.

Hopefully this keeps her busy enough so she forgets about the findings inside of that stupid bull shark.

My new plan is shaping up. I smile. Thank God for Barbara Turkwood. She grabs at the idea and, as usual, runs with it. That woman has trouble making up her mind, so the drawing of plans probably will take as long as the Turkwood's are in the area.

Perfect.

If I'm able to avoid it, I really don't want to hurt Samantha.

She is one determined lady. I know she needs the money, so her agreeing to the project—inevitable. But to hesitate because of the search—well I can't let that happen. Must prolong it. Maybe Sam will forget all about the birthmark. I shake my head. No, I know her. She won't let it drop, no matter how long it will take her.

I have to keep a close eye on her, one way or another.

16

Before Sam left town to go to the cabin, she photocopied the duck birthmark picture and mailed them along with a letter, to both Dr. Mallor and Dr. Vinde. She asked if they recognized or had any way of finding out to whom the mark belonged. This would start her search.

She drove northeast out of Sandpoint on Highway 200 in her four-wheel drive Ford Ranger. The trip would take about a half hour and the scenery around the lake would inspire Sam. Goldie stood on the pickup seat, with her head leaning out the window, ears flapping. The highway curved around the northern part of Lake Pend Oreille, then headed southeast through little towns of Hope and East Hope. Sam passed the peninsula where large, expensive homes and original, majestic log cabins lined the shore looking out over the lake. Since it was a game preserve, deer roamed the yards unafraid. About nine miles beyond the peninsula, she came into Clark Fork.

Goldie sat in the seat, glanced at Sam, and the dog's tail wagged like a metronome, keeping a steady beat against the seat.

"No, we're not going hunting." Sam reached over and rubbed Goldie's pelt. The dog's tail quit thumping and she cocked her head.

Gravel crunched under the tires as Sam drove up Lightning Creek about a mile, maneuvered the pickup onto Cascade Creek Road, and then entered the property. A few hundred yards up the dirt road, she parked next to Ed's pickup. She and Goldie jumped out.

Part of Lake Pend Oreille glistened and the Green Monarch Mountains loomed before Sam. Some trees: larch and others, along with brush blocked the total view.

The landscape architect in her took over. She figured out which plants could be removed. The larch trees, with their yellow needles in the fall, filled her with love and made her smile. She'd keep those in her plans. When they mixed with the reds, the scene would be beautiful.

A bush wiggled.

Goldie barked.

Ed came out from behind the brush. He was dressed in khaki pants and a white, short-sleeved shirt. He wiped his brow with a red bandana.

"Hey, what's with your dog?" Ed walked toward them.

The dog continued barking.

"Goldie, stop." Sam knelt down and scratched behind the dog's ears. "It's Ed."

He reached down and petted Goldie. "Glad you're here, Sam. This is a great place."

"Perfect spot. Where's the cabin?" Sam couldn't see it anywhere.

"Up the road, behind the bend over there. The logs appear to be in good shape. Mark and the Turkwood's aren't here yet."

"Do they want a log house similar to the cabin?"

"They're not sure." Ed sighed. "Want me to come up with some ideas. You, too, for that matter."

"Wonder why Mark didn't beat us here? Sounds as if someone is approaching."

Ed focused his attention behind Sam. "You're right. Here he comes."

A Ford, 4 x 4 Power Stroke pickup pulled up beside Sam's vehicle, making hers look like a Chihuahua next to a St. Bernard.

Mark jumped down from the shiny red diesel. He wore jeans and a red polo shirt. His hair combed to perfection. Sam wondered if he ever looked disheveled.

"Morning everyone. Glad you're both here already. Are the Turkwood's here yet?"

"Ed says no." Goldie stayed near Sam, uttering a low growl. The dog normally didn't act that way with strangers. Maybe Mark wasn't an animal lover and Goldie sensed it.

Mark leaned over to try and pet the dog. "Cute mutt."

Goldie backed up and growled louder, hackles rising.

"Enough!" Sam wondered what Goldie's actions meant. The dog kept her distance.

"Usually dogs approve of me." Mark took a step back and smiled. He took out a cigar and lit it.

Sam opened her mouth to comment, but Ed interrupted. "It's not eight A.M. yet, so I assume the Turkwood's will be here shortly."

"This project will give us a chance to all work together. It'll be fun." Mark surveyed the property and blew a smoke ring.

Sam hated the stench and wished he wouldn't smoke. "You staying with us?" *God, please make him say no.* She waited for Mark's answer.

"For a day or two. Linda's coming for a visit. Then I'll be in and out as needed."

"Let's go see the cabin." Ed strode toward his truck.

The two men climbed into their vehicles. Sam slid behind her pickup steering wheel. Goldie ran ahead as they traveled up the road to the cabin and parked in front.

Sam walked up the squeaky steps onto the porch. "Ed, you're right about these gray-weathered logs on the outside. They do look sturdy, but I noticed the roof needs work." Sam studied the foliage around the cabin. "Appears they need a weed whacker. Plants are choking the house."

"Yeah." Ed skipped a tread. "Need to repair that broken porch board."

Mark came up onto the porch next to Sam. She cupped her hands on the windows and peaked in. Gravel crunched, and she turned around. A black Mercedes convertible rolled to a stop.

A tall white-haired man dressed in dark blue slacks and a light-blue short-sleeved shirt extricated himself from the passenger side.

A woman, wearing designer blue jeans and a sequined low-cut top, opened the driver's door, stood, and slammed it shut. The man and she strode up the steps. "Mark, how great to see you again." She smiled and pulled off her black leather driving gloves. Then she hugged Mark and kissed him on both cheeks.

"Mr. and Mrs. Turkwood, this is Ed Johnson and Samantha Volarie." Mark blew another smoke ring.

"Nice to meet you, Mrs. Turkwood." Sam held out her hand.

She gave Sam a limp handshake. "Call me Barbara."

"I'm Charles." The man cupped Sam's hand with both of his and smiled.

They faced Ed, and Charles shook his hand. Barbara merely nodded. "Shall we go in? Mark, no smoking allowed inside. And I'd appreciate it if you wouldn't smoke around me. Can't stand the smell." She unlocked the door and crossed the threshold.

Sam smiled, glad Barbara felt the same way about the cigar. "Goldie, stay." She gave the hand signal for her dog to sit to the right of the door.

Mark put the stogie out and placed the unused portion in his shirt pocket.

Inside the cabin, the curtains appeared to be new and were pulled aside to let the light in.

"After we talked with Ed," Barbara said, "we had someone come out and clean inside the place, stock the shelves and refrigerator. Afraid the outside needs work, but inside we'll be comfortable. We should be good until Sunday."

"Place looks cozy." Mark glanced around.

Sam did too.

A braided rug laid in the middle of the hardwood floor in the large living room. An antler glass-top coffee table perched on top of the carpet. Above the rock fireplace a moose head with huge antlers stared down at everyone. Sam ran her hand down the over-stuffed leopard colored couch. Two wing chairs flanked it in brown leather.

Four closed doors were off the living room. A big oak table with a flower plastic table cloth had eight chairs around it. In the corner, the kitchen counter separated it from the rest of the room. A large propane refrigerator sat next to the gas stove. Cans of food lined the open board shelves.

"Not much of a kitchen, but we'll survive." Charles smiled.

"If you say so." Barbara motioned toward her husband. "He does the cooking. I stay out of the kitchen."

Barbara Turkwood opened one of the closed doors. "This is our room. You three fight over the other two." She pointed to the door next to her room. "That's the bathroom. Charles, why don't you go fetch our luggage."

Sam pushed open the door on the other side of the bathroom. "I've found my room with the double bed." A big stuffed bear sat in the middle of a pink floral down comforter with matching pillow shams. "There's a bear on my bed with a little welcome sign attached to its paw."

Ed opened the last door. "Guess this is our room, Mark."

Sam wandered over and peeked inside. "Two twin beds for you two with bedspreads. One decorated with different sports and the other with different race cars. Perfect." A small desk and a dresser sat against one wall. A large bookcase filled with paperback books had been built onto the other.

Everyone except Barbara went outside to retrieve their luggage.

The suitcase Sam hauled up the steps, clunked on each one. Goldie still sat by the door. "Stay." Sam smiled at how well-trained her dog was.

"Your dog's welcome inside." Charles leaned down and patted Goldie's head.

"Are you sure?"

"Of course."

"Goldie, come, heal." Sam and her dog went into the bedroom. She threw the suitcase on the bed. "Okay, Goldie, check things out." The dog sniffed every corner, eyeing Sam.

"Yes, Goldie, this is going to be home for a while."

The dog yawned, went over to the foot of the bed, and curled up on the oval carpet, giving an approval of the place.

"Come on, Goldie, I'll unpack later." Sam walked out of the bedroom by Ed and Mark's room. She overheard Mark say, "Yeah, I don't want her to get involved either by chasing after some person who might have been in that shark. Keep her busy out here. She won't have the time."

"Yes, I'll keep her on track."

Blood rushed through Sam's veins. She felt heat rise into her cheeks. The nerve of him to think she would blow this job. *Ed doesn't have to keep me on point. I'm a professional. What is he thinking?*

Before she could vent to them, the Turkwood's came out of their room. Barbara said, "Let's unpack later. We can walk the property and get ideas."

Sam stepped away from Ed's room. Mark came out. "Great idea."

Back in her room, Sam grabbed a pen and notebook.

Everybody exited the cabin. Goldie bounded down the steps and chased a squirrel.

For the next couple of hours, they toured the property.

At one spot, Ed viewed the surroundings and nodded. "This would be a great place for the main house. Sam, a pool over on that side of it?"

"To the right. A good location. Use the native plants for landscaping."

"A good idea." Charles smiled.

"We'll see." Barbara continued farther along.

They discussed one other location and then in front of the old cabin, Ed gave a few remodeling suggestions.

"Yes." Barbara clapped her hands. "And, definitely a new roof."

"Need to get rid of the weeds around the house." Sam shuddered at how close they were to the cabin.

Goldie ran after another squirrel.

"We want to use as many local familiar plants as we can." Charles directed her gaze to the larch trees. "And keep those, if possible."

"Yes." Sam nodded. "I prefer to use the natural flora as much as possible."

The Turkwood's wanted to keep a native look, but have color and ease in gardening.

Sam filled her notebook with their thoughts and her own ideas. Ed and Mark threw some suggestions out. Sam could see this project would entail all her time. This was May. The Turkwood's wanted the house and landscaping finished by the end of August, or by Labor Day at the latest. A quick deadline.

17

The next day, Ed and Sam worked with the Turkwood's on more ideas and on the plans. Mark made minor changes, but basically kept quiet and observed.

Mid-afternoon on Thursday, Charles and Barbara answered a knock at the cabin door. "Frank Collotti. How nice to see you again." She kissed him on both cheeks.

Charles pumped his hand.

"How's everything going?" Frank sauntered into the cabin. "I had to come over this way. Since you called me and told me what you were up to, I thought I would drop by and see if you're really going through with this."

"Ed is marvelous." Barbara strolled over to the table and tapped the plans. "Love his ideas, and the view will be spectacular."

"Hi, Sam." Frank stood behind her at the table. "Barbara told me you'd be doing the landscaping. Ideas coming along?"

"She's incorporated the local flora." Charles traced some of the areas on the drawings. "When this is finished, it'll look natural and yard work won't take all our time."

"Why don't we go over the plans, Mark?" Frank sat next to him.

They reviewed the tentative ideas and made some changes. Sam liked them.

Frank spoke to Mark. "Why don't you come back to Sandpoint. I've some projects I need to discuss with you."

"Go on, Mark." Charles waved toward the door. "We'll work with Ed and Samantha without you. Come back Sunday for dinner. We'll go over what we have then."

"Well, you don't need me at this state, and Linda should be arriving any day now. Okay, I'll be in Sandpoint, looking over property. But I'll definitely come back Sunday." Mark went into the bedroom and five minutes later came out carrying his bag. Frank and he departed in their vehicles.

Sam bet the minute he drove off, he lit his cigar.

Charles barbequed steaks for Thursday night's dinner, along with baked potatoes. Sam tore up lettuce, cut a tomato and chopped up some mushrooms, celery, and a green pepper for a salad.

Friday morning, Sam woke early. She put on jeans and a purple T-shirt. "Come on, Goldie. Let's go for a walk." The dog chased squirrels while Sam inspected all the plants and formed more ideas for landscaping.

Back at the cabin, the smell of pancakes and soft music filled the room.

"Hope you're hungry." Charles smiled as he put a stack of pancakes on a plate in front of her at the table.

"Where'd you go?" Ed took a sip of coffee. "I would have gone with you."

"Your door was closed. Goldie and I walked around the property again. After breakfast, let's get to work. Lots of ideas."

Friday whirred by.

After dinner, they all took the dog out for a stroll, then went to bed.

Sam's hand cramped from drawing.

The next morning, when Sam came out of her room, Ed waited for her in the brown leather chair. He smiled. "Ready for a walk?"

Goldie's tail wagged.

"Guess you didn't want to be passed up this morning." Sam opened the front door.

The dog ran out, nails clicking on the porch, and down the steps.

Sam and Ed toured the property and discussed the plans.

When they returned, Charles made omelets for everyone. Then they worked on the plans until late that night.

"Good night, everyone. I'm bushed." Sam and Goldie went to her room. The dog curled up on the carpet. Sam crawled into bed and fell asleep.

They ate breakfast the next morning and then delved into the plans, making changes, adding new ideas.

Sunday afternoon Sam plopped down on the leopard couch. The Turkwood's were outside taking a walk. "I'm so tired. My hand hurts from writing and drawing. I'm out of ideas. I don't think I'm able to pick up a pencil to draw again."

Ed sprawled in the brown chair, and nodded. "My eyes are crossed. If Barbara changes one more room, I'll throw my pencil at her, if I can even manage that feat."

Goldie nuzzled Sam's arm. The dog held her leash in her jaws and wagged her tail.

"Now?"

The dog's tail wagged faster, while her little butt wiggled along with the tail.

"I think she wants to go out." Ed smiled.

"What was your first clue?" Sam groaned as she stood, leaned down, and snatched the leash from the dog's mouth. Goldie sat, but the lab-whippet body kept wiggling. "Want to come? The exercise will be good for both of us."

"Oh, all right." Ed moaned. "But if you get any more ideas for landscaping, keep them to yourself."

Goldie remained seated as Sam snapped on the leash. Yesterday, they'd smelled a skunk near the cabin, so she kept a tighter rein on her dog.

As they left the cabin and went down the steps, Mark drove up in his red diesel. He jumped out of his pickup. This time, he wore jeans and a blue polo shirt. Sam thought he always looked neat and comfortable.

"Hey, where are you two headed?"

"Nature called." Sam motioned to the dog. "Besides, we're finished and need a break."

"Finished?"

"We've worked night and day." Ed rubbed his hands and arms. "We deserve at least an hour of play."

"Funny."

Linda opened the passenger door and climbed out. She had on a red-flowered sundress with white heeled shoes. Sam felt underdressed wearing her Rider jeans from Wal-Mart and a lavender T-shirt.

"Hi." Linda shivered. "This place is so isolated."

"Where are the Turkwood's?" Mark asked.

"Out walking, too." Sam followed Goldie as the dog tugged on the leash.

"Are they satisfied with the plans?" Mark hurried over to Sam.

She laughed. "Skip them for now. What's happening in the world? We've been listening to mood music all week, have heard no news, and I feel out of touch."

"Linda, go into the cabin. High heels aren't made for walking in the dirt." Mark continued ambling next to Samantha. "Nothing important has happened. Our President has the country well in hand. Same old arguments in Congress."

"What about local news?" Sam wasn't sure she fancied having Mark this close, even if Ed walked along her other side. *At least Linda's back in town.* "I haven't talked to anyone all week. My cell phone died again. The Turkwood's didn't want to run the generator unless we absolutely had to, so I couldn't recharge. At least we have propane lights."

"Sorry. Nothing exciting is happening around here anyway. Oh, I did check on your garden. Hank's taking care of it. He sent a few green tomatoes. Said something about fried green tomatoes being good to eat."

Goldie danced around and bumped Sam's leg. "We need to walk faster. The exercise will be good."

"I'll go back to the cabin, be with Linda, and review the plans while you're gone."

Ed motioned towards the house. "They're inside on the kitchen table. We'll see you when we get back. We need this break."

"Fine, but think about the project. We have to make sure the Turkwood's are pleased."

Sam chased after Goldie as the dog pulled on the leash and sniffed the ground in front of her.

"Turkwood's." Ed followed, shaking his head. "That's all we've thought about. They've changed their ideas so much, I almost quit."

"Me too." When a rabbit darted off, Sam held tight to the leash. Goldie barked and lunged. "No," she told the dog. "Every time Barbara called Mark he'd delete and add ideas also. Why didn't her cell die? Anyway, I thought I'd run out of erasers."

Ed nodded. "Mark could have at least brought us the newspaper. I feel as if I have no idea what's happening in the world."

"I know what you mean. At least we had a portable C.D. player for music. Wonder why the Turkwood's insisted on not leaving the property 'til we finished?"

"They're pressed for time." Ed side-stepped around a huckleberry bush. "They want to get out of here soon."

Goldie tugged harder on the leash. The air smelled fresh and clean. No skunk smells. Sam unsnapped the leash and the dog darted after a small bunny. Leaves crunched as the dog ran through the brush, yipping.

Sam's thoughts turned to her folks and then to her adoption search. She'd been so busy, she hadn't thought of it. If all went well today, she would head back tonight or tomorrow morning, visit her garden, pick up her computer, and surf the Internet. See if she had any hits—anyone looking for her.

While on the Internet, searching, she would also check birthmarks. She wondered if she'd have any mail from either dermatologist.

When they left the trail near the cabin, Sam spotted a blue SUV parked next to Mark's red diesel. "Isn't that Frank Colletti's rig?"

Ed focused his attention on the truck. "Don't know."

A vehicle drove in and parked next to the SUV. "Hey, Paula, Jim, what are you doing here?" Sam smiled. The two climbed out of the car.

Paula hugged Sam. "We went out for a drive and thought we'd check out this project you're working on."

"We just came back from a walk. Come on in."

Goldie raced inside the cabin, screeched to a halt, and growled.

Mark sat at the kitchen table, studying the plans with Linda, the Turkwood's, and Frank. Mark glared at the dog, and then looked at Ed and Samantha. "Hope you had a good walk, cleared your heads. These plans are unacceptable."

Sam's mouth dropped open.

"Why would Samantha's plans not be good?" Jim came up beside her. Paula came up next to him.

"Sorry everyone." Sam put her arm around Paula. "These are my friends, Paula and Jim. They stopped by to say 'hi.' You know Ed, this is Mark, Linda, Frank, and Mr. and Mrs. Turkwood."

Linda smiled. "Hi. Nice seeing you again, Jim."

"Yes." Jim asked, "How did you like the bridge shopping in Sandpoint?"

"Oh, it was so interesting, but not as fun as in Cabo. Did you get anything there?"

"I bet it was fun for you." Jim nodded. "I bought Paula a cute top at one of the boutiques, but you've ruined my surprise."

"I'm sorry. Paula, Jim says you're trying to get pregnant. Any luck?"

"No, not yet, but we're desperate. It will happen."

"I'm sure it will, too, Paula." Sam bit her lip. "Sounds like it's not a good time for you guys to visit."

"No problem." Paula patted Sam's hand. "If you're busy, we'll let you get back to work. We know how important this is to you." She hugged Sam and whispered, "Don't let them get to you. Your ideas are always good."

"Come on, Jim." Paula tugged on his sleeve. "We should leave."

"But we just arrived." Jim yanked away from Paula and strolled over behind Mark and Linda and studied the plans. "Good ideas."

Linda gazed up at him with a furrowed brow. "I thought so, too."

Ed sauntered over to the table. "Okay, so what's wrong with the plans?"

Sam wondered how Ed's voice sounded so calm. She would have shrieked. The Turkwood's loved them before Mark and Frank arrived. Sam wanted to scream, but smiled. "You're kidding, right?"

Barbara tilted her head and gave that sickening smile that Sam knew meant another change was coming. "No, darling, I'm afraid he's not. While Charles and I were walking, we came up with some other ideas."

"She's right." Charles tapped the papers on the table. "Don't wish to change the plans again any more than you, but we're here for a while longer."

Sam's heart picked up its pace—but not from the invigorating walk.

While they discussed some of the changes, Jim and Paula inspected the room. Jim ducked into Sam's room and Paula used the bathroom.

Jim came out. "Cute bear on your bed, Sam."

"I agree," Frank chimed in. "My granddaughter would love that room."

Sam nodded.

"Some of your new ideas sound interesting. You have any more?" Ed pulled up a chair and sat next to Charles.

"A few minor changes to the house." Mark pointed to the drawings. "But the landscaping—"

"We've worked non-stop on these." Sam raised an eyebrow, then smiled at Barbara. "You loved them."

"Well, we've changed our minds." The woman glanced at Mark and then Frank. She looked at Jim and Paula who'd come up to the table again, and shrugged. "It's our prerogative to do that."

"The new ideas make sense, Sam." Frank beckoned her closer. "You have great ones, but I think you'll appreciate the new ideas better."

"Fine." Sam bit her lip. "But how about we run into town for this evening and come back tomorrow?"

Paula clapped her hands. "Great idea. I could make everyone dinner."

"Sorry, darling, we would like nothing better." Barbara harrumphed and waved toward the plans. "But we've got to get this done so we can get to Europe."

"A few more days." Charles grinned. "Then we're out of your hair. Don't you enjoy my cooking?"

"Your food always tastes scrumptious." Sam managed a smile. "I think I've put on a few extra pounds."

"Doesn't look like it to me." Mark squeezed Linda's shoulder. "Honey, why don't you get up so Sam can sit and we can review these new ideas."

Linda stood and stepped back.

Mark rapped on the chair next to him. "That's settled. Sit down, Samantha, and we'll peruse these new suggestions."

"Well, Sam, guess we'd better let you get to work." Jim put an arm around Paula.

"Maybe come back another time." Ed leaned over the plans.

"Might be a good idea." Sam sighed. "But either tomorrow or Tuesday, I'm driving into town to charge my cell phone, check my mail, and get a few things. I won't be gone long." She sat next to Mark in the chair he'd asked Linda to vacate.

"Good-bye everyone." Jim smiled. "I'm sure Sam will come up with some great ideas you'll love."

"Yes." Paula nodded. "She's a great landscaper. See you soon."

"Leaving sounds good." Frank arose. "Linda, would you care for a ride back into town?"

"Thanks, yes I would."

Frank nodded. "Good luck. Come on Linda, we'll leave them to their work."

The four of them left. Sam could hear their clomping down the steps and Linda saying, "Good luck on getting pregnant."

Goldie curled up at Sam's feet.

"Okay, let's see these new ideas." Sam examined the plans.

Everyone sat around the table discussing them. Sam had to admit the changes improved the area and blended with the surroundings even better.

Several hours later, Charles pushed back his chair and fixed dinner. The refrigerator and shelves were stocked with more food. Sam blinked a few times, staring at all the new items. If the Turkwood's had approved of the previous plans, then where did all the supplies come from?

18

Whew. Maybe my luck is changing. Now, I have more time with Samantha away. Barbara Turkwood never makes up her mind.

But, sounds as if Sam wants to come into town. I must not allow that. Not yet. How can I prevent it?

I'll have to put my brain into overdrive. Give it some thought.

I rub my chin. Unfortunately, Samantha is never going to let this drop, no matter how many projects I come up with, or try to avert her actions.

I have to stop her.

An idea forms. I smile, nodding my head. This might work. No matter the outcome, my idea will change her future.

I nod again. Yes, I think this new idea will make a great plan.

A fresh, clever solution. Haven't tried this yet. The other ways did *not* come out right.

This one—it has to work.

I chuckle. I'm so smart. Smarter than she. More brains than all of them.

I can hardly wait.

Success is within my grasp.

19

Mark got out of his chair and rubbed his stomach. "Dinner was great. Why don't we take a walk before we do dishes?"

"A great idea." Barbara grabbed Charles's hand. "Let's go."

"Walking after dinner is good for the digestion." Ed shut off the water at the kitchen sink. "Since it's my turn to do dishes, I'll do them later."

"You all go on." Sam motioned for them to leave. "I'm bushed like Goldie." The dog had already gone to the bedroom to sleep.

Ed walked over and put his arm around her. "Aw, Sam, it won't be the same without you."

She shoved him toward the door. "Go. You'll enjoy it."

When he closed the door, she went to her room and changed into her nightgown for bed. Goldie didn't stir.

Sam crawled into bed, pulled the covers up to her chin, and fell asleep.

Whining, crackling, and coughing woke her up. Goldie's paws were on the bed and the dog whimpered, then barked. Smoke billowed under the door.

Sam threw back the covers and lunged to the floor. She whisked the bedspread off, crawled to the door, and stuffed the spread in front of the jamb to stop the smoke. She placed her hand on the door and removed it quickly when she felt the intense heat.

The others. I have to save them. She screamed, "Fire!" Then listened.

The bedspread. She drug it away and used it on the handle to open the door. Goldie dashed out. More smoke billowed in and filled the room. Sam called for her dog, but the lab disappeared into the smoke and flames. The acrid stench assaulted her.

Sam crouched low and hurried to the Turkwood's room. The door was open. She called out, "Get up! The cabin's on fire!"

No one answered.

The kitchen—ablaze. Fire crept up the walls and surrounded the refrigerator.

The plans lay on the table. Sam snatched them off and coughed uncontrollably. Tears streamed down her face. She rushed to Ed and Mark's room.

No one inside. Barking and screaming came from outside.

The front door stood open and engulfed in flames. The doorframe was also on fire. A loud crack boomed over the sounds of the roaring blaze. A beam crashed down blocking the entrance.

Sam scurried back to her room and slammed the door. She stuffed the bedspread closer to the bottom to block the smoke again, and ran to the window. It wouldn't open. Reaching up, she unlocked it, and heaved upward. The window still wouldn't budge. She wiped snot from her runny nose and dabbed at the tears. The coughing continued, no matter how hard she tried to control it.

By the bed, she dropped the plans and gripped the metal lamp from the nightstand. Back at the window, Sam swung the lamp like a baseball bat and broke the glass.

An explosion blew the bedroom door open. A ball of fire burst into the room. Sam shook her head and threw her hands over her ears, trying to stop the ringing noise that grew louder. It hurt.

Oh, no. The plans. She buckled to the floor and crawled toward the bed to retrieve them. Before Sam could grab the papers, they burst into flames. She covered her mouth, eyes wide open. *Oh, boy.* Sam ran back to the window, and used the lamp to scrape some of the glass from the sill. She stepped on the glass, cutting her feet. She pulled herself up and over, and climbed out.

Shards cut not only her feet, but her legs, hands and arms. She fell from the window and hit her head on a rock.

When Sam awoke, she pushed up onto her hands and knees. She vomited. Dizzy, she dragged herself further from the heat, wincing from the pain. Looking back, she saw the cabin engulfed in flames. The roar almost deafened her. The bottom of her nightgown smoldered.

She rolled over, trying to smother any fire on her. She used her hands and batted at any embers falling around her, preventing a big grass fire. Then she crawled from the heat and the flames. Her last thought before she fell into a black void again: why hadn't they cleared the brush and dried grass from around the cabin?

Sam regained consciousness. Sirens wailed. Loud barking came from the front of the cabin. Screams melded with those sounds. She realized they were her own.

The smoke damaged her throat, and those screams inside her head were muffled on the outside—barely a croak.

The barking became more frantic. *Why hasn't Goldie found me yet?*

The ground trembled. Sirens blared. The grass close to the cabin caught fire and grew closer to her. Sam inched her way toward the flashing lights, but fell into the black void once more.

She woke to someone's voice. "Over here," the man called as he sprayed around her from a hand-held extinguisher.

As Sam opened her eyes wider, a big man bent down, staring at her. "You're going to be okay." He picked her up and carried her away from the heat toward the blinking lights and yelling firemen.

Goldie bounded up, barking.

"Spray water on that side," the man ordered.

He laid Sam down on a stretcher. Another person put an oxygen mask over her nose and mouth.

"We were so worried." Ed leaned over her with a furrowed brow.

Mark waited next to the gurney. "Oh, Samantha, we all thought you were inside. Man, how did that fire start? Did you leave a burner on or something?"

Sam coughed. "What?"

Barbara yelled, "How could the cabin burn down? What did you do?"

The paramedic told the people to stand back. Sam's coughing increased as she tried to speak.

"Talk later." The EMT adjusted the mask.

"Not me," Sam managed to croak out.

Two men lifted the gurney, put Sam into the ambulance, and closed the doors.

"Don't worry." The EMT patted her shoulder. "They'll figure it out."

The ambulance driver raced the vehicle down the road.

20

Sam's arms and legs reminded her of the Return of the Mummy. Bandages covered them from the bottom of her feet to thigh, and hands, which resembled mittens, to her shoulders.

Not only did she suffer the glass cuts from climbing out the window, but she'd been burned from the cinders and flames.

She felt as if sand had been poured down her throat.

The doctor opened her mouth and flashed a light around. "Your throat's been damaged by smoke. You'll be okay though."

Ed, Mark, Paula and Jim crowded around the bed while the doctor explained her injuries. "If all goes well, you can leave by Monday around 5 P.M. I'd rather you stayed one more day."

"No." Sam's voice came out raspy, but firm.

"Samantha, maybe—"

"No, Mark, if the doc will release me Monday night, I'm out of here."

Paula smiled and nodded. "We're taking care of Goldie. You don't need to rush."

"Yes, Samantha." Jim smiled at Paula. "Your dog made it out with no problem. Ed brought Goldie by. We enjoy having that mutt around."

"I'm sorry we didn't find you sooner. I held your dog back from trying to go get you." Ed's eyes lacked the twinkle and his mouth turned down.

"That's why Goldie didn't find me." Sam's voice reminded her of Frank's gravelly, smoking voice. "Thank you for keeping her safe."

"I'm sorry, too." Mark had tears in his eyes. "Not saving you sooner was my fault. I told Ed not to allow Goldie to race off."

"We were afraid your dog would run back inside the cabin into the flames." Ed hovered near the bed.

"No, no, it's okay." Sam swallowed and winced. "I understand."

"Let's let her get some rest." The doctor hung his stethoscope around his neck and shooed them toward the door. "Visitation is tomorrow morning. It's late now. She'll be fine overnight."

They all left the room, and then Sam fell fast asleep.

———

Monday morning, Mark, Linda, Ed, Paula and Jim arrived. The doctor came into the crowded room and examined her. "Are you up to answering some questions?" the doctor asked. "A fire investigator would appreciate speaking with you."

"Send him in."

Soon after the doctor in scrubs departed, a man the same height as Mark entered the room and walked over to the bed. "I'm Arson Investigator Jack Hellman. I have some questions for you."

Before Samantha could say anything, Mark said, "You should have an attorney present."

"I agree, Sam." Ed sighed and looked down at her. "Please, let me call an attorney for you."

"Why? I didn't do anything."

Jim cleared his throat.

Paula touched Sam's shoulder. She fixated on the floor.

"Sam." Ed cupped her face. "Listen to me. The fire was started—"

"Not by me." Sam shook her head as Ed released his hands from her face. She furrowed her brow. "Ask away, Mr. Hellman."

"I'd prefer to talk with you alone." The arson investigator glanced at the others.

"You all heard him." Sam motioned toward the door with her bandaged hand. She croaked out, "All of you wait outside."

"I'm going to go phone an attorney." Ed pulled his cell phone from his pocket and hurried from the room.

"Really, Samantha." Mark lingered. "You shouldn't say anything until you talk with a lawyer."

"Out!" Sam waved him away and watched all of her friends exit the room. *Wonder why they're so concerned for me?*

Hellman came closer to the side of the bed. "They do have a point. You are entitled to an attorney present if you'd prefer."

"Not necessary." Sam swallowed and winced. Talking hurt her throat, but she wanted to get this over with. Her voice didn't sound right, but the words were true.

"Okay." Hellman took out a recorder. "May I record this?"

"Yes." Sam nodded.

The arson investigator spoke into the recorder, giving the date, time, place, and names present. "If you are able, tell me what you remember? You have a knot on your head and fell into unconsciousness for a while."

"That's right." Sam reached up and felt the large bump on her head. It throbbed. "When I fell out of the window I hit a rock."

"Please start at the beginning." Hellman placed the recorder on the little tray table over Sam's bed. He also took out a notebook and pen.

Sam told him who all were at the cabin and what time Frank, Linda, Paula and Jim left. "We changed the plans for the Turkwood's. Then we ate dinner. Afterwards, when the others exited the cabin for a walk, I saw Ed close the door behind him and I went straight to bed."

She cleared her throat and, with both hands, reached for her glass. Her bandages made it hard to clutch the glass.

The investigator came closer and moved the tray closer to her chest so she could sip the water from the straw.

"Thanks. Anyway, the next thing I remember, Goldie barked and woke me up."

"Goldie?" Hellman cocked his head and scrunched his brows together.

"My dog." Sam took another sip. Some of her words were barely a whisper. Her throat felt so raw. "Her paws rested up on the bed and Goldie whined, then barked. Smoke billowed under my closed door. I had no idea of the time."

"When the others went out for their walk, did you go into the kitchen?" Hellman waited for her answer with pen poised above his notebook.

"No, as I told you before, I went straight from the front door to my bedroom. Undressed, donned my pajamas, climbed into bed, and fell asleep. I was wiped out."

"I understand Charles Turkwood did the cooking."

"Yes, he's a great cook." Sam swallowed and took another sip of water, trying to soothe her throat. "He whips up steaks and twice baked potatoes and desserts that make my mouth water just thinking about them. But everything is burned up now."

"When he finished preparing dinner, did he turn off the burners?"

Sam frowned. "Did the fire start in the kitchen area?"

Hellman didn't answer. "Anyone else go into the kitchen area?"

"We ate, then we all helped clear the table and piled our plates and silverware in the sink. It was Ed's turn to wash the dishes, but he said he'd finish when he got back from the walk. I think Charles shut off all the burners. He's very good about that."

"Did you hear anything after you went to bed?" Hellman leaned forward. Even though he was recording the conversation, he still wrote in his notebook. He waited with pen in hand for Sam's answer.

"I'm a sound sleeper." Sam bit her lip. "I don't remember anything. Sorry."

"It's okay. Go on with what happened. Your dog woke you up and smoke came under the closed door. Then what did you do?"

The arson investigator listened as Sam told him about checking the other rooms, trying to save the plans, and then escaping through the window. As she explained everything, he jotted down notes even as the recorder whirred away. She wasn't sure why it was so important for him to do both. Was she in trouble? Should she have talked with a lawyer?

Sam felt the bump on her head. "I think I remember an explosion."

"The propane refrigerator and stove blew." Hellman scribbled on his notepad.

"I managed to crawl through the window, but fell out and hit my head. Memory's kind of fuzzy."

"You're sure you didn't go into the kitchen area?"

"Before the fire? No, I put my plate in the sink along with the others. And, as I stated earlier, I walked from the front door to my bedroom. Why? Did someone say different?"

He perused his notes and flipped a couple of pages back. "The fire started in the kitchen area. Appears as if someone put the tea kettle on and forgot to turn it off." Hellman stared at her. One eyebrow lifted.

"And everyone told you I'm the only one who drinks tea." Sam nodded. "But, I didn't go into the kitchen. I went to the bedroom."

The arson investigator nodded. After making sure no one could overhear, he said, "I know." Hellman leaned closer. "Not a word to anyone, but that's not what started the fire. It was made to look that way."

"Why would someone do that?"

"Not sure, but I'll let the police know my findings. In the meantime, keep this to yourself, and, be careful. You were the only person injured in this fire."

Sam shuddered. "Why?"

"You tell me." Hellman cocked his head.

21

Unbelievable. She's still alive. Samantha is the luckiest person I've ever encountered.

She crawls out the window that I know she can't open. No one sees me when I seal it shut.

My plan—perfect. I cannot risk her coming back to town so soon and still wanting to pursue that stupid birthmark. Why? Abandonment —what an excuse!

Now what do I do?

Maybe with her injuries and the suspicion on her for setting the fire—all that will keep her busy. Too much trouble to even think about that duck mark.

Before the arson investigator talks with Samantha, he asks everyone about the teapot. Now Hellman knows no one drinks tea except Sam. The fire has to be her fault.

Nothing is mentioned about any other way the fire started. So at least part of the plan is working.

This situation demands my close attention. Time to put more of my skills into play. No more screw ups. Let's hope her injuries are severe enough to keep her in the hospital for a few more days.

All her friends are at the hospital, so at least I have a reason to be here. I watch everyone come and go.

Is there a way to get to her in the hospital?

22

When Sam had no answer for Hellman, he closed his notepad and stopped the recorder. He placed both in his pocket. "Be very careful."

As soon as the arson investigator departed, Ed and Mark rushed back into the room. "Are you all right?" Ed came close to her bed. He reached out and gently laid his hand on Sam's shoulder.

"Are you under arrest?" Mark leaned against the foot of the hospital bed.

"Not yet." Sam wondered if one of these men had come back in and set the fire. Why? Her head reeled with the information and throbbed from the lump.

"Where are Linda, Paula and Jim?"

"I told Linda to go back to the hotel." Mark shrugged. "She's not fond of hospitals."

"Jim and Paula went to check on your dog. Paula told me they'd be back later." Ed adjusted her pillow.

With all the talking, Sam's throat felt dry and sore. Her voice croaked. She again thought about Frank Collatti's smoking voice. Would he have set the fire? Why?

"I called an attorney." Ed stroked her shoulder.

Sam pointed to her throat. "I'm tired, I need sleep." She closed her eyes, wanting these two to leave.

"Sure. Get some rest. Come on, Ed, let's leave her alone."

"But—"

"Ed, Samantha's exhausted. She'll be fine."

They both exited the room.

When Sam woke up, Paula sat by her bedside, flipping through a magazine. "You okay?" She arose from the chair and came closer.

"Fine. How's Goldie?"

"Doing okay. Missing you."

"Thanks for watching her again. Please help me with the water. I'm thirsty."

"Here." Paula held the glass while Sam sipped from the straw. "What happened? Ed says you accidentally started the cabin fire."

The cool liquid slid down Sam's throat. *Arson Investigator Hellman told me not to let anyone know the fire wasn't started by the teapot. But Paula is my best friend. It wouldn't hurt to let her know.*

"Don't believe everything you hear." Sam swallowed some more water.

Paula scrunched her eyebrows together.

Even though it hurt to talk, Sam couldn't keep her mouth shut. "I don't know what happened. I went to bed. Goldie woke me up. The cabin was on fire. Goldie dashed out the front door while I made sure everyone else had gotten out. A beam crashed down and blocked the exit to the front. I went out my bedroom window."

"Thank God!" Paula smiled. "The doctor let us know you'd be able to go home tomorrow."

"Doc told me maybe this evening. If I can, I want to get home."

"Jim and I will pick you up with Goldie and take you, whenever the doc says."

"What about Ed?" Sam preferred Paula to take her, but wondered why Ed didn't put up more of a fuss.

"Already told him we'd take you at the time you're released. I'll fix some food so you'll not have to cook for several days."

"Thank you, Paula. That'll be great."

A young-looking man knocked on the door. "Ed Johnson called me and asked me to come see you."

"You're an attorney?" Sam harrumphed. *Did he just graduate from high school?* He combed his black hair to the side, but cut above his ears. When he smiled, his charcoal eyes twinkled. He wore a gray suit, red shirt and purple tie. Sam immediately liked his choice in colors.

"Yes, I'm Philip Hargrove. May we talk alone?"

"Jim and I will be back late this afternoon to see if you get to go home. We'll have Goldie." Paula smiled. "I'll leave you two alone."

The lawyer sat in the chair next to her bed as she explained what Investigator Hellman told her and every step she'd done that night.

"Hellman's right. Don't say anything to anyone about the fire or what the investigator conveyed to you. Appears you're in the clear, but I'll do some research. If they know it was arson and you were set up, you need to be careful."

"Why would someone do this?"

"Could have been an accident, but keep quiet about everything." Hargrove cited a couple of cases to her. "Call me if you need anything further." He set his card down on the service table in front of her.

Sam felt she had been thoroughly briefed. "Thank you, I will."

The attorney strolled out of the room. She studied the card and repeated his name and phone number three times so she'd remember it. Hopefully, she would never need him again.

A half hour later, Frank wandered into her room carrying a vase of flowers. "Heard about your troubles," he said in his gravelly voice. "Sorry." He set the vase down.

"Thank you, Frank." Sam couldn't believe he bought her yellow, pink and orange daisies.

"If you need a good attorney, I can give you a couple of names."

"No thanks. Ed sent one by and we've talked."

"Good. Guess you'll be stuck in the hospital for a few days."

Linda and Mark entered the room. "With those injuries, she should."

"Boy, Mark, I agree with that." Ed followed him in, but came closer to the bed. "How do you like the flowers?"

Sam tilted her head in puzzlement.

"The ones Frank carried in for us." Mark took the card and held it out toward Samantha.

She elevated her bandaged hands, and then eyed Mark. He opened the envelope and read, "For Samantha, Get Well. Ed, Linda and Mark."

I knew Frank wouldn't have brought me flowers. Sam smiled. "Thank you, very thoughtful."

Linda came by the bed and fluffed Sam's pillow. "I knew the daisies would cheer you up. We're so sorry this happened. If there's anything we can do to help…"

"So how much longer in the hospital?" Frank asked.

"Thank you, Linda. Hopefully, Frank, I'm going home tonight."

"Tonight?" Frank's raspy voice asked. "They just don't keep people in these places long enough. I could go talk with them."

"No, no, it's fine. I insisted I go home. I hate hospitals."

Linda smiled. "I don't blame you. They're awful. So full of sick people."

"Doctor wanted her to stay."

"Yes, Ed, and she should." Mark sat on the end of the bed by her feet.

"Paula and Jim will take good care of me at home. I don't want to stay any longer."

"You're sure?"

"Oh, Mark, I believe Sam knows best." Linda patted Sam's shoulder. "If you want to go home and the doctor releases you, that'll be great."

"Thanks. I'll be okay. I miss Goldie, and want to go sleep in my own bed. I promised the doctor I would lie around and rest. Catch up on the news, read my mail, even watch T.V., or something."

"Yes." Ed squeezed her shoulder and grinned. "And I'll come by and check on you. Make sure you're not overdoing."

Frank glanced at his watch. "Well, I'd better go. If you need another lawyer—"

"No, I'm happy with the one I have."

"Have they charged you yet?" Mark got up off the end of the bed and came up the other side and stood next to Linda.

"I've seen the arson investigator once. He hasn't been back."

"Good." Ed avoided eye contact with anyone. "I'm sure it was an accident anyway."

"Of course. It couldn't have been anything else." Mark smiled at her. "Samantha wouldn't set the cabin on fire on purpose." He laid his hand gently on her shoulder.

Samantha shivered from his touch.

Linda raised an eyebrow. Then smiled. "Of course she didn't do it on purpose."

"Careful. Sometimes they charge you anyway." Frank went to the door and glanced over his shoulder. "Get well." He left looking at his watch again.

Mark scrutinized his, too. "Sorry, but Linda and I have to go meet a realtor. Don't go home too early if you're not feeling well." He leaned down and kissed Samantha's forehead. "Take care."

Linda kissed her forehead too and followed Mark, entwining her arm with his.

Sam stared at them as they strolled out arm in arm. Where Mark's lips met her forehead, she felt on fire. She blinked a couple of times and settled her gaze on Ed.

He leaned over and kissed the top of her head. "I planned on taking you home, but Paula insisted."

"You bet she did." Jim smiled as he and Paula walked in.

"That's okay, Ed. You have to work. I'm sorry I couldn't save the plans for the Turkwood's."

Ed kissed her cheek and straightened. "Me, too. But the main thing is you're okay."

Why did that sound like a last-minute statement? "What's going on?"

"Mark had to do some fast-talking with the Turkwood's. They're mad. Upset you burned the cabin."

"Why's everyone believe I did that?"

"Because they're crazy." Paula shrugged.

"They found the teapot on." Ed reached out and brushed a strand of hair behind her ear. "You're the only one who drinks tea."

"I didn't put tea on." Sam crossed her bandaged arms in front of her chest.

"Hey, I'm sure you didn't do it on purpose. No one thinks that, now."

"No one could." Jim clutched Paula's hand.

"Everything will be okay." Paula smiled.

Should I tell them about what Arson Investigator Hellman informed me? It's not fair what Ed and the Turkwood's believe. Hellman's warning blared in her mind, along with her attorney's advice.

"Ed, are the Turkwood's still going ahead with the project?" Sam took a breath and waited for his answer.

"Oh yes. Mark convinced them we could duplicate the plans, and with the cabin down, could even create a better estate."

"Good."

"But I'm not sure they'll keep you as the landscaper. They'll wait and see what the arson investigator comes up with. I'm sorry, Sam."

She sighed. "Oh, perfect. I'm on board with this project and now I might get fired. Even when I didn't do anything. It's not fair."

"No, it's not." Paula shook her head. "We're going to get out of here and let you rest."

"But we'll come back to take you home." Jim smiled.

The three of them strolled from the room. Jim put his arm around Paula as she leaned her head on his shoulder. Ed turned around and gave a little wave.

23

At the hospital, I want to see how easy it will be to get to Samantha.

Flowers—a nice touch.

Too many people in and out of her room. Maybe at night, but she's probably leaving tonight. Stupid hospitals. Why don't they keep people longer?

No problem. I have to use my talent to keep a closer tab on her.

If she is charged with anything to do with the fire, that fact will take care of a lot. But I'm not sure what is happening on that particular front.

Sam doesn't seem too worried about it. This arson investigator is the local fire department's best. Talking around, evidently Jack Hellman is one of the greatest arson investigators they've seen in a long time.

And his report is not finished yet. When I try to learn more, the firemen clam up and won't say much. I do not want to arouse suspicion, so I back off.

Getting Barbara Turkwood to calm down and wait for the report takes a while. But, if Sam isn't going to be charged, I want her working on the plans so she'll keep busy. Not have time to do research on the stupid birthmark. Similar to a nosy reporter, Sam won't leave it alone.

So, she is adopted. Big deal. No reason to search for this guy's identity. Maybe in her mind it is.

I wonder if the thought of her not being able to work on this project will scare her some. Samantha needs the money, now more than ever. Will dollars keep her thoughts occupied? Knowing Sam—No!

I'll keep checking on her. See what she does next.

24

Paula and Jim picked Sam up from the hospital Monday evening at five. Goldie, in the back seat, refrained from jumping on Sam, but gently placed both front paws on her thighs, reached up, and licked Sam's ear.

"Good to see you, too." Sam winced from the paws on her legs. But she smiled for the first time in several hours because she headed home with her dog and friends.

The Queen Anne painted light blue with dark blue trim loomed tall and proud. Sam loved the stained-glass windows and she felt as if she'd been gone for months. Paula rented a wheelchair, and Jim pushed Sam up the makeshift ramp. Paula retrieved the key from under the pot and opened the door. They rolled toward the kitchen. Sam wanted to see her garden out the back.

The wheelchair would be a nuisance, but the doctor ordered her off her feet for a few days. When no one was around, she would see if she could walk. The cuts and burns on her feet weren't that bad, or maybe the good meds kept her pain free.

"Jim, push me over to the back door." Sam tried to open it.

Jim gently shoved her bandaged hands aside and opened the door.

Sam surveyed the yard. "Hank did a great job tending the garden. No weeds." *Probably in better shape than if I'd done it.*

Goldie ran through the yard, sniffing at the lilac bush, the pine tree, and some of the pink rhododendron bushes. The dog went to the fenced vegetable garden area, ran along the fence line and seemed thrilled to be home again, too. Back inside, Goldie raced through the open, swinging doors of the kitchen. Sam could hear the dog running through the house, nails clicking on the hardwood floor. When her sweet whippet-lab returned, the tail wagged non-stop.

Paula wheeled Sam over by the vintage light oak table that had belonged to her mother when she grew up. Sam could still see the patched hole where her mom had drilled into the top by accident. The six matching oak chairs were upholstered with a red rose floral pattern. Paula moved one of the chairs aside and set Sam up close. "We'll be right back." Her friends went out to fetch all the food from the car.

The groceries lined the counter. As Paula stored them in the cabinets and refrigerator, Sam sat in the wheelchair, not objecting. "Man, I'm tired. Jim, why don't you take me to the front room. I'll climb into my comfortable recliner, put my feet up, and relax." She'd bought the La-Z-Boy tan cloth chair when the salesperson had insisted it was the perfect fit for her. She put a floral pillow on it. The recliner was her favorite chair.

"Sure." Jim waited until she transferred into the comfortable seat in the living room, and then walked back to the kitchen.

Sam sat with her feet up and glanced at the stack of mail and newspapers. She held up her hands. They reminded her of when she wore over-stuffed mittens. *Maybe later, I'll go through my mail.* Eventually, she would catch up on her newspapers. She leaned her head back, melted into the soft chair, and fell asleep.

When she woke up, aromas from the kitchen wafted in. She inhaled pork roast and garlic bread. Her stomach growled.

Sam struggled into the wheelchair and tried to push it toward the kitchen. Her hands made it difficult. "Hey, anybody," she yelled. "A little help in here."

Jim hurried into the room and maneuvered her down the hall to the kitchen. The swinging doors sat propped open.

"Surprise!" everyone yelled.

Ed, Mark, and even Frank all sat around the table drinking beer. No Linda present. Goldie was curled near an empty chair, but scrambled up and rushed over to Sam. The dog's tail thumped against her wheelchair as Sam laid her hand on Goldie's head.

"From the look on your face, guess we pulled off your surprise welcome home dinner." Paula grinned from ear to ear. Sam knew she loved giving parties and cooking for them.

"Jim, bring her over here between Ed and me." Mark beckoned. "We saved a spot."

Ed scooted his seat over a bit more so the wheelchair fit.

"We wondered if you would ever wake up." Paula took a plate off the counter. "Hungry?"

"Starved. Where's Linda?"

"She has a headache. Told me to tell you 'Hi.'"

"I'm glad you're hungry." Jim rubbed his stomach. "We are too. Paula's made enough for all of us, and then some."

"Hope you're feeling better." Ed patted her shoulder, which was about the only place on her that didn't ache.

"Somewhat." *I'm amazed that all of these people came into my house and I didn't hear anything.* "Ed, do you know if my computer is fixed?"

"Well, that was the last thing on my mind." Ed blinked and opened his eyes wide. "Haven't called Don."

"Will you call him for me?"

"It's after 6:30." Mark pointed to the wall clock. "Hey, that's an old Coke clock. Wherever did you find it?"

"I shop at antique stores and rummage through old barns. Discovered that one in a barn. Cleaned it up and had it repaired. But don't change the subject." Sam smiled. "Ed, please, I need to find out about my computer."

"Maybe he works late." Paula retrieved the phonebook from the drawer and the receiver from the wall. "I'll look up the number for you, Ed. You call while I get everything on the table."

Ed dialed the number for Sam and put it on speaker. "Hi, Don, this is Samantha Volarie. Is my computer fixed?"

"Hey, where've you been? Tried calling your cell. Your computer's done. You can pick it up anytime."

"Now?"

"If you make it to the shop before seven. After that, I'm closing up and heading out for the week."

"Going fishing or hunting?"

The computer guru laughed. "A little of both."

"Don't lock up. I'll have someone come get it."

Ed hung up.

She turned to Jim. "Please, will you go get my computer?"

"Samantha, how can I refuse you?" Jim stood. "I'll be right back. Then we'll eat."

"Sweetie, there's no rush to go get your computer. My hubby can pick it up next week for you."

"That's right, Samantha." Mark made his point by staring at her hands. "You can't use it anyway."

Sam elevated her bandaged mittens, turning them side to side. "I'll figure something out. Please, Jim."

"No resisting that plea. I'll go."

As Paula's husband started to walk away from the table, Sam said, "Please, make sure you ask Don what was wrong with it."

A half hour later, Sam heard a door open and close.

A few minutes later, Jim entered the kitchen. "Sam, I put your computer in the office. Don explained you were zapped with a virus. Came in through an email. He hadn't seen this one before. Don installed an upgraded virus scan for you."

"That's weird. Thanks for picking it up."

"No problem. Let's eat."

Everyone gobbled down the dinner, except Sam.

"You don't fancy my cooking?"

Sam shrugged. "Sorry, Paula, guess the meds upset my stomach. Not as hungry as I thought. Besides, it's kind of hard with my mitten hands."

"Oh, sorry. Want one of us to feed you?"

"No, Paula. Thanks though." Sam blushed and took a couple more bites of the pork. "Ed, will you hook up my computer for me?"

"Now?"

"Finish eating first. I'm sure no one will mind." She glared at the people around the table, daring anyone to contradict her.

No one opened their mouths.

"Okay." As soon as Ed polished off his peach pie, he shoved back from the table and walked down the hall. Mark pushed Samantha into the office over the carpet situated a foot from the wall. He stopped the chair close to the desk. Jim and Frank followed them into the office. Ed hooked up the computer while everyone watched. Paula stayed in the kitchen to clean up.

"Strange about that virus." Ed switched on the power bar.

"Yes. I'm pretty good about not opening emails or attachments from someone I don't know."

"Well, at least it's fixed." Ed jabbed the button on the computer. Nothing.

"What's wrong?" Sam peered at the black screen.

"Do you have it plugged in?" Frank chuckled as he leaned against the door jamb.

"Very funny." Sam wished everyone would leave.

"Well, …" Jim blushed. "I just set it there."

Ed reached down and plugged in the computer to the surge-protector. "At least I flipped the bar on." He laughed.

The computer hummed into action.

"When Windows comes up, go to Yahoo mail."

A little note popped up: 'No Internet available.'

"Dang it, what now?"

Goldie barked.

"Sshh," Sam knew the dog sensed Sam's anxiety. She petted Goldie's little red head, and waited for Ed to go to settings. "I hate these foul machines. They never work right."

Ed laughed. "Of course, it couldn't be the operator."

Samantha glanced up at Mark who'd stepped closer, staring over her shoulder. She felt his breath on her neck. A sneer crossed his face. She detested it. "Okay, I admit, I'm clueless to these things."

Fifteen minutes passed. Ed still couldn't get on the Internet. "We'll have to call your service provider, see what's up." Ed shoved his chair away from the desk.

Mark yawned. "Why don't you wait until tomorrow. It's getting late."

Sam stared at Ed. "Please call."

He dialed her provider and put the phone on speaker. Sam got an answering machine that said they were closed, but to call an 800 number and maybe a tech could help.

Ed called the number.

Sam explained her problem to the technician.

"Guess you didn't pay your bill."

"I did, too." She gave the tech her account number.

Sam heard tapping of keys. "No, you're delinquent. Seems they shut you off."

"That's not right."

"Computers don't lie."

"No, but operators screw up. I'm sure I have proof I paid."

"Call back if you do."

Ed disconnected and helped Sam look through her records. They called the tech back with the information. "We'll need to see a copy of the cancelled check before we can help you."

"But your office is closed. Why didn't you tell me you couldn't do anything?" Sam wished she could slam down the phone. "Hang up," Sam told Ed. The tech didn't have a chance to answer.

"Calm down." Ed put the computer on sleep.

"Yes." Mark crossed his arms over his chest. "What's so all-fired important anyway?"

"I wanted to do some research."

Paula walked in and sidled up to her husband. "What's wrong?"

"Sam's computer Internet won't work." Jim directed her attention to the screen.

"Well, it's just as well." Paula grabbed the handles on the wheelchair, spun it around, and rolled Sam into the hallway. "You need your rest, and I'm kicking all the men out of here."

"Even me?" Jim frowned and then grinned.

"Especially you." Paula pinched his cheek and smiled.

Ed hovered next to Sam's chair in the hallway by the front door. He raised his wrist and glanced at his watch. "You should rest. Tackle this another day."

"Besides." Mark lifted her bandaged hand gently. "With your hands, you'll have to let someone help you, and we have to work tomorrow."

"Oh, all right." Sam sighed. "I am tired."

One by one, the men said their good-byes and departed. Paula locked the front door, and would stay overnight with Sam, refusing to let her spend the night alone.

25

Sam, still in the hallway, glanced into the living room at her stack of mail and the newspapers.

Paula eyed Sam. "Oh, no." she wagged her finger back and forth. "Those will be there in the morning." She wheeled Sam down the hall toward the back bedroom.

The wood floors flowed into the downstairs bedroom. A queen size bed with a Japanese oak head and foot board perched in the middle of the room. Two matching nightstands sat on either side of the bed and had doilies under matching glass lamps. A highboy dresser adorned one wall and a small closet on another. Old family photos hung throughout the room: one picture of her great grandfather, one with her grandparents, and another photo of her grandmother holding her dad as a baby. A small brown carpet covered the floor on the left side of the bed so Goldie could curl up whenever Sam used this room.

Paula halted the chair inside the room near the foot of the bed. She threw off the bedspread and blanket, grabbed the sheets and made the bed. Then she brought Sam near the nightstand. "You'll be okay down here by yourself?"

"Sure, no problem. You go upstairs and be comfortable in the guest room."

"First, I'll run upstairs and get you a few things." Paula hurried down the hall. Sam heard her run up the stairs and Sam heard her open and close drawers. Soon she came back with a few items Sam would need for her stay downstairs. Paula helped Sam change into pajamas.

"I can't thank you enough for bringing down some clothes and helping me get into bed."

"My pleasure. Now get some sleep." Paula left the room.

In the middle of the night, Sam woke with a start. Goldie waited near the closed bedroom door, growling.

"What is it, girl?" Sam whispered.

The dog fixated on the door and barked once.

Sam slid out of bed and into her chair. She managed to get to the closed door. *Thank God for hardwood floors in this room.* She tried to open the door with her bandaged hands.

Goldie barked again.

CRASH!

Before Sam could try to turn the door knob, she heard whispering, then footsteps. The door opened, knocking Sam's wheelchair backwards.

"What's going on?" Sam stared at Paula.

The dog dashed out the door, barking, and she could hear nails clacking on the hardwood floor as Goldie raced down the hall.

"Hey, Sweetie," a familiar voice said. The dog ceased barking.

Paula pushed Sam down the hall toward the front door.

"Jim? What are you doing here?" Sam saw Goldie's hair standing up along her back.

"Yeah, it's me." Jim patted his heart. "I apologize, Samantha, I ran into the sideboard and knocked a vase over."

"You scared me." Sam felt her heart still beating wildly. She took a deep, calming breath.

"Sorry."

"Why'd you come back?" Paula placed both hands on her hips and tilted her head.

Jim took her hands and kissed each one. "Couldn't sleep. I missed you. Decided to come over and be with you."

"Oh, for Heaven's sake, you two love birds. Take me back to bed, please. Come on, Goldie. Next time, turn on a light."

Paula and Jim rolled Sam back to her room. She collapsed onto her bed. Paula started to close the door. "Leave it open," Sam called out.

⁓

The next morning, Sam woke tired and cranky. Goldie was not by the bed. Aromas of hot cinnamon buns and fresh brewed coffee wafted into the room. It took Sam a minute to get into her wheelchair and follow the odors to the kitchen. Ed, Mark, Paula, and her husband sat around the table, eating. Her dog sat next to Ed as he slipped her a couple of bites.

"What are you doing up so early?" Ed came over and helped roll her to the table.

"We were almost out of here." Mark patted his stomach. "Couldn't miss out on these great buns Paula made."

"Good morning." Sam reached for a bun and then realized she couldn't with her bandaged hands. "If I'm not careful, Paula's food will put back on ten pounds and then some."

"Wouldn't hurt you." Ed leaned over and pecked her on the cheek. "Sorry, but some of us have to go to work today. Ready, Mark?"

"Yes. Glad you're getting around in that wheelchair. Get better, Samantha."

"Good-bye."

A few minutes later, Jim took off, too.

"You going to work now, Paula?"

"I'll change your bandages first. I could take the day off if you want me to."

"As long as you don't close any inside doors, I think I can manage. The hallway, bathroom, kitchen and back bedroom all have hardwood floors, so that'll make it easy."

"How are your hands?" Paula unwrapped the bandages.

A couple of small blisters and a few cuts were healing.

"Wrap them like thick mittens again and I'll manage the wheelchair. They don't hurt too much."

Paula rebandaged both hands, arms, legs and feet. "I lined up your meds so all you have to do is push them off the counter into your mouth. Will make it easier for you. And, don't try to walk yet."

"Yes, Mom." Sam smiled.

"Ok, I'll be back at noon and later for dinner to fix your food." She cut up the buns so Sam could use a fork. "Jim walked Goldie already."

"Great. I'm tired and plan on sleeping most of the day."

"I figured." Paula headed for the front door. "That's what I told the guys." She closed the front door behind her.

Sam propelled herself to the computer room. The area carpet came within one foot from the doorway, but it appeared daunting. She didn't have enough strength to get over it and in front of her desk. Besides, she couldn't manage the keyboard with her hands anyway.

The living room also had an area rug but it was about three feet from the walls. She could get to the stereo cabinet along the side. Sam already had C.D.s in her machine with easy listening music. She had a pen on top of the cabinet and managed to pick it up after grappling a bit, and punched the buttons to get the music going. She sat in her wheelchair and gawked at the stack of newspapers piled on the hardwood floor. She navigated over to them. *Well, I guess if I can't use my computer, I'll get started on my stack of papers.* She could barely reach them, fumbled with the papers, found today's *Daily Bee*, and tried to read.

With her bandaged hands, sometimes she'd turn more than one page at a time. Bobbling with the pages and sections, they slid off her lap and they were too hard to pick up. By the second paper, she gave up and went back down the hall to go to bed. She fell asleep.

Upon awakening, Sam managed to get into her chair and wheeled through the kitchen to the back door. It took a minute, but she managed to open it. Goldie ran outside to pee. When the dog returned, Sam noticed her mail on the counter and scooped it up and set it on the table. With her bandaged hands, she discovered it to be too difficult, but eventually sorted out the junk mail. There was a letter from a Dr. Mallor's office. She couldn't remember a doctor by that name and almost tossed it before noticing "Dermatologist" on the envelope. *Oh, this must be an answer to one of the letters I sent out.*

A container with scissors, pens, etc. sat on the counter. Sam found a letter opener and, back at the table, inserted it into the envelope. Before she could slice it open, the phone rang. She set the opener down and maneuvered her chair over to the phone. After fumbling with the receiver, she answered.

"Hi!" Ed's familiar voice came over the line. "How are you doing?"

"Okay. I can't use the computer because of my bandages. And, I can't roll over the carpet in my wheelchair. I have no Internet. Haven't called yet. I started going through newspapers and fell asleep. I decided to sort my mail."

"Bored already?"

"Everyone's at work, so no one to talk to, and I'm tired of sleeping."

"Want some lunch?"

"Paula will stop by and fix me something. I'm reading my way through back issues of the *Daily Bee*. Began with today's paper and am working backwards."

"That doesn't sound fun. All that old news."

"Old, but something I missed."

"How about something more exciting? I could take the rest of the day off. Maybe take the boat out and we could go to dinner?"

"I'm in a wheelchair and have bandages, remember?"

"I could carry you."

"No, thanks."

"Okay, not a good idea, but I could come over and keep you company."

"Even though I'm tired of sleeping, I'd still probably fall asleep."

"Meds will do that. I could read those papers to you. I bet it's hard with your hands."

"That's for sure."

Paula arrived as Sam hung up from Ed's call. She fixed her a Caesar salad with chicken strips and garlic bread. Her friend set the mail and opener onto the kitchen counter. "Want anything more?"

"Thanks, Paula, but I'm full."

"Then I'll leave. Get some rest."

As Paula was about to close the front door, Ed ran up the porch steps.

"Bye, Paula." He barged into the house and closed the door. "Want me to read the newspaper to you?" Ed smiled.

Sam thought about having him read her mail, but remembered Dr. Mallor's envelope and decided not to share that with Ed.

He pushed her into the living room. The music blared away from the C.D.'s. Sam settled into the recliner. Ed turned down the tunes and picked up a paper. He adjusted his glasses.

"Hey, are those new?"

"Yes, lost my old ones. Jim drove me to the eyeglass place. I still have my prescription, and got new ones. A rush job."

"The black frames are different, but look good on you."

"Thanks. When we got back from the eyeglass store, Jim did some minor adjustments for me. He's multi-talented. He thinks they're perfect for me."

"I agree. I approve of the new look."

Ed read to her. With the drone of his voice and a full stomach, she fell asleep.

⌇⌇⌇

Her eyelids fluttered open. No music. She didn't see Ed, but heard noises in the kitchen.

He came out with a cup of coffee and a cup of tea for her. "Oh, good, you're awake. Why don't we call your Internet provider's office? See if we can get you back on line up and working."

"That would be great."

Ed guided her into the office and used his cell phone to call. He put it on speaker and they talked with a secretary. She asked them for a copy of the paid check. Then they emailed the woman the copy. The lady from the company called back and said she'd received the email. "Let me check with my boss. When he approves everything, you'll have Internet by the evening, or early next morning."

Sam groaned.

Before she could say anything, the secretary said, "I know this is a problem for you, and I'm sorry. We've had a few personnel problems, but they've been resolved. This should not happen again. I'm sorry for the inconvenience."

It was not the woman's fault. Sam decided the poor secretary would probably be getting hassled all day. "It's okay. As long as I'm online by tonight. Thank you."

"That was easy." Ed moved Sam out into the hallway. The dog ran up with a leash in its mouth.

Ed snapped the leash on Goldie's collar. "Come on, girl. Let's go for a walk."

Sam rolled down the hall into the bedroom. She climbed onto the mattress and fell asleep. When she woke up, the smell of lasagna drifted into the room. She slid out of bed, into the chair and wheeled it out of her room to the kitchen doorway. The swinging doors sat propped open. The aromas made her mouth water.

Ed sliced tomatoes and put them in the salad. He looked over. "Hope you're hungry for dinner. Paula made enough so you'd have leftovers. She mentioned something about her and Jim having to go out of town."

"Why didn't she wake me?"

"Jim told her not to and I said you needed the rest. I agreed to make sure you ate. That made her happy. Even Mark volunteered to help out. And, Paula insisted I promise to change your bandages."

Sam glanced around. She hadn't heard anything, and the table was set for two. "Mark's not here, is he?" She shivered and chewed on her lip.

"No."

She thanked God for that. Sam was surprised Paula hadn't conveyed anything earlier to her about having to leave Sandpoint. "Nothing serious?"

"Serious?"

"Why Paula and Jim had to go out of town?"

Ed shrugged. "They didn't seem stressed, and I really didn't ask why. Should I have?"

"No, no, it's okay."

"Don't worry. Paula left plenty of food in the refrigerator and freezer for you, and an army."

Sam laughed. Now if she could manage to do things with her bandaged hands. She wanted to read her mail, but not with Ed around. "Where's my mail?" It no long sat on the kitchen counter.

"Oh, Paula figured it would be difficult for you to open the envelopes. So, while she was here earlier, she slit the letters open for you and pulled them slightly out so you could manage." He motioned out the kitchen swinging doors. "She put them on the maple sideboard table in the hallway so you could reach them easier. Insisted I tell you she didn't read anything."

"Thanks. I'll go check."

"If you're not able to manage," Ed called out after Sam, "I can help."

Sam yelled back, "No, you keep fixing dinner. I'm starved." She found the mail on the sideboard and bumbled with each envelope, sorting through, prioritizing them. Shuffling the envelopes proved to be difficult, but she kept trying.

Ed yelled, "Dinner's ready, unless you want me to help you with the mail."

"No, be right there." Sam didn't want Ed to know *any* of her business and didn't want any help from him. She'd seen an envelope from the bank and didn't want him to see her recent bank statements or know her financials.

Although, she remembered the note in Baja.

Someone already knew.

26

I have to be able to get to Samantha whenever I want. That's not possible with Paula hanging around all of the time.

Knowing how much she wants to get pregnant, sending her off to a fertility clinic is a brilliant idea.

Now I'll be able to keep a much closer eye on Sam without interference from her close friends.

I laugh.

Not sure what my next move is. Hopefully something will present itself.

I smile.

I have lots of patience.

I'm clever.

Spying on her now is much easier.

27

The next morning, Sam decided to see if she could walk. She swallowed her meds and waited about fifteen minutes. She stood holding on to the wheelchair. If she put most of the weight on the outside edges of her feet, standing didn't hurt too bad.

Goldie tilted her head and watched Sam's movements.

With the chair in front of her, Sam took a step, wincing. Even with the meds, pain shot up through her legs and back. She felt it at the base of her neck. But she took another step. Two more and she bit her lip so hard she was afraid she'd draw blood. She plopped into the wheelchair. *Okay, maybe not yet.*

She inhaled deeply, and then, when her breath came under control, she managed her way down the hall to the sideboard where she'd sorted through the mail Paula had stacked and slit open for her. Sam scraped the envelopes onto her lap, and sent her chair racing back to the kitchen.

Goldie followed.

At the oak table, she fumbled with the first envelope. Frustrated, Sam went to the counter and grabbed a pair of tongs from a drawer. She used them to get the contents out of the envelope. One by one she went through all of her mail.

It took her an hour to peruse through the stack. She piled the bills to be paid on one side of the table and threw most of the rest in the trash.

When she finished the last envelope, she stared at the mail.

Something is missing.

Sam pawed through the papers on the kitchen table, rummaged through the trash basket at the end of the counter. Back at the hall table where the mail was originally placed, she studied the floor.

Where is the envelope from Dr. Mallor's office? She rolled back into the kitchen and sorted through the trash again.

Underneath some lettuce leaves near the bottom, she spotted Dr. Mallor's envelope. *How did it get there?* Sam took it out and saw that the envelope was slit, the same as the rest of the mail Paula had opened.

She slipped the tongs into the envelope, pried it apart and peered inside. Nothing. She searched the trash again. When she didn't find the letter, she dumped the trash out onto the floor.

Goldie sniffed at the pile, backed away and sat, eyeing Sam as though the dog's mistress had lost her mind.

With the tongs, Sam dug through the mess. Salad mixings, the mail she'd dumped in, the lasagna she didn't eat last night—that's all she found.

Goldie's ears perked up and the dog uttered a low growl.

"What are you doing?" Ed leaned against the kitchen door jamb.

Sam jumped about an inch from the seat of her chair and felt her racing heart. "You scared me. How did you get in?"

"I knocked, but you didn't answer, so I used the key under your pot. You okay?"

"How'd you know about the key?" Had he seen her use it?

"Paula showed me before she went away."

"Oh."

Ed came in and started picking up the garbage, putting it in the wastebasket. "Looking for something?"

Still holding the envelope in one hand, Sam muttered, "Can't find a letter." The envelope's lettering faced the wrong way, so she hoped Ed couldn't see the name.

Goldie sat by Sam's chair. The dog cocked her head.

"I don't see any letter in here." He finished cleaning up the mess and went to the laundry room. He retrieved the broom and dustpan, and swept the kitchen floor. After putting the wastebasket back at the end of the counter, Ed faced Sam. "Was it important?"

"Don't know." Sam tucked the envelope under her thigh. "What are you doing here?"

"Mark and I have a project out this way, so I dropped by to make sure you felt okay today, and to change your bandages. You doing well?"

"I'm fine. Meds I'm on are great. I have no pain."

"Did you eat?"

Sam bit her lip. She had been so busy, she'd forgotten food.

While Ed browsed in the refrigerator, Sam rolled to her room and put the envelope in the nightstand drawer to the left of the bed and wheeled her chair back to the kitchen.

Ed made a quick scrambled egg mixture and toast. Sam ate. Ed fixed himself a cup of coffee.

"Thanks."

"No problem. Paula made me promise to change your bandages. After digging in the garbage…"

"Okay, let's do it."

Ed put six bandages on Sam's one arm and five on the other arm and wrapped them from under her armpits to her hands, double wrapping the hands to look as if she had mittens on again. Then he bandaged and wrapped her legs and feet. All that wrapping took him a half hour. "Let me check the bump on your head." He palpitated it lightly. "Looks good." Ed read his watch. "If there's nothing else you need, I'm off to work."

"Thanks."

The front door closed and she heard the lock click. Sam decided to search all the garbage cans as best she could. She used the tongs and hoped the letter had been placed in the computer room. But she found nothing from Dr. Mallor.

In the kitchen, she found a pen and jabbed at the buttons on her phone, punching in Dr. Mallor's number. The service answered and a machine said, "I'm sorry, Dr. Mallor's office is closed until Monday. If this is an emergency, dial 911, or leave a message and the office will contact you on Monday."

Sam hung up and went back down the hallway to the door of her computer room and wondered about the thick carpet. She glanced at her hands and feet. She arose and took a step. By bracing herself on the doorframe and desk, she made it to the chair in front of her computer and plopped down.

Now what? She picked up a pencil. Using it, she punched the on button. Her computer whirred to life.

With the pencil, she managed to get to her email account.

There were no emails—all gone.

What the heck? Using her pencil, she poked a bunch of keys.

The emails did not reappear.

Sam called the service provider's technician. "What's going on?"

"Are you back on line?"

"Yes, but how can my emails have disappeared?"

The technician had no answer. "It's not like Hotmail, where, unless you've paid extra, they wipe you out after thirty days. Could you have deleted them by accident?"

With the fire and all that had happened, Sam could not remember when she last saw her emails. "I don't think I deleted them, but anything is possible," she told the tech.

"I don't know what to tell you, but if they're not in your trash file, they're gone, I'm afraid there's no getting them back."

"Oh, great. Modern technology."

"I suppose the Post Office never lost any mail." She heard the tech sigh.

"I get your point. It's just that I had a huge list of emails."

"Sorry, nothing I can do for you."

Sam hung up and focused on her blank screen.

She dialed the first two digits of Paula's home phone and remembered Ed had mentioned they'd gone out of town. She thought about Dr. Mallor's envelope. Had Paula taken Dr. Mallor's letter? Why? *Should I call her cell? No, they needed privacy to make a baby.*

On Google, Sam typed in 'dermatology.' While the computer searched away, she dug around on the desk and found her photos. She opened the one packet and took out the picture of the flesh and skin with the discoloration and laid it on top. She hunted for 'birthmark' on another search engine and the site found seven journals.

The first one listed, *Dermatology Online Journal.* Then Sam went to the Gale Encyclopedia of Medicine under Birthmarks and read:

Birthmarks are noncancerous or benign skin growths made up of fast-growing or poorly formed blood vessels or lymph vessels. Congenital, if found at birth, and acquired, if developed later in life. They are found anywhere on the body. Birthmarks range from faint spots to dark swellings covering wide areas.

Birthmarks also include angiomas, which are a benign skin tumor composed of rapidly growing, small blood or lymph vessels, and vascular malformations, which are poorly formed blood or lymph vessels.

There were so many types: congenital hemangiomas, strawberry marks, cavernous hemangiomas, etc., that Sam's mind whirred with all of the information.

She scrolled through more articles, but found no pictures of a duck birthmark. Sam glanced at her photo. *Who were you?*

Had the person who'd been eaten been out swimming? Had someone dumped the body overboard? Did the tennis shoe belong to the person with the imprint? If it had been an unusual style or size, Sam could start with the shoe. Too bad it was a very common Nike shoe, size eleven. No help there. *I wonder even if the shoe and chunks of human flesh belong together.* Probably, but who knew?

Goldie stood and stretched. The dog perched her head on Sam's lap. "What?" Sam petted the dog. "I've ignored you for too long?"

She shut down the computer and struggled back into her wheelchair. Then she rolled down the hall, went through the swinging kitchen doors, and headed to the back door. She grappled with the doorknob, managed to get it open, and let her dog out. Goldie ran around the yard, sniffing at the oleander and along the garden fence. Over in the corner, the dog squatted.

The air smelled fresh and clean and the sun shone down, warming the earth. Sam wished she could work in her garden.

The phone rang. Sam ignored it, figuring she wouldn't make it in time to answer anyway.

Goldie raced up the back steps and into the kitchen. Sam shoved the door closed.

The phone rang again. This time, Sam wheeled over and answered.

"Samantha, where've you been?"

"Hello, Mark. What's up?"

"Your line's been busy, then no answer. You okay?"

"Thanks for the concern. I made some calls, then I used the computer. When I let my dog out, I ignored the first call because I knew I wouldn't get there in time."

"I was worried."

"Well, Mark, don't be. I'm a big girl. What do you want?" Sam blew out her breath. *Why is he worrying about me?*

"Linda wanted to come by this evening. She wants to make sure you're all right. We'll bring Jalapeño's take out. Have Ed, too."

"Sounds good. I thought Linda didn't enjoy eating Mexican food."

Goldie bumped Sam's chair wanting attention. Sam reached down and scratched the hair on her dog's head.

"She likes American-made Mexican restaurants. Not the ones in Baja. We'll come by around 6:30?"

"Sure. Want me to check with Ed?"

"Already taken care of. He intimated he'd be there anyway to fix you dinner."

"Oh?" Sam stopped stroking the dog and shifted in her wheelchair.

"Paula insisted he made sure you ate. Sounds as if you got your computer working."

"Yes. Finally got to search the Internet."

"Samantha, how could you with your bandaged hands?"

She laughed. "I used a pencil."

"Clever girl. Shouldn't you be resting?"

The dog sauntered over near the back door and drank from her water bowl. Sam needed to feed Goldie. "I had some stuff to do. I wasn't tired."

"If you desire some work, I could keep you busy."

Sam rolled her eyes heavenward. *Desire some work. How sarcastic can he get?* The man drove her nuts. "Thanks, but I'll rest now."

"Okay," Mark said. "Tell us all about your search tonight. Bye."

28

Linda, Mark and Ed showed up with dinner. They sat around Sam's kitchen table. She wolfed down her veggie burrito and sucked her root beer through the straw.

Mark laughed. "Are you starving?"

Sam stared at him as she forked some salad into her mouth. She chewed slowly. *No, I'm nervous having you around.*

"You bored?" Ed took a bite of his enchilada.

After swallowing her bite, she shrugged. "No." She didn't tell her guests she was working on the birthmark, but did confide in them about her searching the adoption records.

"That's so interesting." Linda took a delicate nibble of her salad. "I didn't know you were adopted. Tell me all about it."

Ed scraped his chair back. "If everyone is finished, why don't we move to the front room?"

"Sounds good." Mark pushed Sam's wheelchair down the hall into the living room next to the recliner. Sam transferred over, lifted the lever to pop up the footrest, and felt better when she propped her feet up.

Mark and Linda sat on the soft-material, floral couch. The pattern matched her pillow on the recliner.

Ed pulled a chair over next to Sam. "She likes talking about adoption. She's proud of it."

"Yes. There are several sites on the Internet you register on to see if anyone is looking for you, or you can search for someone. I signed up on those."

"Any response?" Linda entwined her arm through Mark's and smiled.

Sam shook her head. "Not yet. I also found a search angel to help me."

Linda wrinkled her nose. "A search angel?"

"Yes. A person on the Internet who helps you find and connect with adopted relatives. You give them as much information as you can, and they do the research for you."

"Mark, isn't this interesting?" Linda patted his knee.

He nodded.

"Anyway, the search angel suggested I contact Social Services and ask for non-important information. California doesn't give out any names, but they will send me descriptions and any medical history."

"So, you were born in California. And are you going to do that?" Linda raised her eyebrows.

"Yes."

When Samantha finished her adoption search story, Mark frowned. "Think you should be doing this now?"

"Nothing else to do." Sam motioned at her wheelchair. "And no, I don't *want* your work."

"Okay." Mark laughed. "If it's okay with you, it's fine with me."

As if it's any of your business in the first place. Sam opened her mouth to tell him so, but snapped it shut. Linda seemed excited for her. Sam smiled.

"So how does adoption make you feel?" Linda leaned forward. "I'm not sure how I'd handle it."

"Makes me glad that someone wanted me. But also, I have abandonment issues." Sam didn't say out loud: *and that's why I have to figure out who my shark ate.* She wasn't going to mention that part.

"What kind of abandonment issues?" Linda tilted her head, scrunched her eyebrows, and wrinkled her nose.

Man, she looks cute when she does that.

Sam felt Linda was genuinely curious. "Being left on a doorstep, I can't help but feel someone didn't want me. Yes, my adoptive parents love and care for me. But someone didn't. That idea kind of messes with my head. Hence, the need to find out things."

"For example, maybe who was in your shark." Ed nodded. "Explains a lot, don't you think so, Mark?"

The man bit his lip.

Why did Ed have to bring up the shark? Sam wished he hadn't done that and changed the subject. "I'm going to try and find my missing cousin."

"You have a missing cousin?" Linda looked horrified. "Like on the milk cartons?"

"Well, she's not on a milk carton, but Jennifer has been missing for over two years now. No one has heard from her and she always contacted someone in the family."

"Police aren't able to find her?" Mark leaned forward, appearing to be interested in her answer.

Maybe he is interested in this. "No, no trace of her. I'm thinking about hiring a detective to find her."

"Might be a good idea," Ed stroked his chin.

Linda asked a few more questions about adoption and the missing cousin. Then she eyed the pile of papers against the wall and some next the recliner. "You sure have quite a stack of newspapers."

Sam chuckled. "I haven't had a chance to catch up on all of them. I feel so out of touch. Are you sure nothing happened while we were up in isolation?"

Ed scrambled out of his chair. "How about dessert? I'm going to go dish up some."

"If it's fried ice cream, I'm in." Mark smiled.

Ed disappeared around the corner and Sam heard his footsteps in the hallway.

"You were in isolation at the hospital?" Linda shuddered.

Mark clasped her hand. "No, dear, she's talking about being in that cabin over in Clark Fork. No, nothing exciting happened while you were up there."

"Did you tell them about—"

"Linda, that's enough now. They're not talking about the fashion show that went on while they were gone."

Sam noticed Linda squint. Was Mark squeezing her hand too tight? "Did something happen?"

Linda nodded. "I modeled in a fashion show and I saw your friends Paula and Jim. He looks so familiar, but I guess I've never met him."

"That fashion show sounds fun." Sam was saved from further comment when Ed served the fried ice cream. She took a spoonful and so did Ed. Mark reached over for a few bites, and Linda sat there and pouted.

The model-thin woman couldn't eat such things because she would gain too much weight and maybe become a size 2 instead of a 1.

Sam sighed. *Where's this jealousy coming from?*

Linda took the spoon from Mark and took a bite. "This is delicious." She ate no more.

When the ice cream had been totally consumed, Mark arose. "Well, we'd better go. You look tired, Sam."

"I am getting a little sleepy. Thanks for coming."

Mark took Linda's hand as she rose from the couch. They left after Linda hugged Sam.

Ed gathered up the dishes.

"Before you take them to the kitchen, hand me some newspapers, please."

Ed grabbed the top paper, plopped it on her lap. Then he took the dishes into the kitchen to clean up.

Sam, still sitting in the recliner, tried reading the newspaper, but found it too difficult to turn the pages. She gave up, closed her eyes, and fell asleep. She jerked when a hand touched her shoulder.

"Wake up. Let's get you to bed."

Sam opened her eyes and smiled at Ed. "Guess I'm more tired than I thought. Thanks."

She slipped into the wheelchair and Ed pushed her down the hall to the downstairs back bedroom. "Need help?"

"No, I can manage from here. Leave the door open, but when you go outside, please make sure you lock the front door."

"Will do." Ed kissed her cheek. "Bye."

29

Thursday morning, Sam woke to banging on her front door. Goldie ran down the hall, barking.

The pounding continued. Sam donned her robe, maneuvered into her wheelchair and down the hall. She fumbled with the locks, yelling, "Wait a minute. Having a hard time opening this."

She heard someone whisper, "Not likely."

When Sam opened the door, two men waited on the porch.

Goldie stopped barking. The dog sat next to the wheelchair and her tail thumped on the hardwood floor.

"Are you Samantha Volarie?" the older man asked. He wore a wrinkled dark grey suit with a red tie and carried a brown briefcase. His hair was salt and pepper, but his green eyes sparkled.

Sam took a deep breath. "Yes. Who are you?"

"I'm Detective Wayne Kline." The man pulled out his shield. "And this is my partner, Kevin Harrison."

The young man showed his badge. Harrison appeared fresh out of the academy with short-cropped blonde hair, no facial hair, and bright blue eyes. "Ma'am." He eyed her bandages.

"Ms. Volarie, may we come in?"

They moved to enter. Goldie backed up, and her tail wagged harder.

Great watch dog. "Sure, let's go into the living room. If you'd help me."

Detective Kline wheeled Sam to the recliner and waited for her to settle in. Then he sat next to his partner on the couch. Goldie sat next to the chair, and Sam reached over the arm rest and petted her dog.

"If you don't mind my asking, what happened to you?" Detective Harrison pulled a notepad out of his shirt pocket and poised a pen over his pad waiting for her to answer.

Sam told the detectives about the Turkwood's project and cabin fire. "The burns and cuts aren't too serious, but these bandages are a nuisance when you want to open a door or something."

Harrison looked at the floor for a moment. His cheeks turned red.

"If you didn't come about the fire, why *are* you here?"

Detective Kline reached into his briefcase and brought out a tape recorder. "Mind if I set this up?" He put the recorder on the table in front of the couch.

"No, I don't mind." Sam tilted her head. "What do you need it for?"

The detective showed her his palm, wanting her to remain quiet. Then he punched the recorder button. "This is Detective Wayne Kline with Detective Kevin Harrison and Samantha (Sam) Volarie." He also stated the date and time. Then he asked, "Ms. Volarie, did you send some pictures to a Dr. Mallor?"

Sam leaned forward. "Yes."

"Did Dr. Mallor respond?"

"Yes, but I didn't receive his answer."

"Aw, come on, lady." Harrison shook his head and glared at her.

"Excuse me. What is your problem, detective?"

Kline reached out and jabbed Harrison's arm. "Ms. Volarie, why don't you know what Dr. Mallor responded?"

"The letter disappeared. I found the envelope in the trash, but no letter. Never mind that. What's all this about? Tell me, or we're done talking here."

When Sam raised her voice, Goldie got off the floor and her hackles rose. The red hair bristled and Goldie uttered a soft growl.

"It's okay, Goldie." The dog sat back down, but her hair remained at attention.

"Did you get any news while you stayed at this cabin?" Kline glanced at Sam's stack of papers.

"No. It was up a dirt road outside of Clark Fork. No power to the cabin. We worked non-stop. And, again, so?"

"Did you know an Anthony Neal?" Kline pushed the recorder closer to Sam.

"Anthony Neal?"

"Maybe Tony?"

Sam gaped. That was the name of the stupid accountant who'd gotten her into so much financial woes. "Who's he work for?" She bit her lip.

"You haven't read the paper the last couple of weeks?"

"I told you, no." *What could this be about. I don't appreciate the young detective's attitude.* Her gut started churning.

Detective Kline eyed the stack of newspapers again.

"I haven't caught up on my back papers yet." Sam motioned to the pile and held up her hands. "It's kind of hard with bandages."

"Rita Neal's husband went fishing down in Baja. Tony left there, driving home on his own. He never arrived. He's been missing for almost three weeks now."

"Rita Neal?"

"Do you know her?"

"I'm not sure." Sam felt her heart racing. She should ask these detectives to leave right now. Rita and Tony—the couple she had met through Ed. That's how she'd found the stupid accountant.

"What's this have to do with my pictures I sent to Dr. Mallor?" Sam's heart raced. She was getting a bad vibe.

Kline opened his briefcase again, and took out a magazine. He flipped to a marked page, got up, came over to her recliner, and placed it on her lap.

She stared at a picture of a man's hip with a duck birthmark circled in red. Sam perused the article and recognized the by-line: Dr. Fredrick Mallor.

"That's the mark in my pictures." Sam tapped the red circle.

"Yes. And that's Anthony Neal."

"He's from here?"

"Spokane. He's a big shot accountant."

Sam leaned closer to the magazine and skimmed the article. Then she raised her gaze to the detective. "Oh, my God." This magazine had not been on the Internet and it was missing from the library.

"Where'd you take the pictures?" Kline sat back down on the couch.

"In Baja." Sam explained she'd gone there for a fishing contest. "I caught the biggest shark and when they gutted it, it had body parts inside the stomach."

"How did the stomach get opened?" Harrison jotted down something on his notepad. He glared at her, waiting for an answer.

Detective Harrison suspected her of something. Sam shivered. "A dog ripped it open." Then she described how the Baja police weren't interested.

"The police in Mexico may not have been interested, but we are."

"I understand, Detective Harrison." Sam shut her mouth. Then she thought of her financial trouble and the fact she had a picture of this Neal's birthmark. *I haven't done anything wrong, but will these detectives believe me?*

When they delved into her, they would find out she had a connection with this guy. A connection that could be a possible motive to want him dead. Why hadn't she listened to Mark and *not* gotten involved.

"May we see your photos?" Kline shifted on the couch.

Goldie whined. The hackles calmed down, but the dog remained alert.

Sam blinked. "What? Oh, yes. I'll go get them."

She put both arms on the chair and started to rise to get into the wheelchair. The magazine slid to the floor.

Detective Harrison stood, walked around the coffee table and picked the article up, placing it on the glass-topped table in front of the couch. "That's okay, Ma'am. Tell me where they are. I'll get them for you."

She eased back into the chair. "They're in the front parlor. I use it as my office." She pointed across the hall. "Right by my computer."

I don't want the detective to get the photos, but I know one of the packets is right inside my office next to my computer where I can see.

As Detective Kline made small talk, she never took her gaze off Harrison's side. When he came back, the two men sorted through the packet of photos and examined each one. Kline looked up from the pictures. "Why was finding out who this guy was so important to you?"

"I'm over-curious." Sam tilted her head and jutted her chin toward the photos. "So, I snapped shots. Everyone told me it was a waste of time and I shouldn't bother. The body could be anyone. But as usual, I wouldn't listen."

"Why?" Harrison wrote in his notebook.

"A long story, but I can't stand the thought of someone being abandoned."

"And?" Detective Kline coaxed.

"And not trying to discover who that shark ate felt as if someone would be abandoned. They said I'd never figure out who."

"They?" Kline leaned forward. "You mean the police?"

"Them, and Ed, and Mark along with the other men in the fishing group. Even my friends here thought I was nuts."

"Who were these men in Baja with you?"

"I flew down and met up with Ed Johnson. He's a local building architect I do projects with sometimes. I'm a landscape architect. I work at the nursery out in Ponderay."

"You mentioned a 'Mark'?"

"Yes, he put this shark fishing competition together. I met Ed in Baja. This Mark Randall turned out to be a friend of his. They hadn't seen each other in a long time. Mark came with his girlfriend Linda. They were already in Cabo when I arrived.

"The group consisted of eight other men besides him, and then me. We each put up five thousand dollars, and the person who caught the biggest shark won the pot. That would be me."

"Mark Randall?" Detective Harrison wrote in his notebook.

"Yes, Detective, he's a big shot contractor from Los Angeles, I believe." Sam shrugged. "He's here now on the Turkwood project in Clark Fork. That's why I knew nothing about this Anthony Neal being missing. Ed stayed up at the cabin with me."

"That would be Ed Johnson?"

"Yes. As I told you earlier, he's an architect." Sam shifted in her chair, feeling uncomfortable. "Mark's staying at the Edgewater Resort. He came and went from the Clark Fork site. Then we had the fire."

"Mr. Randall didn't tell you about Anthony Neal?"

"No, he reported nothing much was happening in Sandpoint. I think he wanted us to concentrate on the project. It was rather a rush job and important."

Sam caught the look between the two detectives. "Why? Should he have told me? I mean you said Neal is out of Spokane, not Sandpoint. Does Mark know this Anthony Neal? He sure didn't recognize that duck discoloration."

"Are you sure?"

"None of the men seemed to know, and, I believe, they all worked in the construction business in one form or another. From a few different states and different parts of California. Tried to keep me from taking pictures. Most of them acted disgusted with the entire idea. Told me it was such a waste of time."

The young detective scribbled in his notebook, trying to capture every word Sam spoke even though the tape recorder whirred away.

Kline shuffled through the photos again, examining each one. "Dr. Mallor gave us this magazine article." He drew the magazine closer and studied Sam's pictures against the magazine. "The doctor is convinced this is Anthony Neal."

"I don't believe there are two identical birthmarks out there." Detective Harrison rapped on the picture. "Probability—very low. Maybe Mrs. Neal will recognize the tennis shoe."

"It's a size eleven."

Both men gawked at Sam.

"I wrote it down."

"Thank you, Ms. Volarie. And you don't know Tony Neal?"

Now Sam entered into the hard part. If she said no, and they found out, which they would, she'd be in trouble. She chewed on her lip. If she didn't quite biting, she would have a bruise in the morning.

"Ms. Volarie?" Detective Kline looked up from studying the photos, with eyebrows scrunched together, expecting an answer.

Harrison paused with pen over his notebook.

"Maybe. I think I met him and his wife at a party." *At least that's true.* Maybe she wouldn't have to say any more.

"Would you mind coming to the station? We'll type up a statement. The Spokane police are on their way over and want to talk with you also."

"Well—"

"It's not a request." Harrison put his notebook in his pocket and slid the pen in next to it.

"If you're not up to it physically," Kline said, "we could have them come here?"

"No. I need to get dressed. Might take me some time." Sam held up her bandaged hands.

"We'll wait. If you need assistance, I'll call a female officer."

"Thanks, Detective Kline, but I have some sweats in my room in the back. I'll manage."

30

It took Sam a half hour to get ready. The detectives arose as she rolled into the living room.

"Ready, Ms. Volarie?"

"Yes. Goldie, you stay here."

The detectives helped Sam outside, down the make-shift ramp and into the back seat of the car. Harrison folded the wheelchair and set it in the trunk.

At the police station, Detective Kline escorted Sam through the office. Men and women glanced up, then went back to talking with people sitting at their desk or typing on their computers or talking on the phone. The detective brought her into a room with a metal table. Two gray folding chairs sat on one side and a single chair on the other. A big beveled mirror hung on one light green wall. It reminded her of a typical interrogation room seen on television. Sam felt beads of sweat on her forehead. Dampness soaked her armpits. She reached up and with the back of her bandaged hand wiped her forehead before the water dripped into her eyes.

Kline moved the single folding chair aside and maneuvered Sam's wheelchair up to the table. Harrison walked in, and he and Kline sat across the table from her. Kline laid down the magazine article and her pictures. "Are these all the photos from your trip?"

"There were two packets. If Detective Harrison grabbed both, then yes. The ones we perused through at my house are definitely all the ones I took of the shark gutting."

"Harrison?"

"I only saw the one packet."

"We'd prefer to see all the others. May we send someone to your house to pick them up?"

Sam raised an eyebrow at Detective Kline. "Am I under some sort of suspicion for something?"

"No, of course not."

"Then we can go back together."

"Let's get started on your statement. It would save time."

"Look Detective, the man is dead. All I did was take pictures of a shark and its innards. I'm the one who tried to identify the guy. I'm feeling uncomfortable."

"I'm sorry for your discomfort." Detective Kline tapped the magazine. "We want to be able to tell Mrs. Neal what happened to her husband."

"Of course. And, you can now. What do the rest of my photographs have anything to do with it?"

"Look, lady, we can get a search warrant if you don't want to cooperate." Harrison leaned forward and glared at her.

The vehemence in his attitude made Sam flinch backwards. She dropped her lower jaw.

"Harrison, that was uncalled for." Kline pointed to the door. "Take a walk."

The young man scraped his chair back along the tile. He left the room.

Sam inhaled and eyed the big mirror, then spoke to Kline. "I don't know what's going on here, but Detective Harrison's manner scares me." She focused on the doorway where he stomped out. "I'm not feeling well. Something, as they say, is rotten in Sandpoint."

"He's young and eager. I'm sorry for his outburst."

"I'm not stupid, Detective Kline. I bet you didn't bring Dr. Mallor in for his statement. And, this," she waved around the room, "is not me just sitting at your desk."

Sam jabbed her hand toward the mirror. "And I bet that's a two-way. You want to tell me what's really going on. And cut the good cop/bad cop act."

Kline nodded. "You were in Baja; you have photos of Neal. Yet you say you know nothing about his disappearance."

"I couldn't have identified Mr. Neal from that duck imprint. Dr. Mallor performed that feat. I explained I've been isolated from friends, news, and papers for the last week or so.

"And then the arson fire. Check it out. No one else received injuries but me. Talk with Arson Investigator Hellman. I didn't set the fire."

"We'll do that."

"I hadn't heard anything about Neal, and even if I did, I wouldn't have connected my pictures with him, unless you referred to a 'duck birthmark' in the papers."

Detective Kline raised his shoulders. "No, we didn't. And this Mr. Randall didn't tell you about Neal's disappearance?"

"No. Besides, Mr. Randall is from Southern California. And, as I told you, I wasn't alone up at the cabin. Ed Johnson worked with me, along with the Turkwood's. Ask any one of them."

"We will." Kline wrote something in his notebook for the first time.

"Has Neal's disappearance been on the news lately?"

"No."

"So, how could I know about it?" Sam jabbed her chest. "I'm the *one* who has been trying to find out who belongs to this mark." She reached over and shoved the magazine further away from her. "And I don't appreciate being treated as a suspect, because that's how you're making me feel."

She rolled back from the table. "If you want those pictures, I'll be glad to go home with you and get them. But no, you may not send an officer for them. Goldie would go ballistic."

"Goldie?"

"My dog!"

Sam wheeled herself to the door, fumbled with the handle, and managed to open it. Harrison and two other men stood on the other side.

"Ms. Volarie," one of the men said, "we were coming in to speak with you. I heard you, and I'm sorry this is upsetting to you, but Mr. Neal's been missing. Now you show up with photos of a piece of him."

"Unless you're arresting me, give me a ride home to get the other packet. Also, I'm tired. Maybe we could do this later. Then I'd be glad to answer all of your questions, unless you're going to be disrespectful. In that case, I'll call a lawyer and I won't say anything further until I know more why you're acting this way."

"You can't go," Detective Harrison blurted out.

"Excuse me?" Sam glanced at the man who'd told her Mr. Neal had been missing. He wore an expensive black suit with a burgundy tie. Sam figured him for the boss, or a district attorney. Maybe the other man in the blue suit was the district attorney.

"If you'll go back in the room, I'll explain things." The man with the burgundy tie motioned back toward the table.

"Fine." Sam placed her bandaged hands on the wheels of her chair. "But maybe I better call my lawyer."

Mr. Burgundy Tie pushed her back to the table. "Did you know Mr. Neal?"

"I believe once I ask for a lawyer, I don't have to answer any more questions. And you are not supposed to ask me anything."

"That's true. Get a phone for Ms. Volarie to call her lawyer. Do you know an accountant named Neal?"

There was Sam's problem. "Where's that phone?"

The man smiled. "Detective Kline, give the lady her phone call."

The two newly arrived men exited the room. Detective Kline handed her a phone.

Sam stared at it. "May I use the phone book?"

He smiled. "Sure, why not? Harrison get a phone book for Ms. Volarie."

Sam struggled with her hands.

"Oh, here, let me help you." Detective Kline flipped the phone book pages to attorneys.

Sam decided to call the same lawyer who'd seen her in the hospital. Even though she'd repeated his name and number on his card, she couldn't remember his phone number. She feared she would be in trouble once they found out she had dealt with Mr. Neal, but she hadn't done anything wrong. She'd watched too many television cop shows to believe they wouldn't grill her.

Maybe I should call my father. No, I don't want to worry him. My folks don't even know about the fire yet. Besides, her father and mother lived in Florida.

Detective Kline dialed Philip Hargrove's number for her.

The phone rang.

The officer left the room.

She told Mr. Hargrove she needed him at the police station. "Can you stop at my house and pick up a packet of my pictures in my office?" She gave him the address and told him where he'd find the key and the photos. "I have a female, whippet/lab cross by the name of Goldie and my dog won't bother you as long as you call her name out."

Forty-five minutes later, Sam was sitting at a table in another, bigger interrogation room with her attorney. Mr. Hargrove wore the same gray suit, but with a yellow shirt and green tie. He was about four inches taller, so he didn't intimidate her too much. She didn't want to have to call him in the first place, but felt confident in his abilities. Hargrove seemed to know his stuff on the arson issue.

"So, what's the problem, Ms. Volarie?"

"You're my attorney and no one is listening?" Sam looked at the big mirror.

"That's right. When we're finished, they'll come in and talk with us. But I have to know what's going on. Is this more about the fire?"

"No."

Sam told him everything, including the fact that Mr. Neal had been her accountant on a bad investment deal concerning the nursery. She owed well over two hundred thousand dollars because of him. "No one knows I bought the nursery, and then proceeded to lose a bunch of money, not even my father. But someone dropped off a note in my Baja hotel room saying, 'Since I need the money, I should back off.'"

"Okay, so the way I see it," Hargrove said, "you've done nothing wrong, but made a bad business deal with this accountant. Did you see him in Mexico?"

"I didn't even know he was *in* Mexico. I met with him a couple of times at my home, then the deals turned bad. I haven't been able to reach him. I signed up for this trip and was planning on contacting him when I came back from Baja."

"I see."

"Did you pick up the other packet of pictures on your way here?"

He whacked his black briefcase. "Yes. They're in here. Let's call in the big guns."

31

Detectives Harrison and Kline entered the room. The older man, wearing the blue suit, walked in with them. Kline introduced him as Captain Danby. Two other gentlemen Sam hadn't seen before, along with the man in the burgundy tie, also came in.

It felt hard to breathe. If they jammed one more person into the room Sam would pass out. More sweat ran down her sides from underneath her armpits.

The captain put Sam's one packet of photos and the magazine article on the table.

She looked down at her attorney's briefcase and wondered when Hargrove would retrieve her other photos and hand them over.

Captain Danby positioned a tape recorder on the table and switched it on. "Ms. Volarie, I'm sorry my detectives started out on the wrong foot."

"Only one of them." Sam faced Harrison and glared.

Hargrove drummed his fingers on the table three times. A signal her attorney set up earlier for Sam to keep her mouth shut.

"Yes, well…" The captain glanced from Harrison, then back to her. "By the way, this is Detective Paul Oliver and Detective Zeke Barber from the Spokane Police Department."

The two new detectives nodded.

Hargrove cleared his throat. "My client has been cooperating with you and yet you're treating her as a suspect. I have the other photos you asked for. I hope that as we speak, you're not searching her house."

"Searching my home?" Sam's voice rose an octave. Again, Hargrove drummed his fingers three times.

Captain Danby gazed at the other man whom Sam still hadn't been introduced to. She wondered if Hargrove knew him.

Mr. Burgundy Tie nodded. "Mr. Hargrove, Ms. Volarie. You are correct. I'm sorry about the inconvenience and all the subterfuge. However, now that we know Neal is dead, and you happen to have his picture, or at least a piece of him, I hope you understand our predicament."

"Actually, —"

"You have a search warrant?" Hargrove asked, interrupting Sam.

Detective Harrison handed him a paper.

The lawyer read and nodded.

"Why are they searching my house?" Sam asked her attorney.

"Because they can." Hargrove put the warrant on the table.

"The Sandpoint Police are being overzealous." Detective Barber acknowledged Harrison and Kline. "We would rather they had waited until we talked with you and asked for your cooperation, but I'm sure they wanted to prove to us that they were thorough. This is a big case."

"Goldie better be okay when I return." Sam crossed her arms over her chest. "If she's not, I'll have Hargrove sue."

"Goldie?" Detective Barber took out a 3 x 5 notebook.

"Her dog," Kline answered.

"Oh, yes." Barber nodded. "I think the locals told me you have a dog and one of their men has one also. I'm sure he's very good with animals. Your dog is probably following him around right now."

"My dog is pretty protective of my surroundings. I will have Goldie examined. If there's anything—"

"I assure you, Detective Wallace would never hurt a dog or any animal," Kline said.

"You mind telling me—"

Hargrove drummed loudly on the table. Sam closed her mouth and uncrossed her arms from her chest. She pictured her red whippet-lab crossed dog following men around her Queen Anne Victorian.

"What is this about?" Sam's attorney asked.

"Perhaps we should start all over again." Barber wrote something in his notebook.

Sam couldn't keep from talking. "Maybe by introducing the gentleman with the burgundy tie." She pointed at him.

Again, the man bobbed his head up and down.

Barber shrugged and motioned toward the man. "This is Ned Foley, a Spokane Assistant District Attorney. He's here to observe."

"Sorry, I should have introduced him to you." Hargrove patted her arm. "It's okay."

"For you maybe, but I'm wondering how an ADA from Spokane got here so fast. He was outside the interrogation room before you arrived."

"I was already in the neighborhood." Ned Foley smiled.

Sam studied the smile. It made her feel jittery. "Do you suspect me of something? I've already told you all I know."

"Can we go over it one more time?" the ADA asked. "You mentioned you have other photos. Perhaps if you gave us those?"

Hargrove opened his black case, reached inside, drew out the packet, and handed over the other pictures. Detective Barber went through both packets with the others. Nobody talked until they viewed each photo.

"Nice shark." Barber tapped the picture with Sam standing next to the female bull. "Would you mind telling your story from the beginning? Detective Oliver and I haven't had a chance to listen to your other statement on tape. Start with who planned your trip, and all the particulars."

"Who planned the trip? Well, I guess it was Mark's idea."

"Mark?" Barber looked up from jotting something in his notebook.

Sam massaged her temples. "I told this all to the Sandpoint detectives."

"Yes, but we'd appreciate it if you would repeat it for us." Barber smiled.

Sam sighed. "Mark Randall is from L.A. He put this big fishing contest together and Ed, Ed Johnson from here, saw it on the Internet. He knew I liked fishing and suggested if we could get someone to help with the entrance fee, why didn't I sign up for it. I used to go fishing in Cabo with my dad.

"Cabo?" Harrison asked.

"Yes, the tip of Baja Mexico Sur. That little peninsula south of California. Anyway, as I explained earlier, my dad and his cronies lent me $5,000 for this fishing competition and I signed up. I flew to Cabo, met Ed there, and discovered that this Mark Randall was an old-time friend of his. They'd roomed in college together."

"This Mr. Ed Johnson never spoke of Randall before?" Barber stopped writing in his notebook.

"No, not that I recall. Except when I signed up for the contest, he conveyed he had a roommate in college by that name but didn't think it was the same man."

"Was Mr. Randall already in Cabo when you arrived?"

"Yes, I think he arrived the day before with his girlfriend Linda I guess. Making sure all of the arrangements were settled before the others arrived.

"As I explained earlier, the group consisted of ten of us. Each put up the entry fee for a pot of fifty grand. The person catching the biggest shark won. Mark chartered several pangas and put two people in each boat. No one wanted to pair with me, so he became my partner."

"Why didn't anyone want to be your partner?" Detective Barber furrowed his brow and made a note in his little book.

Sam wondered what he wrote since the Sony machine recorded all she told them. "I guess they were shocked when they found out 'Sam' turned out to be a woman and not a man. I signed up under Sam, not Samantha." She tilted her head to one side and raised her shoulder.

"Guess the others were superstitious. Besides, I don't believe they appreciated the idea they might be bested by a female."

"And they were." Kline grinned.

"Yes, I caught a big bull shark. Took me awhile to bring the female fish in. We hauled it back to the dock. I had my picture taken with the shark, and then Enrique, the boat captain, gutted it. My dad and I do a lot of fishing and hunting, so I'm not squeamish. I observed."

"And that's when you spied the chunk of flesh with some sort of mark on it?" Barber made another note on his notepad.

"Yes. Well, no. The contents of the stomach spilled out when a dog ripped it open. All these undigested pieces spewed forth. I spotted a tennis shoe, which still had a foot in it, and then a few other slabs of meat. I examined it all closer and thought I saw a skin discoloration of some sort on one chunk.

"Mark and Ed didn't see it, but I jumped down over the wall and poked through the guts. Something appeared on one of the hunks of undigested meat. I thought it resembled a duck. Everyone else thought I was nuts.

"When I insisted Enrique call the police, he spoke to Mark. If it hadn't been for him telling the boat captain to go ahead, the police would never have been called."

"Was this Mark against calling the police?" Barber asked.

Sam thought a moment. "He wasn't going to until I insisted. Anyway, the Mexican police said it's not unusual for sharks to have parts of bodies in them. Fishermen were lost at sea all the time. Who knows where this shark originated from or when the person had been eaten? They weren't interested in finding out."

"The police didn't do anything?"

"No." Sam wondered if they knew anything about how the Mexican police worked in some towns. "Not until I bullied them into at least checking the hotels to see if anyone was missing. They did that." She pictured the police honcho strutting around, telling her they didn't find anyone.

"And… no one was missing?"

"No, Detective Barber. That's what they told me, and I called around some myself. Got the same answer. Anyway, I flew home and had my pictures printed out."

Foley leaned forward. "Why *did* you take pictures?"

"Because it was the only way to document what I'd seen. The Mexican police had no interest and weren't going to do anything."

"And you had to do this?" The ADA leaned back in his chair and crossed his arms, waiting for her answer.

The men in the room had let Barber and Kline do most of the questioning. The tape recorder whirred away. Sam shifted in her chair and lowered her gaze. "If you must know. I'm adopted. I was left on a doorstep and I have certain abandonment issues because of it. Also, I have a cousin who has never been found after she went missing a couple of years ago. This is too much like abandonment." She took a deep breath and wondered what the ADA thought. She couldn't tell from his expression.

"I assumed that this piece of body belonged to a human being." Sam bit her lip. "Someone out there would be missing this person. I wanted to try and help find out who had been eaten, and let someone know about their death."

"I see." Foley rubbed his chin.

"I don't." Detective Harrison tilted his head.

Detective Kline narrowed his gaze at him and if he'd been a dog, Sam felt he would have growled. That look shut Harrison up.

Sam faced her attorney. "I've always been curious. I even went diving in the spot where I caught the shark."

"What did you find?" Barber scribbled in his notebook again.

She swallowed and looked across the table at the detective. "Sorry to disappoint, but I didn't find the rest of a body."

"Anything?"

Sam thought about the shells, fishing lure, and denim she'd collected, but the stuff she'd found she didn't think had any importance. "Saw a hammerhead shark and found a strip of denim cloth."

"Nothing else?"

She chewed on her lip. "Nothing that stands out." She hesitated. "Maybe a pen, but I don't remember what I did with it. Probably nothing anyway. I came home and was going to start an immediate search, but the Turkwood project came up. Then the fire kept me from it." She held up her bandaged hands.

"I wasn't able to get to my search until now. I've been browsing the Internet on dermatology and looking at birthmarks ever since my computer got fixed and back on line."

"Your computer didn't work?" Barber tilted his head and raised an eyebrow.

Feeling a little more at ease now that the detective was asking the questions again, she scrunched her eyebrows together. "Yes, now that I think about it, all kinds of strange things have been happening to me."

"Strange?"

"Computer problems, emails gone, mail vanished. Anyway, before going to Clark Fork on my project, I sent photos out. Dr. Mallor recognized the mark, and here we are."

"And you don't know Tony Neal or his wife Rita?" the ADA asked.

Sam eyed her attorney and bit her lip. Hargrove nodded. "I guess I think I do know them. Met them at a party."

Barber turned to the ADA. Foley inclined his head. Barber opened a file and pushed a picture across the table toward Sam. "Is this Tony and Rita Neal?"

She stared at the couple, studying the photo.

"Oh, come on." Harrison ran a hand through his hair. "This is ridiculous. Of course she knows these people."

"That's enough." Detective Kline's voice rose an octave.

"If you won't keep quiet, Detective Harrison, I'll ask you to leave." Captain Danby pointed toward the door.

"Ms. Volarie, do you recognize them?" Barber asked.

"Yes, those are the two I met." *They're treating me as a suspect.* She shivered and pictured bars and a small room. "All I tried to do was be a Good Samaritan. With the way this is turning out, I may never try to help someone again."

"I'm sorry you feel that way." ADA Foley cleared his throat and smiled. "We do appreciate what you've done. You've helped us immensely. Mrs. Neal will be much obliged, I'm sure. Rita works with underprivileged children. She teaches them art and tries to get them interested in reading. Sometimes she gives them—"

"Recipes to make." Sam nodded. "I remember she told me all about it at the barbecue."

"When? Which barbecue?" Barber poised his pen over his notebook and waited for the answer.

"Not sure of the date, but you could ask Ed Johnson. It happened at his house."

"Was Mr. Neal your accountant?" Ned Foley asked.

The dreaded question. Sam felt her stomach roil and fought the bile down. Hargrove nodded once again for her to tell her story. She took a deep breath and studied the ADA. "Yes and no. He came to my home a couple of times and gave me some advice."

"Want to elaborate on that?" Foley asked.

"Not at this time." Hargrove reviewed his notes. "I don't believe the question is relevant. Ask her something else."

The ADA shrugged.

Barber jotted down a note.

"Would you please explain for the record where you've been since you got back from Baja." Foley shoved the tape recorder a little closer to her.

Sam waved her appendages. "As you see, I have bandages on my hands and arms, and my legs and feet are wrapped also. I worked at an isolated cabin in Clark Fork for two weeks. Then the cabin burned and I ended up in the hospital. And now I've been at home for a couple of days."

Barber glanced at Foley, and again the ADA inclined his head. "Look, Ms. Volarie, Mr. Neal went down to Baja fishing, supposedly with a client. Mrs. Neal thought maybe whomever Tony met worked in construction in some way or another, but she wasn't sure. She couldn't remember the name of the client, or even if she'd known the name. All she knew—he would meet someone in Cabo and maybe would go shark fishing. Neal flew down, but his wife thought her husband would be driving back with whomever he met there. When he didn't come home as expected, Mrs. Neal called the hotel in Cabo. The front desk informed her that he'd checked out several days ago. They were shocked he had not made it home."

"Mark Randall was already in Baja. I thought he was with Linda, though, and I flew in on Friday." Sam wondered if the man had come in earlier.

"We'll check everything out." Barber looked at the ADA, then asked, "Please tell us who the rest of these men are." He touched the group photo of all of the fishing contestants.

"I don't know all of their full names, but hand me the photo."

Foley set the picture in front of her. For the next few minutes, Sam perused and identified each man.

Barber jotted down the names, and then reviewed the list. "Frank Collotti. Is he from Spokane?"

"Yes. He flew home with us."

"Do you know where anyone else is from?"

Sam tapped each man's photo and gave them cities for the ones she could remember.

"Have you talked with Mr. Randall yet?" Sam asked. *I wonder if he knows Neal? Could he have anything to do with this?*

"We'll take this slow. Don't want anyone to know we're looking into any of this at this point," ADA Foley said. "As a matter of fact, we'll ask you for more cooperation. Don't mention this conversation to anyone."

Hargrove nodded. "We understand. Ms. Volarie won't tell anyone, not even her dog."

Sam scrunched her eyebrows.

Her attorney smiled.

"I won't repeat any of this," Sam agreed.

"Mr. Randall and Mr. Johnson haven't come forward." Foley took the picture of Rita and Neal and placed it in a folder. "And, I believe, they must have seen the news about Neal. Maybe Randall doesn't know him, but you mentioned Johnson does. Anyway, we're being very cautious at this point."

"Well, Ed stayed isolated with me. He might not have heard about Neal either."

"Yes." Detective Barber nodded. "That's a consideration. You and Ed Johnson flew to Baja together?"

Sam hesitated. Barber halted writing his notes and watched her again.

"Tell them everything you know." Her attorney nodded.

"No, Ed and I didn't go together. He went to an architectural conference and met me in Baja. He was standing next to Mark when I arrived. Both were at the airport waiting for me. I never asked Ed when he flew in."

Barber wrote on his pad. "We'll search flight records. Thank you."

"But I don't—"

Hargrove drummed his fingers on the table.

Sam closed her mouth and anticipated more questions.

"When you caught that shark, did anyone act suspicious or as if they recognized anything?"

"Sorry, they all acted suspicious in my eyes by not being interested in finding out who might be in the shark. None of them wanted me to get involved."

"Anything unusual happen after you caught the shark?"

"Well, yes." Sam explained all about what the men said, did, and told them more about her diving incident. As an afterthought, she included the van episode.

"Seems odd." ADA Foley glanced at Barber. "Quite a coincidence Randall and Johnson know each other. We'll talk with Mrs. Neal. See if she recognizes any names on this list. We're suspicious of coincidences."

"You believe Mark or Ed had something to do with this?" Sam blurted out.

"Did Mr. Randall or Mr. Johnson know you were going to try to find out about this body birthmark thing?" Foley tilted his head, eyeing Sam.

"Yes. They both did. So did Frank Collotti. Mark and Frank were against it, but Ed assured me he'd help, even though he really didn't want me to get involved. As I told you before, all the men thought it was a waste of time. Then everything started going haywire."

"How so?" Detective Barber made another note in his little book.

"All sorts of things happened. Mark decided he wanted to stay in Sandpoint and look at property. He got involved in this big project that had to be done right away, which took Ed and me out of town. Before that event, my computer wouldn't work and had to be taken to the shop.

"I was injured in the cabin fire. No one else. Someone made it look like I started it, but I didn't. Arson Investigator Hellman knows this, but asked me not to say anything. The others were all out walking when the fire started.

"When I got out of the hospital, my computer had been fixed, but my server said I didn't pay. While they waited for proof of my payment, I couldn't use the computer for a day. The letter from Dr. Mallor disappeared. Anyway, lots of weird things happened."

"You think someone is responsible?" Barber scribbled more notes.

"I didn't before, but now... I find it truly odd. Too many coincidences. I don't believe in them either. I've seen Mark's pickup, or at least I think I have, leave my street, and then I don't have a server and my emails are gone. If Mark knew all about this Neal mystery, why didn't he say anything? Sure, Neal was from Spokane, but you intimated the articles were in the *Daily Bee*. I find that strange."

"He might not have known him. But we'll investigate." Detective Barber looked at Foley and the man nodded.

"As a matter of fact," Sam said, "Frank Collotti was around for all of the weird happenings."

"We'll check him out, too."

"Now what happens?" Sam shifted in her wheelchair. She felt drained, but still curious.

"We'll type up your statement, include all the strange details you wish, and you'll sign it." The ADA focused on Sam. "Unless you want to add anything?"

Foley lifted an eyebrow, but Hargrove shook his head. "That's her statement."

"Well, then, you must remember to keep this quiet."

"Yes, Mr. Foley, we will." Hargrove nodded to Sam. "Ms. Volarie will not discuss this with anyone."

"I want whoever did this to be caught." Sam sighed. "I won't say a word. Besides, I'm tired. All I want to do is go home and crash."

"Good." ADA Foley gathered up his files.

"I know this sounds naïve, but no one I know could have anything to do with this, but I won't mention this interview to anyone. What about Dr. Mallor?"

"You don't have to worry about him."

"By the way, since Neal is from Spokane and Dr. Mallor is here, why did the doc have a picture of Neal's birthmark?"

Detective Barber laughed. "You are a curious one. Would make a good detective. We asked the same question."

Two seconds of silence passed, so Sam coaxed, "And?"

Foley again inclined his head.

"Neal came over here camping. Got a rash on his back and went to Dr. Mallor. The doc noticed the discoloration and took a picture."

"Hope that satisfies you." The ADA stood. "Now, if you'll wait a bit longer, we'll have your statement transcribed, and you and your attorney will read it over, and you'll sign it."

32

Another forty-five minutes passed at the station. Sam signed her statement. She and her attorney exited the building.

Hargrove drove her home and pulled up in her driveway. "Now, remember, none of this leaves the station." He opened the car door for her and surveyed her house. "I'm impressed with your Queen Anne Victorian. Your stained-glass windows are so colorful and the blue paint color works." Hargrove pushed Sam up the ramp and inside.

Goldie ran to them, tail wagging.

"Your dog is so cute. Whippet and something?"

"Lab."

"Well, if you need anything, give me a call." Hargrove leaned down and scratched the hair on Goldie's head.

"Thanks, I will." Sam closed and locked the door behind him.

The dog still wagged her tail. Sam looked for a sign of anyone around, but saw nothing. She wanted to search each room to see what the police had gone through, but she trembled. Her eyelids felt heavy. Exhausted, she rolled down the hall to the back, guest room, collapsed on to the bed, and fell asleep.

The phone rang.

Sam blinked her eyes. *Now what?* She transferred into her chair and wheeled into the kitchen.

Goldie followed her.

The phone kept ringing.

She fumbled for the receiver. "Hello," she mumbled.

"Where've you been?"

"Mark, can't you say 'hello' first?" Sam yawned.

"Sorry, Samantha. Hello. Where've you been?"

"Sleeping. What's so important?"

"Ed called earlier. There was no answer."

"By now you should know I don't always answer the phone. What's up?"

"Ed wondered where you were when he couldn't reach you," Mark said. "Figured I'd check up on you. Anything wrong?"

Had he been by the house? Maybe someone saw her going to the station. "No, nothing's wrong. Why all of the concern?"

"No reason."

Yeah, right. "I understand the Turkwood project is important to you. I'm sorry I couldn't save the plans. Hopefully the re-creating is going well. Is there something wrong in your life?"

"No, just busy. Why do you ask?"

"I'm trying to figure out why you're so concerned. I'm fine." Sam wished she could go back to bed. "And I'm starting to get weird about all your interest, especially since you hardly know me. Linda okay?"

"She's fine. Flew back to L.A. Got bored with the limited shopping."

Sam bit her lip. *Oh, great, now he has no lady to distract him. But he doesn't need to bug me.*

"Ed was wondering, so I thought I would help him out. You know he's smitten with you. Do you feel the same way?"

"That's none of your business. Ed and I are professionals. Our relationship, whatever it is, shouldn't affect our work; therefore, you shouldn't be concerned about it."

"I'm his friend," Mark said. "What bothers him affects me. When do you think you'll be ready for work?"

"Other than paperwork, I'm caught up at the nursery. Not sure when I'll be able to use my hands well again. What do you have?" Sam needed work to pay back that money. Couldn't believe Neal was dead. Since he gave her bad investment advice, and she wouldn't sue his estate, there was no recourse now.

"Can you reconstruct the Turkwood plans for landscaping on your computer?"

"Probably. Might take a while. I'll have to use a pencil to push buttons." Sam yawned again.

Mark must have heard, because he asked, "Am I boring you?"

"No, I was sleeping."

"Oh, sorry. But now that you're awake, maybe I could come over and help you with the plans?"

Oh, no, I don't want Mark in my home. Not that she thought he had anything to do with Neal's disappearance. Still, he didn't say anything about a headline news story. She wasn't sure he'd even known Anthony Neal. Just because Ed did, didn't mean Mark knew him. She bit her lip. *I wonder if they all went to school together?* "I need some rest."

"How about Ed and I come by for dinner? Ed let me know he would be there anyway and we can go over the plans."

How would Sam keep them both away? "Let's do it in the morning. I'm going to tell Ed not to come over. I'm too tired."

"What did you do all day?"

"Hey, I'm recuperating. Be thankful I'll do it in the morning." Sam couldn't believe all the man thought about was making a buck.

"Okay," Mark said. "In the morning. I'll bring cinnamon buns for breakfast."

They hung up and Sam used a pencil to punch in Ed's number. "Hey, I'm so tired. Don't come tonight. I'm going back to bed and going to sleep."

"Aw, come on, Samantha. You need me."

"No, I *need* rest. How about breakfast?"

"Okay. See you tomorrow morning."

Sam hung up and closed her eyes. She'd found out who the birthmark belonged to, so no more searching.

At least to find whomever was in her shark. Since she managed that feat, maybe it was time to find out where she had come from. She had the name of a search angel. All she needed to do was ask the state for some non-direct information. *Yes, I think it's the right time to commence that search. Maybe I can even hire a private eye to look for Jennifer.* Sam talked to her dog. "Okay, that's my next move."

Sam and Goldie went back to the bedroom.

The dog curled up on the floor.

Sam put on her pajamas, snuggled under the covers, and fell asleep.

33

Friday morning, Sam woke to the aroma of coffee. She sat up. *Oh, my God. I was so tired, I forgot to bring in my outside key so Ed couldn't get in.* It surprised her she'd slept so late. The clock read 9 A.M. She put on her sweats, climbed into the wheelchair, and headed toward the kitchen.

The swinging doors were propped open. Goldie sat in the doorway of the kitchen, staring.

"What's with your dog?" Ed pointed toward Goldie. "Been there ever since we got here."

"I don't know." Sam rolled the wheelchair over to the kitchen table. "How long *have* you been here?"

"Well, Samantha, long enough to make coffee." Mark held up his cup. "But I made you tea." He took the kettle and poured a cup for her. "How are you this morning?"

"Fine." Did Mark now know where the key was, too? What if the police came by and discovered the men here? *Oh, dear, they're going to think I told them about Neal. Maybe I should ask them about him.*

Mark took a couple of steps toward her with the tea. Goldie, who'd followed Sam to the table, stood and growled.

"Goldie, stop that." Sam patted her dog's head. Goldie sat with hackles raised. *What's with my dog?*

Ed handed Sam a plate of scrambled eggs and a cut-up heated cinnamon bun. The frosting ran down the side and Sam's mouth watered from the aroma.

The men settled at the table with their own breakfasts and shoveled the food in. Sam wondered how they could eat so fast.

"You look rested." Ed looked her up and down. He took a sip of his coffee.

Mark took a last bite of his eggs. "Yes, she does." He shoved his char away from the table. "Why don't we go use Samantha's computer?"

"Ed, don't you have work to do?" Sam took a last sip of her tea. Then she finished her cinnamon bun.

"I told the office they could find me here." Ed cleared the table and put the dishes in the sink. He led the way down the hall to the office.

In the room, he switched on Sam's computer and went to her landscaping program.

Mark moved Samantha closer to Ed, and then grabbed a chair and sat next to her. The dog curled up on the carpet far away from Mark, but kept a wary eye.

Both men had not shaved and had red-rimmed eyes. They reminded Sam of someone who had just found out their best friend died. Maybe he had. Sam wondered if the police had questioned them yet. She vowed not to say anything until one of them broached the subject.

Ed opened up Sam's program, and the three of them started recreating the landscaping part of the Turkwood project plans.

An hour sped by. Sam's doorbell rang. Goldie raced from the room, barking. Ed pushed Sam to the front door while Mark hovered against the office door jamb. Sam fumbled with the door handle.

"Here, I'll get it." Ed reached around and opened the door.

Two big men waited on the porch. Sam recognized the Spokane detectives. The dog stopped barking, but wagged her tail. *Great, the detectives will think I'm in here telling all that went on at the station.*

Detective Barber looked at Sam. She shook her head, hoping he got her meaning. Barber asked, "Ms. Volarie?"

"Yes." Sam backed the chair up a bit.

"We're looking for Ed Johnson. His office informed us he'd be here."

"That's me."

"I'm Detective Barber. This is Detective Oliver. We're from the Spokane Police Department. May we have a few minutes of your time?"

Ed glanced back at Mark and down at Sam. "Can this wait? We were in the middle of a work project."

"It's about Anthony Neal."

Sam heard, "Oh, crap," coming from Ed. He must have uttered it under his breath. Mark walked up next to Sam. It was hard to watch both him and Ed at the same time. If she hadn't seen it, she would have missed the slight twitch at the corner of Mark's eye. Ed grimaced.

"Something wrong, Ed?" Mark asked.

Detective Barber eyed him. "Who are you?"

Mark stretched taller. "I'm Mark Randall. Is there a problem?"

"Yes. We need to talk with you, also."

So much for not showing their hand. Now both men would know about Sam's visit. She thought the police would keep it under wraps.

Barber scrutinized his notepad he took from his pocket. "Ms. Volarie, we wish to talk with all three of you."

"At the same time?" Sam tilted her head and scrunched her eyebrows together.

"Well, no." Barber chuckled. "We prefer to interview people one at a time."

Ed laughed. "Why? So they can't get their stories straight."

"Yes, Sir." Detective Oliver nodded. "That's exactly right."

Ed frowned. He turned his head, and mouthed, "I was joking." Back toward the detectives, he asked, "What's Anthony Neal done now?"

"May we come in?"

Ed peered at Sam. She nodded, so Ed beckoned them in and shut the door. Mark wheeled Sam's chair over to the recliner in the living room. The other men followed. Ed chose the floral wing chair. Mark sat on the solid blue chair. Sam managed to climb into her tan recliner. Goldie lay next to her. The dog's tail beat steadily against the cloth of the chair, making a thumping sound.

"Have a seat, Detectives. Would you care for anything?"

"No, thank you, Mr. Johnson." Barber looked at the dog. "Nice animal you have, miss. We have a few questions. Perhaps we could speak with each of you alone for a few minutes."

"Which one of us would you prefer to speak with first?" Ed asked.

Barber swiveled his head toward each person and then settled on Ed. "How about you, Mr. Johnson? Is there some other room we could use?"

"The parlor, which is my office." Sam waved across the hall. "Or in the kitchen toward the back."

"To the kitchen. Let's go back to the kitchen." Ed led the detectives out of the room and down the hall toward the back of the house.

Sam thought it odd that Ed repeated the suggestion of going to the kitchen. *Maybe he's nervous.*

The minute they exited the room, Mark ran a hand through his hair. "Do you know what this is all about?"

"How should I know? Didn't the detective say something about someone named Anthony Neal?"

"That's the name I heard. Do you know him?"

"I think he's Ed's accountant. Works mainly for construction people." Sam waited for Mark to have any sign of recognition. She didn't notice anything. "Do *you* know him?"

Mark stared out the doorway. Sam didn't take her gaze from him. She watched for anything to give her a clue. His body was ramrod stiff. Did he know Neal? She sure couldn't tell from his actions.

Goldie perched on the other side of Sam, staying away from Mark. No tail wagging. What was it about Mark that her dog didn't like? Goldie loved everyone.

The man paced back and forth. *Why is he so agitated?*

The dog didn't budge, but glared at Mark, following his every move.

"Do you *know* an Anthony Neal? Why don't you sit and relax?" Sam couldn't believe Mark spun around so fast.

"You relax. I'm not able to." He continued pacing.

Goldie growled, low and menacingly.

Sam couldn't blame her dog. The man scared her too.

Mark snapped at anything Sam said. When he did, Goldie uttered a growl. *Mark never answered my question whether he knew Neal or not. I think I better sit back, keep my mouth shut, and observe.*

About a half hour later, the men returned. Ed plopped down on the couch. His face, if possible, appeared paler than before.

"How about you going next, Mr. Randall?" Detective Barber motioned toward the hallway.

Again, they left the living room and headed to the kitchen.

Ed didn't look at Sam, but stared out the doorway as Mark had. Goldie went over to Ed. The dog put her head on his knee. He petted Goldie and scratched behind her ears.

Sam chewed on her lips. She couldn't take the silence any longer. "Everything okay?"

He shrugged. "I'm not supposed to say anything to you until they get a chance to talk with you."

"Are we in some kind of trouble?"

"No, everything is fine." Ed turned away, but not before Sam saw something dark in his eyes and heard him mutter, "Nothing is fine."

Time ticked by. Ed looked everywhere but at Sam, and continued petting Goldie.

"Well, at least we could discuss the Turkwood project." Sam thought Ed took a long time to answer.

"No. I can't concentrate. Let's wait 'til the officers are gone."

"Isn't Anthony Neal your accountant?"

Ed strolled over to the window with his back to her, and refused to speak.

It surprised Sam when Ed paced as Mark had and paid no attention to her. *He's acting similar to Mark. Why's he so jittery?*

Another forty-five minutes passed. Detective Barber and Mark came back. "Ms. Volarie, your turn."

Sam transferred into the wheelchair. The detective pushed her down the hall. Goldie trotted alongside. In the kitchen, Sam whispered, "I thought you were going to keep me out of this."

"We have." Detective Oliver made room for her wheelchair.

"We told them both we'd checked records, and found out that the three of you were in Baja." Barber sat at the table. "Said we wanted to know if anyone had seen Neal? We didn't tell them we know he's dead—just that he's missing."

A minute passed. "And?" Sam asked.

"Mr. Johnson told us no, he hadn't seen Mr. Neal, and hadn't heard of Neal's disappearance. Apparently, Mr. Johnson hadn't caught up on any papers either. Although being in the office, his co-workers would probably have mentioned it."

"Did Mark know Mr. Neal?" Sam's curiosity and his actions frustrated her. "He wouldn't say when we were together in the living room."

"Yes, Mr. Johnson told us they all went to school together. He thought Neal and Randall had stayed in touch." Oliver made some notes in his notebook.

"What did Mark say?"

"He was vague at first."

"And?" Sam asked.

Barber scratched his head. "But then he admitted to knowing the man, and that he hadn't seen him in Cabo. We'll check further on that one. We think they were in Cabo at the same time."

"It's a big place." Sam chewed her lip. She hated the habit. Whenever she was nervous she'd end up with bruises on her lip. "If they stayed at different hotels, it's possible they never saw each other."

"Possible." Barber got up and paced. "We tried to find out how much social time they've spent together recently to see if they might have known about Mr. Neal's birthmark. I would think if they were college buddies, they would have known about it."

Sam thought back to her college days. "I have girlfriends, but I couldn't tell you if they had any marks on their bodies or not. Why don't you ask Neal's wife? She'd know."

"That's being taken care of in Spokane." Oliver tilted his head. "What are they doing here? You didn't tell them anything?"

"Mark called after I got back to the house yesterday. Wanted to come over then, but I convinced them to come this morning. We're working on the Turkwood project. Trying to recreate the plans that burned in the fire. The two of them came over for breakfast. They wore bitter expressions on their faces. At first, I felt they'd known I'd been to the police, but they didn't say anything. Then when you two showed up—"

"I saw your head motion." Barber smiled. "I had already told Oliver how to play it."

"Ed wouldn't tell me much when you finished with him." Sam eyed each detective. "Told me he couldn't discuss anything with me until you talked with me."

"That's good." Barber nodded. "But now see if either one will say anything."

"You want me to spy on them?"

"No. Observation is all we ask of you. Let us know if they do or say anything unusual."

"So, all I have to do is keep an eye on their actions?"

"Yes. Mr. Johnson told us he knew Neal and Anthony was his accountant. Randall said Neal did some accounting for him, but he was based in L.A. and used a big firm there. We'll check into it. Anyway, this worked out well. Now maybe the three of you will discuss it."

"Is that all?" Sam asked.

"I think we've been in here long enough." Oliver closed his notebook and placed it in his pocket.

Barber brought Sam back to the living room. "Thank you, Ms. Volarie. Gentlemen, thank you for your time. If we have any more questions, we'll get back to you."

Ed wheeled Sam to the front door. Mark and the two detectives followed. Ed rushed around and opened the door for the officers.

Goldie stood next to Sam's chair. Both detectives leaned down and patted the dog's head. Goldie's tail wagged so hard, her butt wiggled.

"Thanks for your help." Detective Barber and Oliver stepped out onto the porch.

When Ed closed the door, Sam looked up at the two men. "Did you both know Anthony Neal? Mark, was he your accountant and close friend same as Ed?"

Mark tilted his head and studied Samantha. Too late, Sam realized that Ed hadn't told her anything about them being friends or being clients. Detective Barber told her. Had Mark caught it?

"Let's get back to business. My personal life is not up for discussion." Mark marched toward the office.

"Oh, but you think mine is?" Sam gritted her teeth.

Mark spun a 180 and narrowed his gaze at Samantha. Goldie growled.

Ed sighed. "Come on, you two. It's terrible that Tony is missing, but maybe he's deserted his wife. He wasn't all that thrilled with her. Perhaps after being in Baja, he figured there was more to life. Maybe he went through his mid-life crises, and found a way out. We'll probably never know." He glanced at his watch. "We *should* get back to work."

"That was my idea." Mark marched into the office.

"Don't worry about Tony. I'm sure he'll turn up." Ed pushed Sam next to the computer.

She waited for Mark's reaction.

There was none.

34

Not long after the detectives went away, Sam bit her lip and followed Mark's movements as he paced the office parlor. "Are either of you going to add any comments to these plans?" She scrunched her brows together. Neither answered her right away.

Ed typed on the keyboard and put in a few ideas.

Mark stopped by the door, shifted his mouth to one side, and folded his arms across his chest. "No, I've nothing to add. You two are doing fine and don't need my input." He glanced at his watch. "I have a business meeting with the realtor in a half hour. Have to go." He stomped out of the office. Sam heard the front door open and close firmly.

"I don't know about you, but I'm hungry." Ed rubbed his stomach. "How about I fix us a big late lunch or an early dinner?"

"Sounds good." Sam observed Ed as he put the computer to sleep. Then he grabbed the wheelchair and rolled her down the hallway into the kitchen.

Would Ed open up to her and talk about Neal. Sam eyed his movements.

He pulled a pan of lasagna from the refrigerator and put it in the microwave. Ed withdrew a salad and put it on the kitchen table. He set plates and silverware down, retrieved the heated lasagna, and sat next to Sam. They chowed down on the warmed-up lasagna and the salad. Ed talked about the Turkwood project, but nothing else.

Sam couldn't stand it any longer. "What do you think about this Neal guy?"

Ed took a sip of his wine. "Interesting he'd gone to Cabo. But Tony liked fishing. It did surprise me he wasn't in Mark's competition."

"Really? Why?"

"They were pretty tight back in college." Ed picked up his fork to take a bite. "I assumed they'd stayed in close contact. They were always competing. Trying to outdo each other."

"Did Mark say anything to you about Neal in Cabo?"

Ed swallowed his food. "No, we didn't talk much about old times."

"Why would Neal leave his wife?"

"Rita's a strong woman; getting a name for herself. Tony's the kind of guy who likes being in the spotlight. His wife was pushing him out of the light. Maybe he couldn't handle it?"

"Didn't he love Rita?" Sam couldn't believe Ed would say such a thing. At the party the Neal's acted so much in love. Always holding hands, smiling at each other.

"As much as he's capable. He was my accountant, but we weren't that close."

"And Mark didn't say anything to you about his disappearance while we were out at Clark Fork?"

Ed took another bite, chewed slowly, and swallowed. "Why all the interest? You met Tony once at my party."

"Just curious." Sam hadn't told Ed that she'd taken his advice to use Neal. "You know me and abandonment issues. I mean you all went to school together; he was your accountant and friend."

"I wouldn't say friend." Ed shrugged.

"You invited him to your party."

"So were a lot of people I met in business." Ed smiled.

For some reason Sam shivered. No twinkle shone in Ed's eyes. She shook off the chills. "Anyway, Mark must have seen it in the paper."

Sam sucked some water through a straw. "And yet, he never mentioned Tony Neal's disappearance to you. Don't you find that odd?"

"You don't know Mark. If it doesn't make money, he's not much interested. For example, the shark fishing contest. He doesn't go fishing for pleasure, he puts on a competition."

"Yeah, but he didn't make money. In fact, he lost his seed money, didn't he?" Sam took a bite of the lasagna. She wondered if Ed told her everything. His facial expressions said nothing to her.

"I guess. Maybe he didn't make hard cash, however, he did meet nine new contacts. Some of those men will generate lots of money for him. One lives over in Seattle. Frank's in Spokane, and he's already generated big bucks for all of us here, I might add."

"True. I wonder if Frank knew Neal?"

"Probably. Back to making dollars, look at you." Ed waved his hand. "You've also generated big bucks for him."

Sam thought about that for a few seconds. A true fact, but she couldn't drop the issue. "Do you think Mr. Neal went to Cabo to see Mark or maybe even Frank?"

"Who knows?" Ed shifted in his seat. "Would you care for dessert? Paula made a chocolate cake and the thought of it is making my mouth water."

"Come to think of it…" Sam tapped her fork on the table. "Most people who put on competitions aren't in them. Yet Mark partnered with me."

"So?" Ed took a sip from his glass.

"Well, maybe there was supposed to be another man, but he never showed."

"You think it might have been Neal?" Ed choked on his wine.

"Well—"

"No." Ed wiped his chin and cleaned up the wine that spilled from his glass. "Mark would have brought something up. And none of the other fishermen complained. Drop it, Sam. Now you're making stuff up."

"Maybe." Sam didn't say any more. *I think I should mention this to Detective Barber.*

Ed got up, served the cake, and cut two pieces. Rich chocolate aroma wafted by. Sam's stomach roiled. She loved chocolate. She was glad her appetite appeared to be coming back. The meds killed any pain, but made her feel a bit queasy and she didn't get hungry. But, she figured she needed food to keep up her strength.

When they finished eating, Ed cleared the table and put all of the dishes, including those in the sink, in the dishwasher. "Well, Sam, I'd love to stay, but I have some work to get done at home. I'll see you later."

Sam closed and locked the front door. She was getting used to using mitten hands. She gripped the wheels and propelled herself into the living room around the carpet to the stack of papers along the wall. She tried browsing through them. Some were missing. Now that she was stronger, she managed to roll the wheelchair into her office in front of her desk. She used a pencil to turn on her computer and got online. The *Daily Bee*, as many newspapers, existed on the Internet. She found the missing days. Each one contained an article about Anthony Neal on the front page.

Who took those papers, and why? Ed, Mark, and even Frank were in her house, as well as Paula and Jim. Sam couldn't believe Ed, Paula, or Jim could have done it, but they *all* knew Anthony Neal. Paula and Jim were at Ed's party, too.

She finished reading the articles, and then switched over to search the adoption registries. Still, no one was looking for her. Sam wasn't quite ready to widen her search because she wanted to speak with her folks first, not wishing to upset them in any way.

The cuckoo clock chirped six times. She shut off the computer, rolled down the hall to the kitchen, and let Goldie out the back. When the dog returned, Sam, so exhausted and full, prepared for bed.

She pulled the covers up to her chin and closed her eyes. *I should have a phone by this bed.*

The telephone rang.

Sam looked heavenward. *Careful what you think.* She threw back the covers, climbed into the wheelchair and went in the kitchen. She yanked the receiver from the wall. "Hello?"

Silence.

"Is anyone there?" Sam heard background noise and someone breathing.

"Who is this?"

CLICK!

She stared at the phone, then hung up. At the foot of the stairs, she gazed upward. Her gun lay in a locked box in the closet upstairs in her bedroom. Could she make it up to get it?

Goldie's nails clicked on the hardwood and then the dog nuzzled Sam's hand. "Well, girl, I think I better try."

Sam couldn't get a good grip on the banister to walk up, so she turned around and sat on the first step. One by one, she pushed up each tread and worked her way toward the second floor.

The dog ran up and down the stairs following her mistresses progress.

By the time Sam reached the top, sweat ran down her forehead. Her underarms were soaked.

Goldie sat on the carpet by Sam's bedroom door. The dog cocked her head and wagged her tail, waiting.

"Give me a minute. I'm coming." Sam inched forward. She hadn't removed the carpet upstairs, so it was a bit softer crawling.

Huffing and puffing, Sam creeped down the hall into her bedroom. By the closet, she worked her way up the door frame until she was standing. She fumbled with the handle, finally opened the door, and stepped inside. Her metal gun box sat on the top shelf. She managed to get a grip on it and dropped the container to the floor. *How am I going to move this?* She sat down and nudged the box and herself over to the bed. Between her bandaged hands, she hefted the gun box up onto the bedspread.

Sam plopped down and studied her mitten-bandaged hands. She would never be able to pick up the key from her nightstand drawer and open the box.

She flipped her hands back and forth several times, then sighed and used her teeth to get a bandage strip loose. She unwrapped her right hand. The cuts and slight burns were healing. She flexed her fingers. Since she'd taken her meds before bed, she didn't have much pain.

With the key, she opened the grey metal box and pulled out the .38 revolver that her dad gave her. Thank God, she kept it loaded. It would have been difficult to put the bullets in the chamber.

"Now what?" Sam looked down at Goldie.

The dog tilted her head and then lay down and curled up on the blanket next to Sam's side of the bed. Sweat dripped off Sam's forehead. She felt so heavy, she could hardly move. She decided to lie down for a minute to rest for the trip down the stairs. She put the gun under her pillow and pulled the comforter over her. She felt safe under the plaid spread her mother had handcrafted for her.

Soon, Sam tossed and turned, clawing at the covers. She jostled awake from the horrible dream.

Goldie's face peeked over the bed. The dog's paw clawed the bedspread. Goldie growled and glared at the door.

For a minute, Sam thought she was back at the cabin, reliving the horrible fire. She blinked several times, peered around, and realized this was no dream. She was at home in her own bedroom.

The dog ran to the door and growled louder.

"What girl?" Sam sniffed. No smoke smells. She threw off the covers, pulled the gun out from under her pillow, and crawled to the door. She reached up and with her unbandaged hand, opened it. *Didn't I leave this open?*

Goldie raced out the door and down the steps, barking.

Sam on her knees, reached up and flicked on the hall light. She heard a noise and called out, "Who's there?"

No one answered.

The dog ceased barking.

"Goldie, come," Sam yelled.

When the dog didn't return, Sam cried out, "I have a gun." She pulled herself up and took a step toward the stairs. She heard another noise and strained to listen. *I'm sure the back door opened.*

Sam tried to walk to the stairs, but the bandages and pain from her feet kept her from walking well. She dropped to all fours and scurried over to the top. Peering down, she sat on the top step and scooted down one tread at a time to the bottom. In her wheelchair, she placed the gun on her lap and rolled to the kitchen. The sound of a car driving off froze her for a moment, but then she noticed the swinging kitchen door was closed. *I know I left that open.*

With gun in hand, Sam inched forward and shoved the door open. Her dog lay by the open back door, cold air coming in.

"Goldie!" Sam screamed, put the gun on her lap again, and rushed toward her dog.

The furry body didn't move.

Sam clasped the gun and fell out of the chair next to her dog. Shallow breathing came from Goldie. Sam put her hand on the dog's shoulder and wiggled Goldie's body. The dog's eyes glazed over, she shuddered, tried to stand, and collapsed.

Who did this and why? Sam swiped at the tears running down her face and gathered the dog's head in her arms.

I have to get help. She gently laid her dog's head down, crawled back into the chair, and at the phone punched in 911, reporting an intruder. She started to call her vet, when Goldie stood and took a few wobbly steps.

Back over next to her dog, Sam lifted Goldie onto her lap and wheeled alongside the hardwood in the front room over to the window. She clutched the gun in one hand, and watched outside, waiting. Her dog tried to get off her lap. Sam held Goldie in place with her mitten hand.

The police arrived within a few minutes. Detectives Kline and Harrison pulled up right behind the patrol car.

The men piled out of the vehicles, guns drawn. Sam hurried to the front door and opened it before they could run up the stairs, and called, "I think he's gone out the back."

"We'll check." The patrolmen split up and went around the outsides of the house.

Detectives Kline and Harrison tramped up the porch steps to the door. "Sam." Harrison reached out one hand, while the other one somewhat pointed his weapon at her. "May I see your gun?"

Sam fixated on it. "I forgot I had it in my hand." She gave it to the detective, butt first.

Harrison took her .38 revolver and smelled it. "Not fired." He opened the cylinder and ejected the bullets, making sure no cartridges were in it. Then he dropped them in his pocket, and kept her gun.

"I didn't shoot it." Sam looked at Kline.

"Do you have a permit for your gun?"

"Yes. You'll give it back when you leave?" Sam felt glad she had it. Gave her comfort.

Harrison nodded.

Noises from the back of the house quieted them.

Goldie, still on Sam's lap, raised her little head and a low "woof" burst out. The dog tried to move from Sam's lap and fell, in a stupor, to the hallway floor.

Harrison leaned down and picked up the red ball of hair. "What's wrong with Goldie?"

"I think she's been drugged. Breathing is better and moving more. I've seen this before after a friend's dog's surgery when it had been drugged. I found my dog lying by the open back door."

A voice from the rear of the house called out, "It's Officer Jones. Back door's open. We're coming in."

"Search the house," Kline called. He brought Sam into the living room.

Harrison put the dog back on Sam's lap and then went to another room.

Sam petted Goldie. The dog thumped her tail in slow motion.

The patrolmen and Harrison searched the house and walked into the front room.

"We locked the back door." Officer Jones motioned down the hall.

"No sign of anyone in the house." Harrison holstered his weapon.

"What happened?" Kline put his weapon away.

The officers sat on the couch. "Goldie woke me up." Sam patted the dog. "I grabbed my gun and yelled 'Who's there?' The minute I opened my bedroom door, my dog ran downstairs. I heard something, yelled I had a gun, and then a car drove off."

"Did you see the vehicle?" Kline took out his notepad and wrote.

"No. When I made it downstairs to the kitchen, Goldie lay motionless on the floor. I went to her."

"Why were you upstairs?" Harrison glanced at the steps, then her wheelchair.

"Because I received a phone call with no one there. It scared me. Managed to get to my bedroom upstairs where I keep my gun. Exhausted from struggling to reach my room, I stretched out on the bed. Pain meds make me sleepy. I must have passed out."

"How *did* you get up there?" Harrison tilted his head and jerked his chin toward the wheelchair.

"Very slowly and by scooting." Sam rubbed her arms. Her hand ached. "Can't believe how sore I am."

"Is your dog okay?" Kline asked.

Goldie's tail wagged and beat against Sam's lap. The dog licked at the bandages on her hand.

"Think so. Who would do this?"

"You tell us." Harrison pulled out his notepad and pen.

"I don't understand any of this." Sam put a stray hair behind her ear. "You have the pictures."

"Yes, but the killer doesn't know that, unless you told someone?"

"No, Detective Kline, I haven't said a word. You think it's him?" Sam shivered.

Kline shrugged. "If Officer Jones stays with your dog, think you can manage to take a look around downstairs? See if anything is missing."

"If you push the wheelchair over the carpet. Perhaps you can help me re-bandage my hand. There's ointment in the downstairs bathroom."

"Why's it unbandaged?"

"Because, Detective Harrison, I couldn't open my gun lock box with the bandages."

Detective Kline pushed Sam's chair and Harrison walked behind. Room by room, nothing appeared to be missing. "Maybe Goldie and I scared him off before he could get anything."

In the bathroom, Kline smeared the burn cream on Sam's hand.

"Can you bandage my right hand leaving the fingers showing?"

"Sure, if you can handle it."

"Please."

The detective re-bandaged it with her fingers sticking out.

She wiggled them. "Thanks."

They went back into the living room.

Harrison returned the gun and bullets to Sam. She placed them on her lap.

"Perhaps you did scare the person off." Detective Kline stroked his chin.

"Unless that wasn't his reason for being here." Harrison put away his pad and pen.

Kline glanced heavenward and shook his head.

Sam opened her eyes wide. "Oh, no." She looked down at her dog. "You think he's after me?" She shuddered. "Why?"

35

Whew! Too close! I get out in the nick of time. What a cliché but it's the truth.

I stand outside staring at the ornate Queen Anne Victorian. I admire the turrets and scallop details. The light blue paint and darker trim makes the house look striking. So Samantha.

I shake off my reverie and think back when I let Goldie gobble the hot dog with the fast-acting drug inside. I will never hurt an animal, but the dog needs to be quiet.

Sam is too resourceful. How does she manage to make it up the stairs and retrieve her gun? Maybe she really doesn't have it with her.

I cannot take that chance. I know she's a good shot. Has to be since she shot the balls off a deer at 150 yards. But I'm a good shooter too.

Getting into her house—so easy, now that I know where she keeps her key. Not hidden very well. Besides, I laugh because now I have a copy of her key. I can get in whenever I want.

Where are those pictures? I need them. I know she put them in her office. Could she have moved them? Guess I don't know where those photos are. Will have to be more careful. When the cops talk about Neal, chills take over. I've come too far to be caught now.

Damn Neal! Bad advice.

Sam's too curious for her own good. Why dig into something she has no business with?

Sirens wail. Of course, she calls the cops. Goldie's sleepy, but that's all. I better move. If they see me—no that can't happen.

Well, now I must take care of Sam.

Might not be easy, but nothing has scared her off so far. I've tried everything.

No failure this time.

Sorry, Samantha, but your snooping stops now.

I need to plan your death. Make it appear as a suicide? An accident? Getting someone else to kill her appeals to me.

Too bad. Oh, well, the things I do to survive.

36

The next morning Sam dressed and wheeled around, searching the downstairs one more time. She re-loaded her gun and put it in the nightstand drawer on the right of the downstairs bed. In her office, she pawed through the desk to see if anything was missing.

Nothing she could spot.

Is the killer really after me?

She tried calling Paula and Jim. No answer from their home, office, or cell numbers. Where had they gone? It didn't feel right. Paula hadn't mentioned anything about going away.

"Wish you could talk." She looked at Goldie. "Maybe Paula told you where they were going."

The dog tilted her head. The little red tail thumped on the floor. Sam laughed, and knew if the dog could talk Goldie would be jolly and tell her everything.

Sam typed in her password and checked her emails.

Nothing.

Thank God I had Detective Kline rewrap my hand with my fingers sticking out. Wiggling them, she felt freer. Made it easier. She used one finger and dashed off an email saying: Paula, I'm creating a "fisherman" file and it will tell all about the Baja trip. Call me ASAP. *I hope Paula or Jim get in touch with me as soon as possible.*

While Sam sat at her computer, Goldie came to all fours. The hair on the dog's back rose. Goldie growled and dashed out of the room, barking.

The doorbell chimed.

Sam yelled, "Just a second." She rolled the wheelchair to the door, which she unlocked and opened. Mark and Ed were on the porch holding coffee and donuts.

Goldie sniffed in the air and the dog's little butt jiggled.

"Morning, Samantha. Thought you might care for something different to eat." Mark motioned to the pink box Ed held.

"I know you have a sweet tooth." Ed handed her the donuts.

"Thanks." Sam put the box on her lap. "Let's go back to the kitchen."

The dog's nails clipped on the hardwood as she ran ahead.

Around the table, Sam sat close to Ed. Goldie plopped down in between. Mark slid into a chair on the other side. Sam told them nothing about the break-in. "Ed, have you heard from Paula?"

"No, why?" Ed cocked his head, and Sam heard, "Need more food?"

"Ha." She smiled. "Very funny."

"What's funny?" Ed furrowed his brow.

"Needing more food."

"I don't understand."

"Ed, you asked if I needed more food?" Sam scrunched her eyebrows.

"What?" He gave a bite of his donut to the dog. Goldie wolfed it down and begged for more.

"Never mind." Sam patted Ed's knee.

Mark frowned.

"I find it odd Paula left without saying anything." Sam wondered why her friend would do that.

"Maybe it was business?"

Samantha felt uneasy as Mark watched her eat. He took a bite of his own chocolate donut. Sam realized her right hand was wrapped differently with fingers showing. "Why didn't Paula tell me, then?" Sam took another bite of her maple bar.

"Who knows why women do anything. But let me tell you about a new project I have." Mark finished off his donut and droned on about the new business deal.

Sam couldn't concentrate. "Ed, will you change my bandages?"

Mark quit talking and stared.

"Sure." Ed stood. "Let's do it."

In the bathroom, Ed asked, "How come your fingers are sticking out?"

"The other was dirty and I re-did it. Not well, though. You do a great job. Please leave my fingers out again. Easier to do things."

"Of course."

When they went into the kitchen, Mark still sat in the same spot. He was polishing off another chocolate donut.

The phone rang.

Sam raced over to it and picked up the receiver. "Hello."

"Ms. Volarie, Detective Barber here from Spokane. Heard about the break-in. Anything missing?"

"No." Sam turned to the men at the table and smiled. Goldie sat, begging for more donuts from Ed.

"Can you talk, or is someone there?"

"No, I'm fine, thanks. As a matter of fact, Mark and Ed bought me coffee and donuts this morning. They're keeping me company."

"I understand," Barber said. "Call if you have any information."

"Thanks." Sam hung up.

"Who was that?" Ed took a bite of his powdered donut. He swiped the white dust from his chin and then brushed the powder off his chest.

"Neighbor wanting to know if I needed anything. Don't encourage Goldie to beg. Shouldn't you guys be at work?"

"Yes, Samantha." Mark shoved his chair back. "If you're okay, I'll head on out."

Instead of grimacing when he called her Samantha, she kind of liked it now. *Guess I'm getting used to it.* She went with both men to the front door. Goldie padded alongside the wheelchair. Mark leaned down and pecked Sam on the top of her head. "Call if you need anything." He sauntered down the porch steps.

Ed lingered on the porch.

Sam waited with her dog sitting next to her.

"You okay?" Ed cleared his throat.

"Fine."

"I know you, Sam. Something is bothering you. Want me to stay?"

"No, really, Ed, I'm okay." She wanted to yell at him not to leave her, but he acted so weird. He sounded as if he repeated every sentence and his words sounded robotic, so she didn't. Who could she trust? Ed? Mark? Anyone? *What a horrible thing to think. Could Ed have been the person in my house?*

No, probably not, but I can't take any chances.

Ed hugged her, then kissed her cheek, and she heard 'now leave.' Why would he say that? Then Ed strolled down the walkway to his car.

"Have a great day." Sam waved as he drove off.

Back inside, she started to lock the door, when the phone rang. She rushed into the office to answer it. "Hello?"

"Are you alone and doing all right?" Detective Barber asked.

"Yes, I'm fine. I did think of something."

"What?"

"Well, might be nothing, but Mark was my partner."

"Yes, I remember you told us that fact before. So?"

"From what I'm familiar with is that the person who sponsors the contest isn't involved in it. And I wondered if there might have been another person signed up who didn't show?"

"And," Barber said, "maybe that person was Anthony Neal."

"Or someone else."

"We'll check it out. Good point, Ms. Volarie."

Sam hung up and signed into her computer. She clicked on Google Search, wanting to look for her birth parents, but this urgency inside of her… She typed in the name 'Mark Randall' and hit 'Search.'

Goldie curled up on the floor and closed her eyes.

Sam spent over an hour reading everything about Mark. She typed in Anthony Neal and several other names, which took another hour. She copied and pasted all the information into a file on her computer, labeled it "the fishermen," and put the folder on her desktop. Because of her bandaged hands, even though Ed left fingers showing, this took forever. *If something happens to me, maybe this file will prove to be useful.*

Her stomach grumbled. Sam glanced at the clock and saw both hands on the 12. The dog jumped up. Sam pushed away from the computer, leaving the monitor on, and went to the kitchen to fix lunch. After she finished eating, she would revisit the Internet and do some research on adoption. Maybe even look for a private eye. Goldie followed her to the kitchen, the dog's tail wagged non-stop. Sam switched the burner on for hot water. As she searched the refrigerator for sandwich ingredients, the doorbell rang.

Goldie ran out of the kitchen. Sam heard nails clicking down the hallway. Before Sam could leave the kitchen, she heard, "Sam, you home?"

Oh, my God, I forgot to lock the door. I have to be more careful.

She poked her head from the doorway. Mark and Ed were inside the front door by the entrance to her computer room. Goldie stood in the office doorway, growling. "Yes, now what?"

"Took pity on you." Mark held up a bag. "We brought you lunch."

"You guys trying to fatten me up? Bring it on back." The tea kettle whistled and Sam went to the stove and turned off the burner.

Both men entered the kitchen with bags of burgers and fries, Sam's favorite comfort food. The dog sat in the kitchen doorway with head cocked to one side.

Before the three of them could sit down to eat, the doorbell rang again.

Goldie rushed down the hall, barking.

"I'll get it." Ed headed out of the kitchen.

When he came back, Frank followed him. The old man handed her a bouquet of yellow daisies. "Thought I would see how you are."

"Doing well, thank you. The flowers are lovely. Want to join us?" Sam held her breath. *Please say no.*

"Don't mind if I do. I have a project I need to go over with Mark, anyway."

Ed found a vase for the flowers and set them on the table.

Everyone sat around eating the burgers and fries, and they discussed the future project, which was another house with a pool and landscaping.

The dog curled up at Sam's feet.

Mark finished his last bite of hamburger. "Mind if we use your computer, Samantha?"

"I guess it'll be okay." *Hope this will get them out of the house faster.*

Ed, Mark, and Frank went into her office. Sam threw the bags and wrappers into the garbage. Goldie stayed watching her, probably hoping for her to drop some food. She let the dog out back.

When she finished in the kitchen, with Goldie back inside, Sam wheeled down the hallway to the office doorway. The men huddled around the computer looking at some architectural designs.

Ed hit print and papers spewed out of the printer. Mark handed them to Frank.

"Thanks, Mark." Frank tapped the papers. "That should do it. I'll work up a proposal and get a copy to you. Appreciate the lunch, Sam. Feel better."

After Frank said good-bye, Sam heard the front door close.

Mark got up and laid his hand on Sam's shoulder. "Nice of you to let us use your computer and printer, Sam, but it's time for us to go." He tightened his grip on her shoulder for a brief tender moment, and then stepped outside into the hallway.

Ed kissed her on the cheek. "See you later."

"Bye."

The men departed and closed the front door.

From the office, Sam heard the door lock click. She noticed her computer desktop screen and "the fishermen" file. She groaned. *Oh, my God, did they see it?* If she knew more about computers, she could check to see if they'd looked. She thought her program recorded the date, but that wouldn't help. She opened the folder. Down on the left side it gave the date and time. The time when she'd worked on it. Could the time have been altered?

I'm being paranoid again. Goldie bumped her leg, leash in mouth.

"Need to go out again?"

The dog wagged her tail.

"Okay." Sam shut off her computer. "I'm ready to go out and get some fresh air, too."

37

My view is from a van a few blocks down the street. What is Samantha doing? The fishermen file seems dangerous. Why is she so curious? Will she make the connection?

Taking that chance is not an option. The other "accidents" didn't work. Risky to do it here, but what choice do I have?

All I work for can disappear. I won't let that happen.

Sam's door opens. My luck is changing. She is outside. What is she up to?

She rolls out onto the porch and looks down the stairs. The 4 x 8 plywood goes down part of the steps. Will she try to roll down on her own? Is she that strong?

Goldie barks.

Sam tilts her head from side to side as she studies the steps a bit longer. She hooks the leash on the dog. I watch her shrug and then she gives the wheelchair a push.

The wheelchair races down and Goldie runs alongside. I envision Sam crashing out into the street and getting hit by a car. That's perfect. No more troubles. And, I don't have to do a thing.

The dog stops and the wheelchair makes a sharp turn at the bottom and comes to a screeching halt by the sidewalk. Sam pats her dog on the head, and has the mutt lead her down the cement walkway.

Samantha goes in the opposite direction from where I watch. She disappears around the corner. Must follow her. I pull out and drive at a turtle's pace around the corner. I spot Sam up ahead and stop by the curb.

No cars are on the street. Can I get away with it?

I close my eyes and picture jamming my foot on the accelerator and running into her. I open my eyes. I lift my foot up to put on the gas.

Just then, an old man comes out of his house. Sam halts the wheelchair, waves and rolls up to the bottom of his porch. Goldie sits by her side, and Samantha talks with the guy. An animated discussion ensues and then the old guy walks down the steps, grabs her chair, and turns it around. He pulls it up the porch steps. The man's face turns red as he pulls her up each step, and he looks my way. I swear he sees me. He has a strawberry birthmark on the side of his cheek. He furrows his brow, turns redder, and finally he gets her to the top. They all go inside.

Did the man really see me well enough to identify me? If I can make out the red mark on his cheek, he surly could see me. I can't take that chance.

I better drive around the block. Back near Sam's house, I park a block away.

The street is deserted, so I rush up the path to her front porch. No one sees. I don't have to grab the key from under the flower pot. I take my copy out of my pocket and slip inside.

At her computer, on the desktop I click on "the fishermen" file. I see the list of men and all the information on each one, including what she'd found out about Anthony Neal.

Oh, Samantha, why won't you quit searching? This won't do. I have to stop her at any cost. I'll fix her. One way or another, I *will* get her.

38

After having a cup of coffee with old-man Rogers, Sam finished her walk with Goldie. Poor Rogers, he was so lonely. After his wife died, he didn't have many friends. He told Sam too many people stared at the red mark on his face. Made him feel self-conscious.

Every time Sam and Goldie strolled by, the old man invited them in. Her dog loved him because he always handed out doggy cookies.

The fresh air invigorated Sam, but she felt as if her body carried an extra fifty pounds. It ached. Wheeling back home, she crossed the street from the park. A van came barreling down on her. As it started to pass, Goldie ran backwards, yanking on the leash that Sam had tied to the chair. The dog pulled her back away from the vehicle.

The driver's face blurred as the van raced past, never slowing down. Rap music boomed, making Sam's head pound.

She shivered. *The van in Baja, now this van.*

Goldie licked her hand. *Breathe in, breathe out.* "Enough. I'm not getting paranoid. Probably a stupid kid. Let's get home."

At the bottom of the steps, Sam stared at the top of the porch. *How will I get back up?*

She sat in the chair, thinking for about two minutes. *I got it.* She tightened the leash onto the front of the wheelchair. "Goldie, pull." At the same time, Sam pushed on the wheels. It took a couple of tries, but they managed to get to the top. *That only took a half hour.*

On the porch, Sam turned the chair to face the street. She studied it. No vans or strange cars. *Must have been a mishap with a distracted teen.*

She took the key from under the pot, went inside, and locked the front door behind her. She rolled around the house and checked each window she could get to downstairs, making sure they were locked. Her dog followed her around as Sam jiggled the windows and the back door.

Maybe I should call the police?

Loud music had blared from the van. *Am I being too scared? Imagining things? Probably nothing. Bet the driver didn't even see me.*

39

That stupid mutt pulls her away from the van. She is *so* lucky.

I think that old man is going to be a problem. While Sam tries to figure out how to get up her porch, I'm going to go see that old man.

What to do? Kill him? Make him forget?

Have to hurry though. I must take care of him before Sam. When she dies, his memory might be a problem for me.

I don't want to have to do this, but can't take any chances now. I have to get this done and still have plenty of time for Samantha.

He's around the corner from her, so she won't know what's happening.

My plan is good. It'll work.

The man likes company and visitors. I don't park near the house.

I make sure no one notices me as I walk up his steps. I knock on the door.

"Oh, hi." The man smiles. "Come on in." He opens the door and beckons me inside.

I know him. So, it's easy. I avoid looking at the big strawberry birthmark on his face. I know he's self-conscious about it.

We go into the kitchen and he fixes me something to drink. I help him carry the cups to the table. I slip the drugs into his coffee. He doesn't suspect anything. "How's everything with you?"

Old man Rogers grins. "Couldn't be better. One of my oldest friends is coming by in about an hour."

Perfect.

Someone will find him. Sam will hear sirens, but that happens.

We chat for awhile. I look at my watch. It's taking longer than I thought.

The man finishes his drink and gets up to put the cups in the sink. He stumbles. Old man Rogers turns to me and then falls flat on his ugly face.

The cups crash to the floor and shatter. What a racket!

I wait a few minutes as he twitches on the floor, and then rise to walk over when there's no more movement or groaning from him. I check his pulse.

Nothing.

As I sweep up the mess, the phone rings.

I freeze.

Three rings, four, five, and the answering machine comes on. A call to remind him of a doctor's appointment.

Won't be needing that.

I put the shards from the broken mugs into a bag. I wash up the other cups that are in the sink and put them in the drainer. Only two—it'll appear as Sam's and his mugs. I put the towel I used to dry in my bag and as I'm hanging up a new one, the doorbell rings.

Must be the old friend. This presents an excitement I didn't need.

I slip out the back with my bag of broken cups and towel, I hurry across the yard to the gate in the back. I dash down the alley and go around the corner. I climb into the van and pull away from the curb.

That's close.

Now, on to the next part of my plan.

I whistle as I drive. With the mark on his face, and if they figure out he's a murder victim, maybe they'll dub me as the Birthmark Killer.

It's all coming together.

40

Sam drank some tea that calmed her nerves, and settled down to her computer. Goldie curled up next to the desk on the carpet. The computer screen was on.

Didn't I turn this off before I left? I guess being almost run down by the van wiped my memory.

What time did I create the fishermen file? She knew approximately, but not the exact minutes. *Why didn't I write it down?*

Her new cell phone needed to be charged so she plugged it into the charger next to the computer. Ed had bought this one after her cell had burned in the cabin fire.

I'm so pooped. Her own bed upstairs would be so comfortable. The one downstairs hurt her back. As before, she scooted backwards up each step, the dog tracking her.

On the way up the treads, she heard sirens. *Wonder who that's for?*

By the time she got to her room, she forgot about the wailing sirens. The bed beckoned her. She lay down and glanced around her room, so glad to be in it. "What the heck is that?" she asked her dog.

Goldie's head tilted and the dog perched her paws on the bed. Goldie barked.

Sam crawled over to the vent on the wall. She peered between the slats. An envelope. *How did that get in there?*

She needed a screwdriver, but the thought of scooting back down to look for one exhausted her. *Wait a minute, I used one last month to replace an outlet cover. It should be in my nightstand.* She managed to get around to the other side of the bed and rummaged through the drawer. "Here it is."

The dog observed her every movement.

The vent on the wall seemed so far away. Getting back over there proved tiresome and struggling to do so took all her energy. The cover became another challenge. Hard to remove from the vent. It felt as if it took an eternity to untwist all the fasteners. The screwdriver made a good pry bar. The vent cover fell to the floor. Inside—a thick envelope. She pinched the edge and held it up. *Who put this in my vent?*

She crawled back to the bed and sat on it, thinking hard. The detective TV shows suggested wearing rubber gloves for this, but they were downstairs. Wrapped hands would prevent using them anyway. She slipped the screwdriver under the flap and carefully opened the envelope, pulling out several sheets of typed paper with the tips of her fingers.

When she read what was written, she cried out, "Oh, my God."

The first impulse was to shred this. Sam looked toward the door. If she had been hit by the van and the police had found this, they would assume she'd killed Anthony Neal.

Who knew about this? *I hid this deep on my computer. This is an account of what Neal did to get me into financial trouble.*

The police would call this a motive.

Goldie growled.

The doorbell rang.

41

Goldie barked. "No! Stay!" *God, please don't let my dog run downstairs barking. I don't know who's at the door and I don't want them to know Goldie and I are here.* Whoever was at the door, Sam didn't want them inside.

She reminded herself to breathe, and waited.

The bell rang again. *Thank God I remembered to keep the key from outside.* She reached in her pocket and fondled the cold metal.

Silence.

Had whoever rang the doorbell fled?

She tilted her head, straining to listen. Would Goldie give any sign? The dog settled down and curled up by the side of the bed.

Goldie pricked up her ears, and uttered a low growl.

Banging came from the back door.

"Goldie, stay." Sam ogled the packet.

The last people to use her computer, besides her, were Frank, Ed, and Mark.

Ed had taken her computer to his trusted friend Don. Maybe Neal had done something similar to him and his computer business. *No that's paranoia talking. I hadn't created the fishermen file yet or uploaded pictures.*

Call the police, or no? No, their focus would be on her then because she lied.

The dog's head dropped back down on crossed-over paws, eyes wide open, watching Sam.

No one had knocked or rung any bells for several minutes. Sam chewed on her lip. Was the person who had been at the door gone? She clasped the papers by the edges and managed to stuff them back in the envelope.

Should I put the packet back where I found it?

Big brown eyes blinked twice and continued to follow Sam's movements. Goldie's soulful eyes stared.

Sam knew what she needed to do. "All right, girl." She replaced the cover on the vent and returned the screw driver to her drawer.

With the edge of the envelope between her fingers, she crawled to the top of the stairs, sat and scooted toward the bottom, dragging the envelope behind her.

Her dog ran past her to the bottom, and looked up, tail wagging.

"Glad somebody is happy," Sam muttered. "I'm coming."

Even though exhausted, she climbed into her chair. She grabbed the wheels and propelled herself down the hall and into the computer room. She put the packet on her desk. Rummaging through a drawer, she found a post office mailer, stuffed the envelope inside, and addressed the packet to her father. She shoved the mailer underneath a stack of old magazines. *I'm going to call my attorney.* She picked up the receiver to punch in his numbers.

The telephone was dead.

42

As Sam reached for her charging cell phone, Goldie ran out of the office toward the front door. Ignoring her phone, Sam rolled after her dog. Its nose sniffed the front door, but with tail wagging.

Sam got closer and heard, "This is where she keeps the key. It's not here."

"Maybe we should knock."

"Don't want to wake her if she's asleep."

"I'm not sure this is a good idea."

"Paula, is that you?" Sam called through the door.

"Are you up?"

Sam unlocked the door. Paula and Jim, on the porch, held up bags of Chinese take-out. "Where have you two been?"

Paula hugged her, and they strolled into the hallway. Jim locked the door behind them, with a loud click. "What do you mean?" Paula asked. "Didn't Ed tell you?"

"He said you were going away, but you didn't tell him where."

"Oh, he never listens." Paula patted Goldie's head. "We went to Seattle to a fertility clinic. Well at least I did. Jim had another out-of-town client and a hypnotism class he had to attend."

"Yes, Samantha, and we both wanted to come check on you and bring you dinner. I'm starved. Let's eat."

Jim pushed the wheelchair to the kitchen and Paula set out the boxes of Chinese take-out.

Jim put plates and silverware on the table and sat next to Paula to eat.

"So, how are you doing on your hypnotism? I know it doesn't work on me." Sam took a bite of fried rice, spilling some kernels onto the floor, which Goldie gobbled up.

"You're too strong, but I've helped people lose weight, stop smoking."

"Yes." Paula nodded. "If you could only get me pregnant with it."

Jim shrugged. "Doesn't work for everything. Don't worry, we'll get you pregnant." He smiled.

"I'm sure it will happen soon." Sam admired the way the two of them loved each other. One day someone would look at her the way Jim eyed Paula.

Sam finished eating. "The food was great, but I'm really tired."

"No problem. Jim, help me clean up and then we'll get Samantha to bed."

While they were in the kitchen, the phone rang. Paula answered and handed it to Sam. "Hello." Sam listened. "No, I heard sirens earlier. Dead? Oh, my God. Goldie and I visited with him a few hours ago. No, I'm fine. Paula and Jim are here. Talk with you later. Thanks for letting me know." She gave Paula the phone to hang up.

"What's wrong?" Jim put the utensils in the dishwasher and empty boxes in the trash.

"That was Detective Kline. You know old man Rogers that gives a cookie to Goldie every time we walk. The detective says he's dead."

"Oh, Sam, I'm so sorry." Paula gave her a hug. "He was nice to both of you."

"What a shame." Jim shut the dishwasher door.

"Yes. They're not sure of the causes yet."

Paula gasped. "Do they suspect foul play?"

"Not sure, but Detective Kline asked me an odd question after I told him I'd visited with the old man today."

"What?" Jim folded his arms over his chest.

"Asked if I had any birthmarks on me?"

"That is odd." Paula shook her head. "Why would he ask that?"

"Well, I find a chunk of flesh with a duck imprint. Now old-man Rogers is dead and he had that horrible strawberry mark on his face."

"What, these detectives think someone's going around killing people with birthmarks?" Jim chuckled. "Really odd. You don't have one, do you?"

"No, just a big mole on my buttocks."

"Too bad about Rogers, but he was old. Maybe he just dropped dead." Paula wiped down the counter.

"Probably that's it," Sam said.

Paula and Jim finished cleaning up the kitchen, fed Goldie, and then Jim moved the wheelchair toward the back, downstairs bedroom. Paula followed. "Everything else okay with you, Sam?"

"Well…" Sam wanted to tell them everything, but for some reason she hesitated. Who had been outside earlier? Paula and Jim? She felt beads of sweat pop out on her forehead. Her skin tingled. *Am I an idiot, or what?*

"Something up?" Jim rolled her over near the bed.

"No, I'm just tired, I guess. Losing old man Rogers is hard."

"We should get some sleep." Jim walked to the doorway. "Paula and I will stay over if that's okay? We'll talk in the morning."

"Sounds good to me. Guest room is all yours." Sam sighed. Relief flooded her, knowing Paula and Jim would spend the night. *I won't be alone. I'm sure it wasn't them out on the porch earlier.*

Paula helped Sam get into bed. "Wait 'til you hear what I found out at the clinic."

"Not now, Paula. Samantha needs her rest."

"I can hardly wait to hear about it in the morning."

Paula kept the door open. Goldie curled up by the side of the bed.

Sam's eyes closed. She breathed deeply. She and the dog fell asleep.

43

Man, it's getting crowded in Sam's house. How can I pull this off? The key is now inside. Doesn't matter because I have a copy. Besides, it's easy to break into a Victorian house. There's a window that is easily jimmied open. No one looks in closets, specifically the one in the guest room upstairs. I'm very patient.

The drug-laced meat for Goldie is in place. The dog is not a problem.

Now, I need to worry about Paula. Her hearing is excellent, unlike her partner.

I laugh. Don't have to worry about him.

They'll never suspect me. Samantha and I are close. Why would I have any reason to harm her?

I know she suspects Frank Collotti. That old guy looks at me funny. I think he's figuring things out. Since I can't have that, I take care of it.

I keep my eyes closed and remember back to earlier today when I snuck away. Finding his pickup truck—easy. No one's around. I slip underneath and slice his break line.

Calling him and sending him on a steep, winding road—brilliant idea. I follow at a distance. His truck goes into a slide. He corrects too much and the vehicle flips over, and over, and over.

An empty road and no one around. When I pull over and walk up to the truck, I notice it's mangled. I know nobody can survive that mashed mess.

Blood oozes out the broken window and Frank smells like copper. He's covered in the red liquid. His shirt is torn and he has some sort of discoloration on his shoulder. Maybe it's a birthmark. I laugh. Yes, the Birthmark Killer strikes again. Has a nice ring to it.

I feel for a pulse.

No way.

He opens his eye. It rolls in his head. He gasps and then lets out his last breath.

No more heartbeat.

I get in my vehicle and drive back the way I came. I round the bend and a car passes me.

I avert my face, gun the engine, and speed down the road.

Not sure if the person saw me.

Thankfully, I'm not in my own vehicle.

No one will figure it's me. Let Samantha believe Frank is doing all of this to her. He could very well be the one.

Except, now he's dead.

Maybe Frank knows Neal and has trouble with him. I hope so. Sam mentions Frank's possible involvement to the cops. She suspects him, and now maybe the cops do too.

Frank Collotti.

I laugh.

Damn, Anthony Neal.

Samantha didn't tell me she fell prey to his scheme as I did. A good reason for her to want him dead. When Sam's gone, the police will find that paperwork. It's hidden in the vent, but I have a plan to have it discovered.

She's the perfect suspect. She has good reason to want Neal dead. So do I, and a few others, too.

But, I point all leads to Samantha.

Too bad she must die.

Won't be easy, but it has to be done now.

Too curious for her own good, and I need a patsy, or....

A soft snore erupts.

Everyone is asleep now.

It's time.

All quiet.

Slip out from the closet. Make no sound.

Paula's breathing heavy. It's cute she snores a bit.

Tiptoe down the hall, and take the steps one at a time on their outer edges to make no noise.

The aroma of hot dogs for Goldie permeates the air.

Perhaps I'll keep Sam's cute red dog as my pet.

I smile, but then frown. I'll miss Samantha, but this is her fault. Who digs through fish guts, finds something like a birthmark, and insists on discovering who it belongs to? She should have left it alone.

I creep down the steps and hurry along the hallway toward the downstairs bedroom door where Samantha is sleeping. Have to be very quiet as it's open. Goldie has great hearing and a keen sense of smell.

I make it to the doorway. Sam's in bed asleep. No one else in the room.

Killing Samantha is too bad, but it is necessary for my survival.

44

Sam awoke from a horrible dream. Goldie was on all fours, growling. The dog's head cocked and Goldie fixated on the open bedroom doorway. Then the tail wagged, thumping against the side of the bed. A familiar figure walked forward.

"Jim, what are you doing in my room?" Sam shook her head, trying to dispel the sleep cobwebs, and scrunched her eyebrows. *Come on, wake up!*

"Thought I heard something." He stepped toward the bed.

Something came down on his head. Jim crumpled to the floor.

"Why did you do that?" Sam asked the figure that stood behind Jim.

"Couldn't… let… him… hurt… you."

Goldie ran to the end of the bed and sniffed Jim's limp body.

Sam threw back the covers.

"No! Stay there."

"But…"

The man leaned down, holding his hand up and out. "No, don't…"

Sam, frozen in place, smelled hot dogs.

Why is he here in my room? The sleepy fog elevated from her mind. No jolly smile. His eyes watered and drooped. No twinkle there. Ed dragged Jim over to the corner and propped him up. His chin rested on his chest. Sam couldn't tell if Jim was out cold or dazed.

Ed shifted in front of Jim and blocked her view. "No, I don't want to." Ed straightened and jerked his way over toward Sam with something in his hand.

Goldie staggered and fell to the floor.

Sam opened her mouth to scream.

Too late.

Ed jammed a white handkerchief against Sam's face. The stench of ether assaulted her, and she tried not to breathe.

Her eyelids grew heavy. *I don't want to die like this.*

~~~~~~~

Before she had to take in a breath, someone yelled, "No!"

Ed was yanked away from her. The hankie fell to the bed. She inhaled deeply, fighting off the drug.

Two men struggled.

"Stop. Why would you try and hurt Samantha? You're crazy."

Vaguely aware of a fight, Sam opened her eyes. A figure hit Ed. But he fought back. *Oh, my God, that's Mark.* Ed punched him in the gut. Both men fell to the floor. The two men pummeled each other.

Everything to Sam played out in slow-motion. She heard, "Hit him harder. Don't let him ruin everything." *I have to get to the gun.* Sam rolled over and extended her hand toward the nightstand to the right of the bed.

Wait, is that my hand? She turned her hand over and over. It was wrapped funny. *Never mind, I need the gun.* She kept reaching and found the drawer knob. She pulled on it, creating a small opening, and reached inside.

The two men arose from the floor, still boxing each other. Blood ran down Mark's face. Ed's nose—swollen and bleeding. But his new black-rimmed glasses were still on. His face contorted.

"This is not happening!" He threw another blow to Mark's stomach. The men fell on the bed, pinning Sam's legs.

She screamed. Her hand—inches from the gun, but she couldn't grab it. "Oh, God, help me."

Sirens wailed in the distance. Could those be for her?

"Paula, Jim, wake up. Someone, call the police." Sam yelled and struggled to clasp the gun, but also kept an eye on the men.

Ed's eyes widened and his mouth formed an "O". Reminded Sam of a cartoon character where a light bulb went on. He crawled toward the nightstand.

How did he know my gun's here?

Mark clutched the back of his shirt and tried to prevent him from reaching the drawer.

"No!" Sam hit Ed and gripped the gun.

His hand surrounded her wrist. "Squeeze hard," she heard. Ed tightened his grip.

Pain shot through Sam's arm, all the way up to her shoulder and down to her fingers. Her hand opened, releasing her grip.

The gun dropped to the floor.

Mark threw Ed to the opposite side of the bed, and flung himself to the floor to retrieve the gun.

Ed scrambled up and grabbed Sam around the throat in a chokehold.

Her eyes widened.

Mark came up with the gun and aimed it at Ed. "Enough!"

Sam heard a faint, "No." Ed dragged Sam further away from Mark. "Give me the gun."

"Ed, please stop this."

From the corner where Jim sat propped up, Sam heard a groan. *Come on, Jim wake up. Help us. Where's Paula?*

Ed's chokehold tightened. Sam struggled to breathe. Her breaths sounded ragged.

Movement in the doorway caught Sam's eye.

Paula was wide-eyed. She screamed, and ran back down the hall.

"Oh, damn," Ed muttered.

But Sam didn't think it sounded like him. He acted so strange.

"It's over, Ed." Mark waved the gun. "Paula will call the police, if she hasn't already. Hear those sirens? They're getting closer. Let Samantha go."

Ed leaned his chin on the top of Sam's head. If she'd been in another circumstance, it could have been a romantic gesture, endearing. She felt something wet on her hair. Was he crying?

"You had to find out who your shark ate." More wetness dripped on her hair.

Sam clawed at Ed's arms.

"Quit." He pulled her from the bed. Her legs hit the floor. Pain radiated up her spine. Stars brightened her vision. She bit her lip and willed herself not to pass out.

Ed sat the two of them on the floor, Sam between his legs. He still did not release the hold around her neck.

Sirens wailed louder. Tires screeched. Footsteps pounded up the porch and down the hall.

Detectives Kline and Harrison burst through the doorway. Guns pointed at Ed and Mark.

"Drop the gun." Kline looked at one man, then the other.

Harrison glanced over to the corner. He took a couple of side steps toward Jim.

I hope he's okay. Sam watched with wide eyes.

"Mr. Johnson, let her go," Detective Kline demanded.

Ed sniffed. "I can't. Have… to… finish… this."

Sam frowned. *There's that robotic voice again.* She tried to remain calm, thinking. What could she do?

"It's already over." Harrison turned to Mark. "Lower your weapon, or I'll shoot."

Mark laid the gun down on the bed, raised both arms. "It's not me, it's him." He focused on Ed. "Help her."

Kline inched closer to Ed and Sam. Ed's arms tightened. She rocked side to side.

"Let her go now. You won't stop anything by killing her."

Sam's eyes widened as she stared at the big, black hole of Kline's gun. If he fired, it would blow Ed's head apart.

Ed positioned Sam so she covered more of his body.

Sam rasped out, "Please, Ed, don't." Tears ran down her cheeks and dripped onto his arm.

Ed's hold lessened. Sam could breathe better. Movement came from the other side of the bed.

Kline yelled, "No!" His gun wavered.

Mark dove across the bed, slammed into Sam and Ed.

The detectives hurried over and pulled Mark away from Ed. Five police officers crowded into the room.

One officer helped Sam up and into her wheelchair. He rushed her out the doorway and down the hall.

Halfway down, Paula ran over to her. "Are you okay?"

The officer rolled Sam out the front door with Paula walking beside her wheelchair. Two ambulances, parked outside, waited with several paramedics. Two men scurried over to her.

"I'm okay. What's happening inside?"

"I don't know." Paula looked toward the porch.

Gunshots exploded.

"No!" Sam screamed.

Paula clasped her arm. They both stared at the front door.

Two officers helped Jim out. He held his head and needed help walking, but blood seeped out no bullet holes. Paula ran to his side. The officers put him in the ambulance. Paula climbed in beside him. The driver gunned the engine and the vehicle shot forward, tires squealing as the driver raced off.

Then another officer, grasping Mark's arm, escorted him out of the house. Blood ran down his face.

Detective Harrison came to the doorway and yelled, "Need a paramedic in here. Hurry!"

Two paramedics with a gurney and a couple of officers hurried up onto the porch and inside the Queen Anne house.

Mark and the officer escorting him stopped next to Sam.

"What happened?"

A paramedic wiped blood from Mark's face. Sam wanted to help, but couldn't.

"I'm sorry." Mark patted her shoulder. "He got away from the detective and lunged for the gun on the bed." Mark furrowed his brow. "I don't know why he did that. The cops had no choice but to shoot him when he aimed the gun toward Jim.

Paramedics carried a stretcher down the porch steps and toward another ambulance that just arrived. Detective Kline followed. The paramedics opened the back doors and hoisted the gurney inside.

"Will he make it?" Mark called out.

One paramedic looked at Detective Kline. "Doesn't look good." He scrambled in and the ambulance driver, with sirens blaring, peeled out and careened down the street. The group stared after the vehicle.

45

Detective Kline asked Sam, "What happened here?"

Harrison stayed on the porch, glancing down the hall and then back outside.

Sam explained about someone banging on her door, but she didn't answer. Then Jim and Paula came in last minute to eat dinner and spend the night. "When I woke up, Jim was inside my room. Then Ed conked him on the head and tried to chloroform me. Suddenly Mark showed up. They fought, and then you and other police officers ran into the room." She faced Mark. "How did you get here?"

She bit her lip. The chaos that had ensued shook her to the core. She felt cold, but curious. How had Mark arrived in time to save her?

Mark interrupted her thoughts. "Ed and I came by the house earlier. We tried to see you. No one answered. I told him you were probably sleeping. We had separate vehicles and we drove off. Something didn't set right with me. Ed behaved so odd. Didn't want me to come by with him. Then I noticed he made a strange turn. Didn't think much of it. Saw Paula and Jim drive by. Figured they were heading to your place.

"To be honest," Mark ran a hand through his hair, "I suspected Jim. Something Linda mentioned about him being in Cabo or thought she saw him there. I decided to come back to your house. Heard noises inside and couldn't get in the front door, but the kitchen door was unlocked. The rest, you know."

"I can't believe you think Ed killed Neal."

"Believe it, Ms. Volarie," Kline nodded. "He confessed before he made a dive for the gun."

"Why?"

Kline frowned. "He said, and I quote: 'We killed him for the same reason Sam could have.' Do you know what he means?"

"Me?" Sam blushed.

Detective Harrison came down the steps and walked over to them. "That's what Johnson said. You know what he meant?"

"Not sure. That's not the man I know." Sam chewed on her lip. *Oh, God, guess I have to call my attorney again.* What if the police find the envelope? Will they believe she had nothing to do with it?

"Samantha, you look too pale." Mark put his arm around her. "I'm sorry about Ed. I'm sure it's a shock."

Sam's stomach felt as if it did a flip-flop. She gazed up at Mark. His face had cuts and bruises. His eyes glistened and his smirk or smile no longer appeared on his face. But that's not what upset her.

Before she could say anything, Detectives Barber and Oliver arrived. They jumped out of their vehicle and hurried over.

Barber studied Sam. "You okay? When Kline called and told us there was a ruckus at your place, we zoomed over from Spokane."

Kline nodded. "Ed Johnson killed Neal. Tried to kill Ms. Volarie."

"What? Johnson killed Neal?" Barber pulled out his notebook.

"Yes, I was shocked, too." Sam shivered. "I was convinced Frank Collotti was trying to kill me. He showed up at every strange event."

"Frank Collotti?" Barber paged through his notebook. "Couldn't be him. He was killed today in a single car crash that's under suspicion."

Frank's dead!" Sam blinked several times at Mark.

"Did you know he had a birthmark on his shoulder?" Detective Barber asked.

"No. What's that have to do with anything?"

"The press is calling Neal's, Rogers, and Collotti's deaths, The Birthmark Kills. They think someone is killing people due to their birthmark. Dubbed the killer as the Birthmark Killer."

"That's crazy detective. Is there any proof that Roger's or Collotti's deaths were anything but accidents?" Mark asked. "And when did you find out Neal was killed? You told us he was missing. That's the duck birthmark in Sam's shark."

Detective Barber shrugged. "Still an on-going investigation."

"Oh, my God. Do you think Ed killed them?"

"We'll delve deeper into Collotti's and Roger's death. Might be a connection." Barber jotted down a note.

"Detectives, I think Samantha should be taken to the hospital. Ed had quite a chokehold on her." Mark nestled her against him. "Her color is bad, and she's sweating. I'd feel better if a doctor checked her out."

"Yes." Kline stroked his chin. "Be a good idea. Don't worry, Miss Volarie. We'll be here at the house, processing. No one will enter that we don't log in."

Both Harrison and Kline turned, walked up the steps, and entered the house.

"Oliver, you stay here. I'll go to the hospital with her." Barber yelled, "Paramedic over here."

"Really, I'm fine." Her voice was barely a whisper. "I'll stay here." Sam didn't want to leave. *What if they find the mailer?* She hadn't sealed it.

The paramedic checked her vitals. "We should take you to the hospital. Your blood pressure is high and your neck is very red."

"Come on, Sam. The police will keep your house safe."

"Oh, my God, Goldie. Where's my dog? We have to help her."

Harrison walked out carrying the dog. "Goldie will be okay. I'll keep a close eye on your dog and take her to the vet if needed.

The paramedic guided Sam toward the rig. They lifted her inside and then Mark and Detective Barber climbed in with Sam.

Oliver closed the doors and pounded on the outside. The ambulance driver revved the engine and raced the vehicle down the street.

At the hospital, Sam spotted Paula and Jim in the cubicle next to her in the ER. "How's Jim?"

When the nurse started to close the curtain, Sam held up her hand. "Wait."

Paula stood next to Jim's bed and rubbed his shoulder. She smiled at Sam. "He has a slight concussion, but will be all right."

"I'm sorry, but I'm closing the curtain." The nurse pulled it across.

Detective Barber stayed at the foot of Sam's bed. Mark was near her left side trying to be close to her, but out of the way. He no longer had the smirk on his face and she thought his eyes glistened with tears. *Unbelievable that Ed killed Neal and tried to kill me. Why would he do it? Doesn't sound like the man I knew.*

An ER doctor with a stethoscope around his neck walked in. He examined her and gently palpitated Sam's throat. "You'll have some bruising, but no permanent damage. Vocal chords might be sore and hoarse, but your throat will heal in a few days." He unwrapped her bandages on her arms and legs, checking on her burns.

Sam winced when the doctor felt the palm of her hand. "You're healing well, but I'm going to have the nurse re-bandage everything, including your hands."

"Please have the nurse wrap my hands so my fingers show."

"I'll have her leave a couple out, but I want your fingers from middle to pinkie covered. Right fingers look okay to leave out. You heal fast. Keep applying the burn cream and re-bandage every day."

"Thanks, Doctor."

Paula and Jim walked past. "You okay, Sam?" Jim had a bandage around his head and Paula held onto his arm.

"I'm good. How about you?"

Paula smiled again. "Thank God, he has a hard head. I'm taking him home. Doc told me to keep him awake for several hours. We'll be up late."

Detective Barber spoke to Paula. "Detective Harrison will come by your house. He might be bringing Sam's dog and will need a statement from you."

Paula nodded. She and Jim departed.

When the nurse finished wrapping Sam's burns, the doctor came back in. He looked over her chart and signed release papers for Sam.

Detective Barber and Mark kept quiet for the entire examination. Sam signed the release papers.

"We'll go to the police station." Barber cleared his throat. "Your house is a crime scene, and we have to ask you some questions. Mr. Randall, you'll have to come, too."

"I planned on it. I won't leave Samantha."

"Do I need an attorney?" Sam gazed into Mark's eyes, waiting for his answer.

"You're not in any trouble," Barber said. "You were attacked."

"Maybe you should call one just in case." Mark helped her get into the wheelchair.

"Of course." Barber nodded. "It's your right."

Detective Oliver arrived at the hospital as Mark pushed Sam out through the front doors with Barber walking alongside. He pulled Barber away from them and whispered to him. The detective scrunched his eyebrows at Sam. "Oliver will drive us to the station."

They all scrambled into the car. Oliver put Sam's chair in the trunk and then he pulled away from the curb. Sam felt cold from the silence in the vehicle.

She couldn't stand the quiet, so she asked Mark, "Where's Linda?"

"She went back to L.A. Doesn't appreciate the small-town living and she made it clear if I stayed in Sandpoint, I could find another girlfriend."

"I'm sorry."

"I'm not." Mark smiled.

Sam felt tingles go up and down her arms when Mark reached over and patted her hand.

At the police station, the detectives seated her and Mark in an interrogation room. "Okay, I think I should call my attorney."

They handed her a phone and she punched in Hargrove's number. By now she'd memorized it.

When she asked him to come to the station, her attorney said, "Don't say anything until I get there."

Sam told Detectives Barber, Oliver, and Kline, who'd just come in, Hargrove's instructions. "Where's Detective Harrison, by the way?"

"He took your dog to the vet. So, he'll be heading to Paula and Jim's after to obtain a report about the incident from them and will leave Goldie there. We'll wait for your attorney. Would you care for some tea?" Kline asked.

To stall for time, and to keep awake, Sam nodded. "That would be great, thanks."

The attorney arrived within fifteen minutes. "I need to speak to my client alone first, before we get started?"

"All right." The detectives stepped out.

Mark asked, "Want me to stay?"

Sam didn't have a chance to answer. Hargrove pointed to the door. "Best if you wait for us in the reception area, please."

"I think the officers wanted to talk with me, too."

"I can't represent you both."

"I don't think I need an attorney. They'll just take my statement. I'll meet you in the reception area."

When Mark looked at Sam, she nodded. She wanted him to stay. For some reason she felt safer when he stood near.

The door closed behind him.

Hargrove sat next to Sam. "What's the problem now?"

"Ed, or someone, hid a packet in my house explaining all about my financial mess that Neal got me into—a motive for his murder." Sam explained how she noticed it behind a vent cover in the wall in her upstairs bedroom, put the papers in a mailer, and wrote her father's address on the outside. "I hid it in my office. Not sure if I sealed it or not."

"And, if the police find it, and it's open, will they check?" Hargrove nodded. "Answer is, probably, yes."

Sam felt sick to her stomach. "Detective Oliver, who came from the crime scene, whispered something to Barber and he eyed me funny. Before Ed killed himself, he said, "*We* had reason to kill Neal.""

"Okay, let's allow the detectives in and see what they have to ask. Remember my signal of drumming my fingers on the table. Don't say a word when I do that." Her attorney walked over to the door and opened it. "Come in, gentlemen." He went back around the table and sat next to Sam.

Detectives Barber, Oliver, and Kline strolled in, along with the ADA she'd talked with earlier. Ned Foley carried an envelope. It sent chills down Sam's spine.

She gasped.

Her attorney drummed his fingers on the table. She kept quiet until spoken to.

46

Foley sat across from Sam and slammed the envelope he carried onto the table. His index digit tapped on the paper to a staccato beat.

Sam swallowed, but remained silent as her attorney kept drumming his right fingers on the table.

Detective Barber cleared his throat. "Ms. Volarie, is there anything you'd care to say?"

Hargrove quit drumming. "Did you have questions for my client?"

The ADA jabbed several times on the envelope. He shoved it a little closer toward Sam.

She stared at it, felt sweat dripping down her armpits, but kept her mouth closed.

"This is ridiculous," Oliver blurted out.

Barber glared at him. Oliver didn't say another word. "Ms. Volarie, we found that envelope," the detective tapped the one on the table, "in your office. One of the officers knocked over a stack of magazines. The envelope tumbled onto the floor. It was not sealed and the papers slid out." The detective stopped and stared at Sam.

Hargrove leaned forward. "And?"

"I've seen the contents." Foley glowered. "Do you have anything to tell us?"

Her attorney continued drumming his fingers.

Detective Barber waited. "Maybe I should just ask. Did you conspire with Ed to kill Neal?"

Sam gasped. "What? No, I did not. Why would you think that?"

The ADA focused on the envelope. "Those papers show motive for Neal's death, and Mr. Johnson said, 'we'."

"I thought Detective Barber said Neal's death might have something to do with birthmark's and tied with old-man Rogers and Collotti's deaths."

Foley glared at Barber.

The detective cleared his throat. "The press is trying to tie the deaths together. When they found out Neal was identified by his birthmark and then Rogers and Collotti have birthmarks too, they're calling whoever had a hand in their deaths, The Birthmark Killer."

The ADA tapped on the envelope. "But this gives us another motive. And, we're not sure the other two are related. You don't have anything against people with birthmarks, do you, Ms. Volarie?"

"No, of course not."

"Then explain about this paperwork."

Hargrove leaned back in his chair and cleared his throat. "Ms. Volarie, now you tell them what you told me."

Sam took a deep breath. "I bought the nursery and Neal gave me some very bad investment advice where, as you see from that information you found, I lost a substantial amount of money. I met with him twice. But I did not meet him in, see him in, or even know he'd gone to Cabo." She explained how and where she'd found the envelope in her vent in her upstairs bedroom wall. Told the police about her note in Cabo.

"Do you still have the note?" Barber flipped a page in his notebook.

"No, it disappeared in Cabo."

"Convenient," Detective Oliver crossed his arms over his chest.

Foley leveled a stare at him.

Sam sighed. "If I'd killed Neal, why would Ed confess, or why would I try and find out who was in my shark?"

"She has a point, gentlemen." Her attorney nodded.

Someone knocked on the door. An officer came in, handed the assistant district attorney a slip of paper, then turned around. Not waiting for an answer, the policeman departed from the room.

Foley perused the note. "That's strange."

"What?" Detective Barber asked.

Foley looked up. "Ms. Volarie, Mr. Hargrove, please excuse us for a minute." The ADA got up. "Detectives, may we have a word." He stepped out of the room.

The detectives glanced at one another, then rose and followed Foley out into the hallway, closing the door behind them.

Hargrove faced Sam with a raised eyebrow. "Something else you need to tell me?"

She opened her eyes wide. "I've told you everything. What do you think?"

"No idea. But Mr. Foley seemed confused."

"I thought so too."

"When they come back in, let them talk first."

Sam and her attorney waited for what she felt was an eternity. *Will they charge me? I didn't do anything, but that file makes me appear guilty. Not to mention the fact I didn't say anything about it.*

Sam chewed on her lip and gawked at the closed door. Her lips were bruised from all the biting. "What's taking so long?"

Hargrove kept staring across the table where the detectives sat earlier.

The door opened and Detective Barber sauntered back in. No one else followed.

"It seems we have our killer. We tore Ed's home apart and found more evidence. The file we found in your house—we figure Ed planted it there to make you look as guilty as him. Evidently, he fell for the same bad advice you did. He got angry because he couldn't get his money back and killed Neal. Dumped him in the ocean." The detective ran a hand through his hair. "Sorry for any inconvenience. You're free to leave the station, but stick around town. We may have more questions."

Sam gaped at him. Was he going to say more? No. He shrugged and motioned toward the open door.

"Thank you, Detective. My client will be available for any further questions."

"And, I'm afraid, Ms. Volarie, your home's a crime scene. You'll have to stay elsewhere."

"No problem. I'm sure I can stay with Paula and Jim. They have Goldie anyway."

"Fine." Barber started to say something, but closed his mouth. He pursed it as if he'd swallowed a very tart lime.

Hargrove arose, clutched the handles on Sam's wheelchair, and hustled her out the door.

Detective Oliver slouched against the wall in the hallway next to Foley. Sam didn't see any sign of Harrison or Kline. The assistant district attorney and the detective nodded as Sam and her attorney hurried by.

Mark paced in the reception area and rushed over. "They took my statement. Everything okay with you?"

"Let's get out of here." Hargrove pushed the wheelchair faster.

In the car, Mark sat in the back while Sam's attorney drove.

"May I at least go by my house, get my new cell phone, and a few clothes?"

"It's after midnight." Hargrove frowned. "Will your friends let you stay?"

"I'm sure they will."

"I'll call Detective Kline and see about getting a few things out of your house now, but probably won't be 'til tomorrow morning. Let's get you settled somewhere."

47

They parked in front of Paula and Jim's Queen Anne Victorian. Their house was painted a dark grey with black trim, and the tower frowned down on Sam, giving her the creeps. She bit her lip, but remembered Paula had made the tower room into a girl's cave. Or a woman's "inside she shed" as Paula always corrected Sam. A light shone from the front window.

Hargrove and Mark hauled Sam onto Paula and Jim's porch. Her attorney rang the bell.

A minute later, the porch light came on and Paula opened the door. "Sam, are you all right?" she tugged her robe tighter around her waist.

Goldie ran out and licked Sam's fingers.

Sam stroked her dog. "I'm fine. But I'm not allowed to go back to my house. I know it's late, but may I stay here?"

Jim walked up behind Paula in his robe. "Of course. Paula's keeping me awake for my concussion. Come on inside."

Mark rolled Sam's wheelchair into the living room.

Hargrove waited next to Sam's chair. "Now you have a safe place to stay, I'll go call and see if I they'll let me get some of your things from your house, but don't count on it. I'll call you in a few minutes if you'll still be up?"

"You want a cup of coffee or something?" Paula asked.

"No, no it's late. Thanks."

Sam clasped her attorney's hand. "Thank you. Thank you for everything. I appreciate all you've done."

"No problem. It's my job." Hargrove nodded. "Is there anything else you need?"

"No, I'll be fine here."

"Okay, then. I'll let you know if I'm successful in getting any of your stuff." Hargrove wrote down Paula's number and she saw him out the door.

When she returned to the living room, Jim said, "Tell us what happened at the station."

"Let's sit down. Jim should be off his feet." Paula guided her husband onto the brown leather couch. "Do you want anything to eat or drink?" She hovered over Sam.

"No, thanks. Sit, Paula. Jim, how are you?"

"Fine. As Paula pointed out, I have a hard head. Now, spill the beans."

"Okay, I'll tell you what went on at the precinct."

Mark pulled over a brown chair next to Sam's wheelchair and sat. Paula and Jim were across on the couch. Goldie curled up at Sam's feet.

Sam explained about the envelope, the bad investment she had made from Neal's advice, and how she thought she'd be arrested.

Mark sat quietly by her side through the entire monologue. Sam appreciated that he was near her and being patient. She smiled at him.

"Is there more?" Paula asked.

"Yes." Sam continued, "Then, Mr. Foley received a note. He went out of the room with the detectives."

"You must have been so scared." Paula grabbed Jim's hand. "So, what happened?"

"Detective Barber came back in and told us they had their killer. They searched Ed's place and found evidence he tried to frame me."

"Sam, I'm so sorry." Jim adjusted the bandage on his head.

"That's awful." Paula went and hugged Sam. "I'm so sad for you. Thought Ed seemed nice. May I get you anything?"

"Nothing for me, thanks." Mark shook his head.

"How about you, Sam?"

"No, I'm okay, Paula. Just shocked. Wasn't like Ed. So, what did you say to Detective Harrison when he brought Goldie by?"

"We didn't know much." Paula gazed at Jim. "I was sleeping, heard a commotion and came downstairs." She turned to Sam. "Saw you, Mark and Ed and screamed. Called 911."

"Yes." Jim nodded. "I'd come downstairs. Thought I heard something and wanted to check on you. Then everything got fuzzy. Guess Ed hit me over the head." He reached up and adjusted his bandage again. He yawned.

"Oh, no, Doc told me you have to stay awake." Paula touched his knee.

The phone rang.

Paula answered, listened, and hung up. "Sorry. Hargrove said he couldn't get into your house to get any clothes or your cell phone. Maybe tomorrow."

"Okay. I'm glad Ed didn't hurt you too bad, Jim." Sam fidgeted in her wheelchair and yawned. "Can't believe it. I'm so exhausted. Think I can crash now?"

"Of course. Let's get you into the bedroom." As Paula pushed the chair from the room, Sam yelled over her shoulder, "Good night, guys."

Goldie padded alongside down the hall to the guest room. It was set up similar to Sam's. A double bed, night stands, and hardwood floor.

Sam heard Mark yell, "Get some sleep." She also heard him ask, "May I sleep on your couch? I don't want to leave her."

She wasn't sure what Jim answered, as Paula closed the downstairs bedroom door.

Paula helped Sam onto the bed. She lay on top. Paula flipped half the floral bedspread over onto her. "You going to be able to sleep? I can give you one of my pills or something."

"No. I'll be okay. Just so tired."

"You're safe here." Paula patted her shoulder. "Get some rest." She closed the door on the way out.

Goldie curled up alongside on the little brown rug next to the bed.

Sam closed her eyes, but sleep refused to come. She pictured the fight in her mind. It ran frame by frame. She couldn't get over how Ed acted so strangely. Didn't even sound like him at times.

Why did he kill Neal over losing money? Was he that messed up? She found it too hard to believe.

Goldie stood and padded around the bed, sniffed at the door, and paced. Then the dog came over to the bed and placed her chin on the spread.

Sam reached over and petted her dog's head. "Am I keeping you awake? Sorry, girl, it's so hard for me to believe Ed did any of this."

Goldie whined.

"You agree with me. Well, in the morning when we wake up, I'll go to the police and find out what evidence they do have. Okay, girl, that's decided. Let's get some sleep."

The dog did 360-degree circles and settled down on the rug again.

Sam rolled over and closed her eyes.

48

It's about time. Everything works out. The police believe Ed is Neal's killer and Samantha's problems are over. They don't know for sure if Rogers or Collotti's deaths are an accident or not.

I sneak down the hall and hear her talking to Goldie. Why can't the woman leave everything alone?

She won't drop it. How am I going to stop her now? Let me think. I'm in the clear, but if she refuses to let it go…

No, I have to stop her. If only Ed could have killed her. Didn't have good enough control over him.

Maybe I could burn the house down? I tried it once, but she escaped.

Have to make it appear as an accident. If not, I'll be a suspect. Can't have that. I'm not a suspect now.

Come on brain, come up with something.

Maybe I'll make it appear as if someone else did it? That worked before.

I sit at the kitchen table.

A plan forms.

Yes, that might work.

I smile.

Damn, Neal and his bad investment advice. Guess Sam did the same thing as I did.

Sorry, Samantha, but I have to do this.

49

Sam's eyelids flew open. Mark leaned over her and his hand clamped over her mouth. She tried to scream.

Mark, in a low voice, spoke in her ear. "Shh. You're not safe here. We need to get you out of this house." He removed his hand.

"What do you mean?" Sam whispered.

Mark brought a finger to his lips. Then he threw back the bedspread and motioned Sam to get into the wheelchair. Goldie was nowhere in sight.

Sam's eyes widened. "Where's my dog?"

"Outside. Hurry."

Still groggy from sleep, Sam didn't understand any of this, but for some reason she trusted Mark. Without another word, she got into the wheelchair. Mark pushed her out of the room, down the hall toward the front door. Sam felt a chill run down her back. *I trusted Ed, too.*

They were about to open the door, when a voice said, "Where are you going?"

Mark halted. He squeezed Sam's shoulder. Then he turned around, leaving her facing the door. In front of the wheelchair, Sam heard Mark say, "Out on the porch for some fresh air."

"Why don't we go out to the back yard? It'll be more private there."

The voice made Sam shiver. She gritted her teeth.

"The front porch has that nice swing on it. Sorry if we woke you." Mark didn't move.

Mark reached back and squeezed her shoulder a little tighter than before. Sam shivered.

"Don't you think the back yard would be better, Samantha? That's where Goldie is."

She craned her head around, trying to see, but Mark blocked her vision. "The swing *is* comfortable." She wanted out the front door.

"Let's go to the back yard. I'm sure your dog wants to see you. Let's go now!"

Mark spun the wheelchair around. Sam's eyes widened and her mouth fell open. *Where's my dog? This is not happening!*

Jim stood in the hallway pointing a gun at them. "This is not how it was supposed to go. I was free. Samantha, you couldn't let it go. And you, Mark, insisted on spending the night. Now I have to deal with both of you. Move!"

Mark rolled the wheelchair slowly toward the back of the house.

I'll swat the gun out of Jim's hand as we go by. He was too smart. He backed up into the kitchen and waited far enough away.

"Open the door and don't call out. If either of you makes a sound, I'll shoot. I'm as good a shot as you are Sam, and you know it."

Sam reached for the doorknob. "Why, Jim?"

"I'm sure you're smart enough to figure it out."

"You lost money with Neal's bad investment advice too, and I bet Paula doesn't know."

"See, I knew you were intelligent. Now quit stalling and join Goldie outside. And don't scream when you see your dog. Goldie's not dead. I drugged the mutt. I'd never hurt your dog, or any other animal, because they can't talk. Why wouldn't you drop it? I was not a suspect. Because of hypnotizing Ed, everyone thought he killed Neal."

"But…"

"Enough. Open the door and get outside."

"Where's Paula?"

"She's upstairs, sleeping. I slipped her one of her pills. I have to finish this. I'm sorry, Samantha, but you wouldn't leave it alone."

Sam opened the door and Mark moved her chair out onto the porch. She saw Goldie's still form lying under the big, larch tree. Tears formed. Sam couldn't help it. Jim had rigged a ramp down the stairs.

"Hold on, Samantha!" Mark shoved the wheelchair hard. She went flying down the incline.

When she hit the bottom, someone jumped out and pulled her from the chair, getting her out of the way.

"Freeze. Don't move!"

Sam heard struggling on the porch, then a gunshot.

"Keep quiet, Miss Volarie. It's me, Detective Oliver." He covered Sam's body. She could only hear the commotion.

"Drop the gun. Call an ambulance. Oliver, you and Detective Harrison get Ms. Volarie and her dog out of here."

"No," Sam yelled. "Who's hurt?"

Oliver picked her up and put her in the wheelchair, and rushed her toward the back gate. Harrison lifted Goldie into his arms and carried the dog alongside.

"Stop. Who's been shot?" Sam couldn't get them to even slow down.

Oliver went through the gate where a van idled. He and Harrison loaded her and Goldie inside. Tires squealed and the officer in the driver's seat sped off.

"Where are we going?"

"We're taking Goldie to the vet to make sure she's okay. You're not hurt, are you?"

"A little rattled from being tackled to the ground, but no, Detective Oliver. What's going on? Do you know who fired the gun? Anyone hurt?"

Oliver sat in the passenger seat and looked over his shoulder at her. "Sorry, I know as much as you do. The plan was to get you safe."

"Plan?" The van had no back windows and Sam felt closed in.

"Yes, I'm sorry, but we used you as bait."

"What?" Sam couldn't believe it. Why would they set her up?

"We'll explain later." Harrison, who sat in the back with Sam, held Goldie's still form. "When we saw your dog, I called the vet. He's waiting for us. Let's get Goldie checked out."

50

"Your dog will be okay, Samantha." The vet stroked the red hair. "Goldie was drugged and will sleep it off. I do want to keep your dog overnight though to make sure."

Detective Oliver received a call. "Yes, we'll be right there." He hung up. "We have to go."

He, Sam, and Detective Harrison loaded back into the van and the police officer drove off.

Oliver leaned over and told the driver to head to the hospital.

"Why are we going there?"

"Detective Barber instructed us to bring you to the hospital. Wants to make sure you're okay, and to answer some questions."

"Who was injured?"

"Barber will explain everything."

Sam took a deep breath. *Why won't they tell me what's going on? This is so frustrating. Unbelievable Jim was behind this whole thing.*

Sandpoint is a small town and it didn't take long to get to the hospital from the vet's office. Oliver helped her into the wheelchair and propelled her through the ER doors. Harrison followed. Sam didn't see Mark or anyone inside the waiting room. The nurse waived Oliver through the next set of double doors. Sam saw Detective Barber standing outside of one of the cubicles, along with Detective Kline.

Oliver pushed her over toward Barber. A nurse stopped him before the next cubicle and motioned him to enter the empty one.

"I'm fine." Sam tried to get out of the wheelchair, but the nurse kept her seated. "Who's in that cubicle? Tell me what's going on!"

Detective Barber came over. "Please let them check you out. Then we'll talk."

"Is Mark okay? What about Jim? Is Paula here?"

The nurse helped Sam up onto the bed. Then she wrapped a blood pressure cuff around Sam's arm and pumped it up.

Barber took a deep breath. "I'm sorry it went down this way, but Foley wanted to make sure we had the correct killer this time. He was convinced we could keep you safe, so we sent you away and told you your place was a crime scene. The ADA figured you'd go straight to your friend's house to stay. He was right. I didn't want it to go this way, but I have to go along with my bosses."

"What are you talking about?" Sam heard beeping from a machine in the next cubicle.

Mark walked into view. He had his arm in a sling. "They should have told us, or at least me." He glared at the detective.

"Are you hurt?" Sam's eyes widened, staring at the sling. "Were you shot?"

Mark rubbed his bicep. "No, hurt my arm tackling Jim."

"I don't understand any of this."

The nurse finished taking Sam's vitals and the doctor came in. After he reviewed the results, he listened to Sam's heart. "Appears you're okay. You should take it easy for a day or so." The doctor put down the chart and strode to the next cubicle.

Mark sidled over and sat on the edge of the bed. "I'm so sorry about Jim."

"What about him?" Sam looked from Mark to Detective Barber. Oliver walked out of the room and stood in front of the next cubicle, along with Kline and Harrison, as if they were on guard.

Before Barber could answer, Sam heard a flat-line noise from the machine next door. A scream exploded from the curtained off cubicle. Then sobbing erupted.

Sam felt chills run down her spine. She tried to get up, but Mark kept her down. "Let her grieve a minute. Then you can go over to her. I'm sure the doctors did everything they could to try and save him, but couldn't."

"Jim?" Tears streamed down Sam's face.

Barber cleared his throat. "Yes. When he and Mark tussled, the gun went off and he was shot in the stomach. Not much anyone could do for him. I'm sorry."

"Why? How did Jim do this?"

"Paula did get a confession out of him," Barber said. "We already figured it was he who had done all of this and not Ed."

"How?" Sam waited for Barber's answer.

"Well, we examined Ed's new glasses which were a sophisticated type of spyware. Jim could see and hear, and even give Ed instructions through the earpiece that was inconspicuous on the glasses." The detective cleared his throat. "We traced everything back to Jim. He hypnotized Ed and told him what to do through the earpiece. That's why Johnson behaved so odd."

"So, when I heard things from Ed and he acted confused, it was really Jim speaking?"

"Yes." Barber nodded. "Evidently, he didn't have full control over Johnson. That's why you are still alive. Johnson fought hard not to hurt you. Jim was into Neal as you were, but a bit more. We also discovered a Bic pen in your laundry room."

"I found a Bic pen on my dive in Baja."

"Yes, so you told us. It gave us the final clue."

"The pen had writing on it. With everything that's happened, I forgot all about it. What did it say?"

Barber glanced over at the curtained-off cubicle. "Hypnotism. Are you susceptible?"

"Oh, my God. That's Jim's pen. He had those printed up. I would have figured it out. So, Jim was in Cabo?"

"Yes. Tried to run you down in the van there and here. For what it's worth, he apologized to Paula for trying to hurt you."

Sam leaned forward and stared at the detective. "Burned down the cabin?"

"Afraid so. He came back after Paula and he'd left. Said it was pure luck everyone went for a walk but you."

"He tried to make Ed look guilty and planted evidence in my house?"

"All true." Detective Barber shrugged. "Would have worked too, if Mark hadn't come along and messed everything up by fighting with Ed in your house."

"What about Rogers and Collotti?"

"He said he had to kill them because he couldn't take any chances they'd figure out he did it when he killed you. Was afraid Rogers saw him in the van, and Collotti seemed suspicious. He laughed about the press calling him the Birthmark Killer. Since we tracked everything back to Jim, with his hypnotism background, we figured out his plan. Let you loose, believing you'd go there and he would try to kill you again. I didn't approve of the idea, but…"

"You should have told me so I could have kept a better eye on her." Mark furrowed his brow.

"Couldn't tell anyone. Weren't sure who was responsible or working with each other."

Sam couldn't believe Jim didn't have other options. She gazed at Mark. "How did you know to get me out of the house?"

"I couldn't sleep very well and I saw Jim go down the hall to your room and carry Goldie out." Mark sighed. "Scared me, so I wanted to get you away."

"Paula must be devastated." Sam still heard sobs coming from near her. "May I see her now?"

Mark helped Sam up and into the wheelchair. He pushed her to the next cubicle. Paula was draped over Jim, crying hysterically. Jim's eyes were closed and his skin was grey. The coppery smell of blood assaulted Sam. Blood was all over the floor. Sam's heart ached for her friend.

"Paula, I'm so sorry." Sam cleared her throat. "What do I need to do to help you?"

Her friend looked up with tears streaming down her face. "Why couldn't he have told me we were broke? I would have forgiven him."

The pain in her voice was almost more than Sam could bear. She didn't know what to say. Sam held out her arms.

Paula left Jim and rushed into Sam's outstretched arms. She sobbed on Sam's shoulder. "I'm pregnant," Paula whispered.

Sam pushed Paula away from her shoulder and cupped her face in her hands. Tears ran down both women's faces. "We'll deal with this together. You'll make a great mom and I know you can handle anything. I'll be right there with you every step of the way."

"You have many friends here, Paula, that will help you." Mark smiled a sincere smile, no longer a sneer. "I've decided to stay in Sandpoint, and I'll be there for you, too."

Paula looked back at her husband's body. The nurse covered it with a sheet. Then Paula stood tall. "I'm so sorry Jim flipped out on you." She patted her stomach. "We'll make this right."

Sam clasped her hand and Mark took the other one. "We'll do this together." Sam squeezed Paula's hand.

Detective Barber cleared his throat. "I'm sorry for your loss, but we still have to take statements from you all."

Sam shook her head, glaring at him.

Barber held up his hands. "We'll meet you at the Sandpoint station tomorrow. Paula, your house is a crime scene, but Ms. Volarie, if you stay out of the back bedroom, you may all go back to that house. See you tomorrow, but we already know most everything and figure you don't know much."

"Thank you, Detective, for everything. Come on, Paula, Mark, let's get out of here."

About the Author

J. A. Winrich lives and writes in Southern Arizona. A member of Sisters in Crime and the Society of Southwestern Authors, Santa Cruz Valley Chapter.

See website: www.writerjaw.com

Connect With Me:

Follow me on Twitter: https://twitter.com/JulieAWinrich

Friend me on Facebook:
https://www.facebook.com/JulieAWinrichWriter/

Subscribe to my blog: https://writerjaw.com/subscribe/

Other books by J. A. Winrich

Night Terror

Vanity Killed

www.ingramcontent.com/pod-product-compliance
Lightning Source LLC
Chambersburg PA
CBHW071136170626
46809CB00002B/640